THE LONE TREE

A Historical Novel by
James D. Yoder

Faced with rejection,
starvation, and the horror of a plague,
a teen-age girl struggles to preserve
her family and her faith.

INFINITY
PUBLISHING.COM

Copyright © 2008 by James D. Yoder

ISBN 978-0-7414-4922-1

Published by:

PUBLISHING.COM

*Info@buybooksontheweb.com
www.buybooksontheweb.com
Toll-free (877) BUY BOOK
Local Phone (610) 941-9999
Fax (610) 941-9959*

Printed in the United States of America

Published November 2012

To those who love the church, and to those
who have great love for trees.

…and he shall be like a tree planted by
the rivers of water, that bringeth forth his
fruit in his season; his leaf also shall not
wither; and whatsoever he doeth shall prosper.
(Psalm 1:3)

PROLOGUE

The Lone Tree story is based upon historical events. The decrees of the Russian government forced Mennonites from Polish-Russia to emigrate or lose their historical faith and practice. This resulted in a great migration from Russia to Kansas in 1874. Among these immigrants were the 700 from the village of Antanofka.

This historical novel is a recreation of how it might have been as lived by the Becker family, especially through the viewpoint of seventeen-year-old Lusanna Becker.

This community, which had struggled financially, left their province in December, 1874. Though they had been encouraged to do so by their bishop, Tobias Unruh, they received guidance that proved to be problematic and even fatal for their well-being.

Though receiving help from several Mennonite Aid groups in America, the immigrants did not have sufficient funds to complete the trip. Surviving the treacherous North Atlantic in winter, they arrived in Philadelphia on Christmas Day, 1874. Here the plans for their journey to Kansas were bungled.

By the time they arrived in Kansas, they had had nothing but bread to eat for five days. When they arrived in Hutchinson, a town that had first agreed to receive them, they were met with rejection. Forced onto boxcars, they were transported to Florence, Kansas, where they were unloaded. The temperature was fourteen degrees below zero.

Lusanna Becker and her family are crowded into a building selected by the Santa Fe Railroad. Here the 700 suffered from the ravages of smallpox, cholera, and near-starvation.

Legend has it that of these Antanofkan Mennonites, 300 died and are buried at the western edge of a cemetery in Florence, Kansas. Records report that as many as twelve bodies were placed into a single grave. Visitors to the cemetery may see a stone marker memorializing their burials with an inset, which Leslie B. Allison of Florence, Kansas, in her article in *Kanhistique*, November, 1993, p. 9, describes as a Russian bear. However, Mennonite historian, Keith Sprunger, after inspecting it, identified it as a lamb, which is more in character with the immigrants' Anabaptist theology.

When Lusanna Becker left her village of Antanofka, she said good-bye to her favorite tree, a large and commanding poplar near her home. Through her journey to Kansas, and throughout her suffering in Florence, she kept hoping to find another tree to love in Kansas.

In the spring of 1875, the survivors, grouped as families, settled upon land in McPherson County. Each family received forty acres within the section called the Lone Tree Township, named after a giant cottonwood tree. The Lone Tree provided shelter for early settlers and travelers on the Santa Fe Trail. It became a reference point, providing shade, and welcome rest by Running Turkey Creek. A post office, called Lone Tree, was built nearby. Within a few miles one found the Lone Tree School, and finally, after a few years, The Lone Tree Church of God in Christ Mennonite Church.

My friend, Jacob Goering, of North Newton, Kansas, grew up near the giant tree, often fishing and playing there. He has written and lectured about this tree. A granite marker, placed by members of the C.B. and Adina Goering family, and the McPherson County Historical Society, with descriptive text, has been placed near the tree site. (Exit 54 on I-35, east one-quarter of a mile on Comanche Rd.)

Though the tree survived prairie fires, drought, and the ravages of storms and time, it finally succumbed to civilization. In the mid-1930s an oil drilling crew allowed salt water to drain into the creek, an action which killed the tree and flora along *Running Turkey Creek.*

1

GOOD BYE, BASHA
September, 1872

Lusanna Becker crouched on the worn brick floor of their thatched house and barn in Polish Russia.

Though she was fifteen, she could not completely control the twitching in her arms as she clutched her four-year-old brother, Benjamin, close to her. She heard a rustle as her mother, Catherine, slipped into the room from her bedroom, "God help us, we are alone and an outlaw band descends upon us in this darkness. Keep your heads low." She drew her nightgown close to her thin body as she slid to the floor.

Lusanna's mother was named after Catherine the Great of Mother Russia, who had welcomed their people onto her lands a century ago, granting them freedom to establish their German villages, schools, and peaceful churches.

Responding eagerly, her people were scattered in villages throughout south Russia and here in the Polish province called Wohlynien; land snatched up by greedy Russia.

Lusanna felt the warmth of Benjamin's small frame and his heart thumping as he snuggled against her. The boy, disturbed from his sleep and in his nightdress, lifted his head in the darkness, pierced only by dim coals showing through the grate of the large brick Russian oven behind them in the hallway. Odors of smoked sausages and ham drifted from the wide chimney.

"Will Father and Andrias be safe, Lusanna?" the boy asked.

"They surely reached safety in Ostrog by now. Hush, Benjamin. We have to be quiet."

Neighs of horses and fast-clopping hooves echoed in spite of the foggy darkness. Lusanna ran a thin hand through Benjamin's tousled hair, hoping to calm him.

The Russian wall clock, her mother's wedding present, with its pendulum big as a pancake, and its hanging brass weights, struck midnight. But there was another sound which worried Lusanna even more, the nervous clanking of a cow bell coming from inside the barn adjoining their house.

"Don't give yourself away, Basha," she whispered. Basha, their source of milk for morning porridge of ground millet or rye, butter and cheese. Lusanna could smell the loaf of rye bread on a cupboard, baked late yesterday, coarse, but quite nourishing.

The increasing wind outside carried the chilling sounds.

"I wish Basha would stand still." Mother Catherine's voice quivered. Lusanna could faintly see her hunched form on the floor before the chair Father Joseph had made for her, bending its arms and rockers after he had soaked them. He had taken pride in his work.

"I'll sneak out and try to calm her," Lusanna whispered. If I stay with her, I can hold her bell.

"No. Lusanna, I *forbid it*. You know Cornelius Wedel stayed out too long in the night air. He is still not over the fever," her mother rasped. The frame of a loom squeaked as her body nudged it.

Lusanna realized the desperation of their situation. Strange riders and horses stomping and neighing in the rutted street. Coarse yells of Tartar-like ruffians catching in the wind, their voices muffled by the heavy fog. She knew that they were bent on thievery. She could see in her mind their wool brimless hats pulled low, shoulder capes or worn blankets extending in the wind, faces hard-set as they raised their long wooden lances, weighted at each end. She heard

4

the crash of glass, no doubt vodka bottles shattering on their gate post.

She realized that the drunken thieves were raiding their village as much for fun as for the opportunity to steal a cow or two, a horse or even, should they be bold enough to break down the door, scoop up what pantry goods, woolens and linens they could snatch..

Lusanna dared not focus her mind on other kinds of violence. *What if they stole their small supply of ham and sausage? What if the thieves shoved their way in, crashing the wooden looms and her spinning wheel?*

Lusanna realized that they, the Beckers, by being thrifty, had enough. Just enough, little excess. Neither were they highly educated as they had all attended their own school until each had passed level four. She knew quite well that they endured hardships under government officials who raised their land lease dues yearly without pity for the brethren's petitions.

The yells and stomping horse feet drew nearer.

"Mother, I am going to slip out to the barn, Basha keeps..."

"Stay in the room, Lusanna. Whatever you do don't go outside, the night air is foul, filled with sickness:" Her mother's voice wobbled in a hoarse whisper.

Lusanna recalled her father's words. "One-half of all we make goes to the Russian government. If only we could own our own pieces of land like our brethren in other villages are allowed."

Even Lusanna knew that was not possible. Russian noblemen refused to sell the Crown land to Mennonites in this part of the empire. Nor did they sell it to the small Jewish villages to their east, whose people were even poorer than they. She had fleeting thoughts of Esther and Laban Hershkovitch, teenagers like Andrias and herself. She swallowed a lump in her throat, remembering that their people were bullied, their villages sacked, sometimes even burned.

And what about the poor peasant Musicks adrift in this lonely world? They suffered even more than the Jews or the Mennonites. No wonder so many of them staggered on the road to Ostrog in drunkenness and despair.

Now father and Andrias were on their way to the city of Ostrog, their green and red Russian wagon loaded with a half-dozen sacks of grain and a twenty-foot roll of the linen cloth. She had spun the carded flax. The shuttles flew and clanked when she and Andrias were at the looms. They hoped to sell both linen and grain for a few more rubles than the village miller and merchants in Waldheim were allowed to pay.

"It's against the law to sell our grain to mills in Ostrog, but we will risk the two-day journey," Father had said last evening at candlelight as his dark brown eyes stared straight at Mother's drawn face, his shock of graying hair raked back by his work-worn fingers. The candle light had flickered as if shuddering at his words.

Lusanna worried, knowing why her father risked such a law and could be fined. Didn't the Bible say "obey those who rule over you?"

What if the law was an unjust law?

Mother had looked at him in silence. She swallowed and drew a trembling hand from beneath her chin and across her lips. Lusanna knew that she did not want Benjamin and her to see the worry in her eyes. The sadness in her mother's eyes seemed perpetual, however, her heart still ached from the burial of three babes who had died before Lusanna's birth, buried in the church cemetery.

Brother Andrias, now fourteen, rested an arm sheathed in a patched blouse-sleeved shirt before his wooden bowl, emptied now of his borsch. He cleared his throat to announce, "Father, I'm going with you this time." He straightened in his doublet vest, made of coarse homespun wool.

The wind carried the laughter and horses' neighs, now louder. Sounds of splintering wood reached her ears.

Had the marauding thieves broken down the Buller's door?

Next Lusanna heard her mother's whispers: "Our Father who art in heaven...." She heard a screech as her mother's back, through a sudden move, had nudged one of the two linen looms in the darkened room against her spinning wheel.

It had been this way for three years now, each year the Russian noose drawing tighter.

"You will have ten years to emigrate or decide to become like good Russian citizens. It's laughable that we continue your sons the benefit of not going to war. We will take over your schools. A joke, your schools perpetuating your low German language, your German catechism and Bibles. No more hymn singing and ignorant teachers."

The official representative of the Crown had sneered at them.

Their Elder, Tobias Unruh, however, when hearing these words, pulled at his graying beard and with tears in his eyes, surveyed his Antanofka congregation and spoke: "Perhaps it's time to consider Cornelius Jansen's words and consider emigrating to America where some of our people from Russia and Prussia already reside. Surely we must consider it."

The two presiding ministers, brothers Eck, and Koehn, appeared startled, their chins dropping.

Murmurs rippled through the assembly.

Move? Those fortunate to own a few acres for oats or barley, sell it? Who will buy such low-lying swampy land? Everyone knows the lies of the deceitful government officials. Who can trust them? Surely Bohemian vagabonds will steal our property, anyway.

They had turned distraught faces to each other. But then Elder Unruh reached out his arm as if to calm them and said: What if God wants to do a new thing with us? Isn't that possible, if we trust His guidance?

Who believed those words?

Lusanna had knelt then, along with all the other women, while elder Tobias and several of the brethren prayed earnestly to the heavenly Father in whom they had placed their confidence.

Could *she* believe it? This *new thing*? Did it mean there could actually be an ocean voyage to America, to the place called Kansas, where a few of their people from their northern colonies had already settled? *How could it be?*

Wouldn't it be as miraculous as the Israelites crossing the Red Sea?

Father, though, guiding the horses and wagon, on the way home from the meeting, betrayed his anxiety. "How can we emigrate to America? How? Less than half of us have land to sell. Over half of our people could not pay for ship passage, even if they sold all they possess, and. there are over 700 of us here in Antanofka.

***

Next morning, the grayness hung as if the sun refused to show itself above the oaks, slowly revealing their outlines. Across the rutted road, a hundred feet from their front door, a lone poplar tree towered as if searching for the sun. Sticks from the stork's nest atop their chimney poked dimly through the heavy air.

Lusanna glanced through the small kitchen window, looking down the rutted village street. She hurriedly tied her apron strings and reached for the poker to stir the fire in the Russian oven. The storeroom door squeaked open as Mother Catherine, holding an empty and battered milk pail, stepped into the dimly-lighted kitchen. Odors of barn manure and old straw drifted to Lusanna's nostrils.

Lusanna knew in her heart that the news would be grim. She lifted her eyes to her mother's drawn face, kerchief tied under her chin. Her grey-green eyes wide opened.

"Lusanna," Catherine's voice faltered. "They stole Basha! Theives cut the leather strap from around her neck. They threw the bell by the open barn door."

Lusanna watched her mother turn, clutching her home-spun apron up to her eyes to wipe away the tears.

Oh, God, Lusanna thought. *Where are Father and Andrias?*

Now Benjamin will have to eat his porridge with only water.

2

LUSANNA RESISTED THE THOUGHT

This will be my last year in this school, Lusanna vowed to herself, having just turned sixteen. *I'm ready to emigrate to Kansas. Anything to get away from this.* By *this*, Lusanna meant sitting at this plank table only two chairs away from schoolmaster Heinrich's chair. Male students, including Andrias, stared at her from the opposite side of the table.

Her mother often spoke with pity about Heinrich and his widowed mother, Gerda. Sure, the few rubles that a schoolteacher earned, plus his summer job of cowherd, put a little food on their table. Nevertheless, Gerda hobbled along on her corns sucking her lower lip, face set as if the thatched roof had just fallen in. Lusanna figured it was because Agathe Foth broke her engagement with gangling Heinrich, leaving him standing with his elbows akimbo, mouth open, having to endure the snickers of the teenage boys.

Lusanna sat stiffly, her chestnut braids pinned tightly around her head. She wore the homespun dress, dyed with walnuts, that her mother had made for her birthday present.

That day they had broken the rule of eating no wheat, except for funerals or weddings. Her mother had surprised her with a dish of boiled wheat and milk and a honeyed syrup made out of stewed carrots. Of course, Mother had to get the milk from good-natured Frieda Kohn, three houses down the village road. This was their way, sharing and loaning in good will through the hard times. Now they shared a cow with the Kohns, whose children were grown and married and had households of their own. Catherine

10

bartered carrots and turnips from her garden in exchange for the Kohns' fresh milk.

Lusanna felt a surge of grief thinking of Basha. *Where was she? Did the raiders butcher her that evening? Did they beat her with their long lances until she dropped?*

She and Andrias had walked at least four miles, that fateful morning, searching the ditches alongside the road for any sign of her. It had been a futile effort.

Lusanna and Andrias were thankful for the opportunity to learn to read and write. Lusanna was now in the fourth curriculum, which consisted of the study of the entire Bible, of course in German. She pushed her slate aside, lifting her worn leather Bible from underneath.

What passage would schoolmaster Heinrich assign her today?

She had always complied, hadn't she? Weren't there only just two more chairs and then she would be sitting next to the teacher himself? On her right side sat black-haired Elise Wedel, a good friend. Next to her sat red-headed Agnes Unruh, slouching as if she was through memorizing Psalm 100, her moon face contented as a Guernsey's in a field of buttercups. Agnes didn't seem to mind at all, having the honor of sitting next to the lanky schoolmaster. The finest scholars moved up, taking their turns sitting next to Heinrich Schmidt. They didn't mention his garlic breath or how he breathed with his mouth open, a gap in his yellow front teeth.

I wish we didn't have to sit around this table plastered so close to each other. Lusanna realized that she resisted the thought of moving ever closer to schoolmaster Heinrich. *Would it really be an honor to sit there?*

Should I be diligent as a Christian and show myself approved unto God by, renewing my mind, a workwoman who "needeth not be ashamed," according to St. Paul?

She knew that if she kept up mastering the lessons, memorizing with ease and perfection, what was in store. It was only a matter of hours before Elise or Agnes stumbled

11

over a verse or sang off-key during the singing lessons and would be forced off their perches, moving her ever closer.

Even worse schoolmaster Heinrich kept licking his long, fleshy lips, a crooked smile on his face each time Lusanna decreased her distance to his chair. *This was the way it was done. Be true to tradition. Best scholars move closer to the teacher's chair. Do not question it. Consider myself fortunate to be able to cipher and read. Smile and be delighted to show my classmates how the schoolmaster takes delight in my steady advance to the front. After all, about 80 percent of Russian population can neither read or write.*

Lusanna sat straight and swallowed as the teacher called her name.

"*Fraulein* Lusanna, would you read our lesson today from II Samuel, Chapter 11?" He cleared phlegm from his throat. His Adam's apple bobbed.

So, he was being formal today. *Fraulein* Lusanna. She surveyed him, one long-fingered hand on the table, the other, chapped and coarse, holding a pointer. His eyes, though gleaming, were tinged with a yellow cast. Perhaps Kansas wouldn't be so bad after all, she thought to herself. *But maybe Heinrich would set up schoolteaching there.*

Yes, she was a church member. She had taken her vows with the deepest commitment, receiving the waters of baptism, kissed appropriately by the elder's stout wife, Helena. *Would this be prideful, receiving such honors from the schoolmaster?*

She certainly thought Henry Voth got the big head when he landed at the teacher's side across from her.

Lusanna stood obediently, her hands trembling, and began to read. Though she had studied the passage only the evening before by the light of the candle and the open hearth of the oven, it never occurred to her that any teacher would call upon her to read *this passage* out loud in front of her peers.

She lifted her chin. A chill crept over her neck and shoulders.

"And it came to pass, in an eveningtide that David arose from off his bed, and walked upon the roof of the king's house, and from the roof he saw a woman…"

Oh, Mother, what shall I do? Father, come here to tell me whether to read or not. Are there any angels hovering above me to give me a nudge?

Franz Peters, directly opposite her on the boys' side, stifled a snicker, making out as if he was wiping his nose with the butt of his hand.

Her eyes flashed to her brother Andrias's face. His cheeks were scarlet. She could hear his toe tapping on the puncheon floor. Andrias knew his Bible well.

Schoolmaster Heinrich's face clouded, his eyes narrowed. He slapped a stout hickory stick, cracking it on the boy's side of the table.

Would someone be dismissed from school over this?

To save both herself and her brother, Lusanna braced herself. *Hadn't she learned fearlessly to wring a chicken's neck and hold it out so that its blood did not splash against her apron?* She would read the German Bible with perfection, honoring God, the scribes who put the shameful words down on parchment, and herself, if this was what the schoolmaster required.

Again she lifted her chin and swallowed. *Read the passage perfectly. Get this day over and go home and knead dough. Knead dough.*

She plowed through the difficult passage, Uriah's wife, Bathsheba, her tub of water out on the roof. The betrayal. David, placing Uriah in the heat of the battle. The sorrowful ending: "And when the wife of Uriah heard that Uriah was dead, she mourned for him…"

Schoolmaster Heinrich held up his hand for her to stop. "I commend you. Fraulein Lusanna, you read the German perfectly." His smile broadened as he dug a dingy handkerchief from his breast pocket to wipe his lips. "You may continue to read."

Which should it be? Act dumb and tangle the syllables? Tell the schoolmaster, who seemed to be enjoying the situation far too much, that she was ill and needed to race to the outside privy?

Why hadn't all this anguish among her people about scraping enough money together for passage to America come to fruition? Oh, to be on a windswept prairie in that place called Kansas. Anything better than this.

But then, she knew he would only call upon her tomorrow, or the next day, if she skipped a day. He might even make her stay after school where she would be forced to sit there, he, breathing into her face, giving her private instruction, a soiled finger pointing to another passage. She knew that he saw through her as a cat sees the mouse behind a sunbeam.

"Read on, Lusanna." His smile broadened.

Before she continued with the verses, she shot a glance across the table and saw Carl Jantz looking at her with his large soulful eyes, like the archangel's eyes in a picture in her Bible.

The thought flashed across her mind *Carl sympathizes with me.* She caught a glimpse at the purple hand-crocheted bookmark laying across his Bible.

With her eyes back upon her Bible page, Lusanna read on.

***

Stepping briskly along the dusty village road alongside Andrias, Lusanna focused a weary eye upon the majestic poplar tree across from their thatched-roofed house, barn, and storage shed. Its branches seemed to beckon her in the wind as light from the afternoon sun gilded the leaves. *Had she been as sturdy as that tree this day? Wasn't the Psalmist the one who had written about a tree and water?*

The verse about the righteous person flowed through her mind.

And he shall be like a tree, planted by rivers of water that bringeth forth his fruit in his season; his leaf also shall not wither; and whatsoever he doeth shall prosper.

Andrias stumbled on a clod in the road. His silence communicated to her the embarrassment they both had felt at the predicament the hollow-chested schoolmaster had put Lusanna through. Even worse. Elise had been careless in her multiplication tables and lost her chair and had to move back. Lusanna, obeying the teacher, who pointed with his index finger, moved one chair closer.

As she had predicted, during the hymn singing, careless Agnes dropped the whole stack of song books, trying to keep up with the schoolmaster's demands. He never even gave her a chance. "To the back end of the table, Agnes," Heinrich commanded, forehead lined by his frown.

"For our scholar, Fraulein Becker." The schoolmaster's face changed from a frown to a beaming smile. He rested a hand on the chair back as Lusanna, cheeks crimson, eyes downcast, slipped over to the seat already warmed by Agnes Unruh's wide bottom.

***

Lusanna stopped, her feet in the yellow road dust. She grabbed Andrias by his shirt sleeve, slid her hand down to his calloused palm. "Andrias, I forbid you to mention the events of this day to Mother or Father. Do you hear me? I *absolutely* forbid it."

"But Lusanna," Andrias grinned, "You've been honored, perched as you are beside the schoolmaster. And I must tell you that Elise whispered to me during recess, 'Schoomaster Heinrich wants to marry Lusanna'"

Andrias took off running to join a group of boys straggling along behind, legs of his homespun trousers ballooning, his laughter drifting in the wind.

Ahead, the stalwart poplar, its roots sucking nourishment from mother earth, beckoned her homeward.

To Lusanna's surprise she saw Carl Jantz edge toward the road ditch and step up onto the road, his blue cloth cap tipped back.

"Wait, Lusanna," he called.

15

Though aware a girl her age didn't walk with someone of the opposite sex, not of the family, unattended by an adult, nevertheless, considering the events at school, she turned and smiled. "Hello, Carl."

She wanted to say more, but considered it improper - something like, "I surely appreciated your sympathetic look when the schoolmaster asked me to read that passage."

"Lusanna," he matched his step to hers as they sauntered toward the houses ahead. "Lusanna, you did the right thing, plowing on ahead in that passage. I want you to know I think schoolmaster Heinrich was out of line asking you to read it out loud and in front of us all like that." His head turned, eyes focusing upon her blue-green ones.

"I, I," Lusanna realized that her cheeks were flushed, discussing the subject with a boy from her very own church. "I thank you, Carl, for your words of understanding." Her toe scraped a clod.

Her heart lightened as the day's humiliations disappeared in the light of Carl's care, and in the light shining in his dark-blue eyes. "Lusanna, as far as I'm concerned, I'll put a stop to any rumors spread in the community about this, that passage and all."

Lusanna wished she could just reach out and clasp his hand. But before she could turn her head away, she felt his warm flesh against her hand and something drop into her palm.

"Good-bye, Lusanna. I'll see you in class Monday." Carl turned to head toward his own thatched roof.

Opening her palm, Lusanna's eyes focused upon the small purple cross that had lain across his Bible during the hour of her trial.

Lusanna closed her hand around it, a smile at her lips.

3

ELDER TOBIAS SPEAKS

Lusanna's father, Joseph, lifted his long cross-cut saw, the teeth shiny from sawing logs in the forest. He hung it on wooden pegs in the storage shed. Both he and Andrias had earned a handful of rubles from forestry work, money which Catherine would store in a brown crock with a tightly-fitting lid, shoved under their bed. The rubles would be added to what they had earned from selling linen, whose weaving had involved all the family members in its making. First they had to pull the flax out of their small patch of land just when it was starting to turn yellow.

Both Lusanna and Andrias had then taken it upon themselves to then yank the stalks through a plank where nails were driven, combing out the seeds. Their mother saved these for remedies when someone was ill.

Next, Catherine and Lusanna soaked the stalks until the outside was almost rotten, stacking them up like one would shock bundles of rye or oats. After they had seasoned, Andrias and she beat the bundles with a flax breaker, a flail, until all the outer shells had come off.

Finally, Catherine and Lusanna took over drawing handfuls of fiber through the hetchel, a kind of a curry comb, combing it out silky and fine.

Then in candlelight in the evenings, the great oven toasting their backs, Catherine and Lusanna took turns at the spinning wheel, spinning the soft carded flax into yarn.

Andrias labored at his loom as Lusanna handed him a skein of yarn, his shuttle flying like a mouse escaping their cat.

Joseph's back ached from drawing the saw the long hours of the day. Yet, he was thankful that many of their people could earn a meager living through lumbering. He knew that Andrias's muscles, too, would be more than weary, his legs and arms sore. He had stood faithfully through the long hours in a pit, the giant log stretched across, while he drew the saw upward and Andrias pulled it down, sawing the oak boards clean and even.

He brushed sawdust from his patched coat. Sour odors from the boards clung to his clothes. Cabbage and onion smells drifted from underneath the kitchen door. His mouth watered. *Maybe Catherine fixed potato pancakes, too.*

Joseph's mind focused on the recent meeting of most of the members of their Antanofka congregation. Their minister, Samuel Kohn, eyes wide in anticipation, introduced Elder Tobias Unruh who had just returned from his trip to America, traveling with eleven other leaders from their Russian and Polish colonies. Like Joshua, their purpose had been to spy out the land, come back and report whether or not such a country would be suitable for settling. *It would be good news, wouldn't it?*

"Brethren," the elder began.

Members lifted anxious faces, opening their ears to hear the elder's report. Joseph knew that many of the folks on the benches would be saying to themselves: Elder Tobias surely looks like he prospered on the journey.

So he did, stocky, filling out a suit obviously purchased from a merchant, something that only a few of them could do. His graying beard and hair combed, black bow tie at his neck.

"We are saddened that not all of our people listen to our guidance. There are some in our colonies who have been wooed by Count Tod von Leben, sent out by the Czar to win us over to the Russian ways. They have offered our young men jobs in forestry and in sanitation instead of entering the military, if we continue to stay. Von Leben has been here in the village of Antanofka. You know his words. Do not be deceived. We cannot compromise our principles and work with the Russian military."

There were murmurs and heads nodding, indicating that the listeners were affirming the elder's words. He tugged at his lapels and continued.

"You would not believe the wonders of America and the welcome I received from our people there and from President Grant when I met with him at his summer home on Long Island Sound."

Meeting with a president? How could it be? Joseph cleared his throat and nudged Andrias to be certain that he was listening.

"I am impressed by the simplicity of that man, a general and one who led his troops to a great victory in the war between the American North and the South. He received us in an ordinary suit, no ornamentation, no badges, braid or military insignias. He encouraged us to emigrate..."

"What about war? Being drafted in America?" whispered Andrias, dark eyes focused upon the esteemed elder. Joseph knew that this matter certainly concerned Andrias.

"The American president assured us that his country would not have a war for at least 50 years, maybe longer. Those of our belief could then petition the government, which promises to give us serious hearing."

Heads nodded. Some braced their chins with their hands. Others looked at each other in doubt.

"I and the eleven other delegates from our colonies traveled across the continent, oh, my brethren, *such a land.* Some of the brethren traveled to Canada, to the great plains of the province of Manitoba.

"The trains that carried us farther west were beyond description. I could scarcely believe their speed, the comfort of the cars. We traveled over a work of wonder, an iron bridge spanning a great falls, called Niagara. It was almost more than I could comprehend.

"I and another delegation arrived in the marvelous states of Pennsylvania and Ohio, where Swiss and German Mennonites have resided for more than a century. What a blessed country. I felt like Joshua surveying the land of promise.

"Oh, could I only have brought back to you, not just a cluster of grapes, but *bushels* of fruit - apples, peaches, pears, plums. Everywhere throughout the countryside were well-kept gardens, our own Mennonite people welcoming us. I cannot even describe to you the beauty of their farmsteads and the insides of their homes, the great barns filled with hay, granaries bulging with wheat and oats."

Necks stretched. Worn hands clasped. Women, heads covered with the traditional black bonnets called *haubes*, ribbons tied religiously beneath their chins, lifted solemn faces.

Even little Benjamin listened, mouth open.

"At a place called Summerfield, Illinois, beautiful name, our brothers met us there and entertained us in their homes built of both wood and stone with basements stocked with barrels of wine and crocks of preserved meats and pickles. Many of the houses were two stories, bedrooms enough for all their many children. Some of the houses had *three* stories, broad windows allowing in the freshest air since Eden, the purest sunlight. And oh," he added, "the land, the beautiful black, loamy soil, edged by great forests. We can have wheat fields five times bigger than any present ones. I cannot tell you enough about the finest horses, beef cattle and milk cows on the pastures and in the barnyards.

Sounds of happy exclamations swept through the assembly. Folks leaned even farther forward.

"I can tell you that many of our brothers are now working on our behalf. There is an Aid Society, a Mennonite Board of Guardians, and even the Quakers interested and willing to assist us in our journey.

"One of our very own, Cornelius Janzen, who was expelled by the Russian Crown, now labors faithfully in our behalf."

Well, yes, thought Joseph Becker, Cornelius Janzen was an untiring worker in behalf of their colonies, feeling that it was their duty to witness for Christ, the Prince of Peace, not relinquishing the Lord's command to "put away the sword."

Joseph felt a tinge of sadness at how Cornelius and his wife were now refugees, forced to emigrate to America to continue their lives there. The Russian Crown would have no more of Cornelius Janzen encouraging their communities in Polish Russia or Russia to pack up and leave. Joseph was aware that the government officials would consider that a great loss for Mother Russia.

Assist us? How? How could such a thing be possible? Wouldn't there be several thousand from their colonies who would emigrate? Surely Elder Tobias is speaking of loans which we would have to pay back.

Joseph leaned forward to catch the words.

The elder clasped pudgy hands before his buttoned vest, continuing.

"Why, sisters," He surveyed the uplifted heads on the women's side, "Standing in one place, I could count seven kinds of wild rose bushes blooming, wild flowers, gooseberries, strawberries and blackberries grew everywhere. Hickory nuts, walnuts, nuts of many kinds stored in pantries and basements."

By now, thought Joseph, mouths surely must be watering. No wonder Tobia's vest fitted him so snugly.

"Brethren such as C. B. Schmidt, who works with the American railroads, will help us with transport. Christian Krehbiel, and Bernard Warkentine, a recent but wealthy immigrant to America, are working on our behalf. But we have to do our duty. We have to respond. We must begin selling what we own, make the required shipping trunks or boxes. We must band together, united more than *ever* before."

For a period of time, Joseph Becker failed to hear the elder's report, focused as his mind was upon their predicament. Only a few rented acres. The buildings, house, old, decades old. The roof lines sagged on many of their village houses. Most of them had scanty livestock, a few cows, taken to the village commons to pasture in the summertime, led by schoolmaster Heinrich, eking out a few more kopecks in addition to his paltry teacher's salary. Here and there a small flock of sheep. A few teams of horses, or oxen. A handful of neighing goats, hutches of rabbits, pigs who ate the weeds of summer, providing them with sausages and pork. Gaggles of geese, a few flocks of ducks.

What would it all amount to as they made their attempts to sell their buildings, their stock and fowl? The Russian peasants, though they might look with longing eyes, were surely too poor to bargain and buy as they spent their extra kopeks on vodka.

Jews from a colony to the east might purchase their livestock, bargaining for good prices, then having them made kosher by their Rabbi.

Joseph was assured of one thing: they would receive absolutely *no help* from the Russians. In fact, wouldn't they goad the Bohemians to flock to their villages and simply claim as their own the property that hadn't sold?

Elder Tobias's last words startled Joseph even more.

"I have been notified last week that already our people in the village of Gruental have sold their property and applied for passports. Brethren and Sisters, they plan to leave in March. Our prayers must go with them."

So the migration has begun. The poor land renters, lumbermen, weavers, and day laborers, the millers, give or take a few, were left to ponder. *How can we do it?*

***

Mother Catherine and Joseph rocked on the wagon seat, Joseph guiding the team on their way back to their place. They rode mostly in silence.

"Can *we* do it, Joseph?"

Joseph saw the tears tracing the lines in Catherine's face. He realized the tears were for the infants buried behind the church. He knew she was thinking, *How can I leave them?*

He was certain of the words flowing through Catherine's mind. His heart, too, ached.

Those days are with the silent dead,
With me, they're living still.

Catherine spoke again. "True, our life is hard here, Joseph, but I married you before God and our people for better or for worse. It doesn't sound like, at least from Elder Tobias, that such a move to Kansas would be for *worse*, does it?"

Joseph's heart warmed at the faint smile on her lips.

He focused his eyes upon her gray-green ones, now wide open as if seeking his trust and confidence. He reached out with his right arm and drew her close to him, noting the thinness of her frame. A wind rustled the maples and undergrowth across the road from them. A fecund earthy smell rose from the woods. A solitary frog chirruped.

"No, Tobias's words did not sound like *worse* to me, Catherine, my dear, dear wife. Though, I must confess, and don't tell anybody, I think he was a bit flowery in his descriptions of the new lands."

"You noticed it, too? I'm wondering, though, how Andrias and Lusanna feel about such a discussion, such plans - it could be a great upheaval. This is the only home they've known. Isn't it hard to uproot people their ages?"

"Young people adjust well, Catherine. Especially if the choices are toward what is fulfilling and good. Sure, they would be losing their home here, some of their Jewish friends. And, maybe not all of our congregation would decide to go." Joseph cleared his throat.

Catherine's body swayed. She drew a thin shawl around her shoulders, obviously pondering his words.

The horses drew near their barnyard and stopped.

23

"Tobias, Tobias. In the book of *Tobit*, wasn't he the one who was blinded by pigeon-dung?" Catherine asked, her eyes searching her husband's face.

"Well, I don't know about that, Catherine, but I'd just say that Elder Unruh has a very big responsibility right now. He is our *Kirchenspiel*, our bishop, all this turmoil and over twenty congregations under his care.

4

HE WOULDN'T STAY BEHIND, WOULD HE?

The next morning, Lusanna, digging parsnips from the little patch at the side of the house, lifted her head to see Elise Wedel fidgeting with the garden gate. She stood, hand on her aching back, grateful for an excuse to stand. She noticed that Elise carried a small jar in her hands. "What a welcome surprise, Elise, good morning."

"Good morning to *you*, Lusanna." Elise's cheeks blossomed red as her smile broadened, showing white teeth. "And, may I add, Lusanna, congratulations on your *achievement.*" Elise giggled.

Lusanna felt the blood rush to her neck. Her toe dug into fresh-turned earth, which smelled of mold and the spicy mixture of bruised herbs. "You mean, you mean -" she hoped Elise didn't mean…

"Yes, I mean your arrival at schoolmaster Heinrich's elbow. Are you his handmaiden now?" Her giggle turned into a loud he-haw. "But before I forget, Mama sent your mother this jar of currant jelly."

Lusanna, ignoring the laughter, reached for the jar. "Thank you for Mother's favorite jelly, Elise, our currant bushes hardly produced anything this season. But I have a question to ask you. You *really do* know your multiplication tables, don't you?" Lusanna grinned slyly.

"My multiplication tables? Why, Lusanna, isn't nine times eight *ninety one?*" She bent over and slapped a thigh.

"You know better than that. If you don't stop teasing me, I'll *never* speak to you again. And, if you do happen to be on a great ship steaming through the ocean to America, standing by a deck rail beside me, I'll let on like I don't even know who you are." Lusanna held her own sides as she, too, broke into gales of laughter.

Elise, not yet unwilling to let go goading Lusanna, got in another dig. "That'd be all right, Lusanna. No need for me to be beside you at the ship's rail. Schoolmaster Heinrich will be by your side, anyway." She lifted her head and howled.

Their laughter startled the grackles who swarmed away from a pear tree. Lusanna's mother stepped briskly out of her kitchen door to the side of the house by the parsnip patch.

"For you, Mother, from Elise's mother." Lusanna, feet half-buried in the sandy soil, handed the jelly to her mother. She tried to arrange her face in a manner befitting a faithful Christian, one who was circumspect, not suffering fools.

"Why," Catherine's eyes brightened, "do tell your mother thank you, Elise. I'm pleased to see you girls enjoying each other." Catherine's eyes lifted from their faces to the thatched roofs to the south, the poplars moving gently in the morning wind, men's breeches and homespun shirts blowing on the clothesline.

"Why don't you girls sit awhile on the stoop and I'll make some mint tea."

"Why, if you don't mind, that'd be nice," Elise clasped her chapped hands before her.

So they sat, in their homespun gray and brown garb, sipping the hot tea. Elise obviously had sense enough to know when she'd gone far enough with her teasing, sobered herself so as to enter sensible conservation with Lusanna's mother.

They chatted about Elise's family, her mother Helena, who had just recovered from a fever, her father, Amos, off in the woods with son Benjamin to join Andrias and Joseph in lumbering. Lusanna was pleased her mother allowed a little visit and a spell of rest, knowing that the minutes would quickly roll by. The verse about "workers who needeth not be ashamed" was always nudging an edge of their minds.

Odors of Catherine's potato noodles, cooking with a bit of smoked meat drifted toward the stoop. The conversation hung in the air. Elise's face grew pensive.

"Are you folks starting to pack? Quite a few of our people are more than unsettled by Elder Tobias encouraging us to emigrate." Elise shuffled her feet.

"Well," Lusanna said, "Father talked about it last night after he read the scriptures and led the prayers. Since Andrias will soon be old enough to be drafted, emigrating to America is a serious consideration in our family."

"But is it the Lord's will?" Elise asked.

"That's the question, isn't it, Elise? How does one know?" Lusanna raked back a strand of hair.

"If only it weren't the changes in the government policies, the military, the taxes and all. I love many things about living here, Lusanna. It's the only home you and I have ever known. I'd miss our storks who come every spring. I don't think there would be storks in that place called Kansas."

"I think you're right, Elise. Maybe only buzzards." Lusanna giggled.

"What has it been, seventy or eighty years, our people here? Wouldn't we be disrupted for even a greater unknown? Father said that the idea of young men entering forestry projects and doing sanitation work may just be a reasonable compromise instead of the military. Besides," he said, "we've been able to buy a few acres of land, and that's a big step forward for us."

At Elise's words, both Lusanna and Catherine grew silent. Feet shuffled. Tea mugs clunked on the stoop as they set them down. A drift of wind carried the spicy scents of the woods to the southeast.

Lusanna felt a tug within her breast as she thought of Elise's brother Jacob and his dark brown eyes, his tender spirit, the way he, like Carl Jantz had looked at her when she was required to move close to the schoolmaster? *Surely not Jacob. Elise and Jacob wouldn't stay behind, would they?*

"Oh, Elise, your father may surely want to consider *that* again. You know how the government keeps commitments. It could be a dangerous placement of our faith, our young men compromising like that." Lusanna remembered her father once, in a low voice, mentioning that two of the brethren from one of their northern colonies had been snatched up, buried in a prison somewhere in Siberia.

They sat pensive and silent, their anxieties betrayed by the thought of resettling so far away. To Lusanna, it seemed a fantasy, a dreamy, hazy wonderland of fresh showers, great meadows and grasslands with sweet winds, and most of all, all those strawberries, and other fruits Elder Tobias raved about. She shifted her feet, feeling a tension created by Elise's sobering comments about her brother, Jacob and the new Russian military alternatives.

Now what? Whither would the Lord lead them?

"Father urged Andrias *not* to compromise by believing the Russians. I saw Father looking over our livestock and our buildings. It seemed to me that he knew that all of us would soon be saying good-bye to the only home we've ever known," Lusanna added.

"My father said the same thing, Lusanna. But he also said that such a move would be a great unsettling, a great risk. He also said that Elder Tobias is a bit windy. Anyway, you know, Lusanna," added Elise, "not all of the people in our village will do such a risky thing."

A chill swept through Lusanna's entire body. Her eyes shifted aside.

How can I leave the only home I've ever known for such a strange-sounding place as Kansas? Haven't we heard rumors that out on those plains there are folks called Indians who scalp people?

Lusanna reached out to give Elise a tight hug. Tears stung her eyes.

5

WE'LL BE SAYING GOOD-BYE
October, 1874

In every house, hustle, bustle and hurry. Prayers ascended in faith and with faltering faith. Sounds of hammers pounding nails echoed throughout the village as heads of households and their carpenter sons sawed sturdy boards, planing them, nailing them according to the directions given. Each grown person sailing to America would be allowed *one* *chest* of approximately three feet by three feet, twenty-seven cubic feet per adult.

Andrias could hear the pings as blacksmith Ezra Buller, down the village street, pounded hot iron strips, shaping them into strong bands to bind the chests the men were feverishly making.

He recalled how his mother's face fell when Father described this matter to her. "Joseph, why, Joseph, why, why, why, I can't take the things I..." Tears glistened in her eyes as she turned to look at her Russian clock, its pendulum swinging.

Andrias noticed his father's face grow even more solemn as he strode over to put his arm around her, something he rarely saw his father do in his presence.

Andrias's little brother, Benjamin, lifted his brown eyes to his father's face, "Papa, won't we need a little wooden house for Dutch?" The black and white sheep dog had crept close to Benjamin's leg where he lay down.

"No, Benjamin. No, we won't be able to take Dutch. We won't be allowed to take pets. Besides, people who move into our houses will take good care of him. He will have a good home."

Andrias could see his father sigh. *What words did he have for Benjamin? How to soften such a matter?* He swallowed a lump in his throat as he watched his father lay down his hammer, lean over and put his arm around his little brother.

"Benjamin," he said, "we will all be leaving many things behind. Some of our favorite things. We'll be saying good-bye to this land and our home here. See how Mother and Lusanna are packing and sorting inside? They, too, will leave many of their things behind. Of course, we will try to sell as much of our property as we can."

"And you, too, Papa, you'll leave our horses behind?" Benjamin's dark eyes searched his father's face.

"Yes, my son, Felka and Gazilya both, but they will be cared for, we pray. I've already sold them to a Jewish man who has a market wagon. He has a good heart."

Andrias's heart stirred when his father began to hum a few of the words of the hymn they'd sung at church last night: *Guide me, O Thou Great Jehovah, Pilgrim through this barren land.*

A part of him anticipated the journey ahead like a frisky horse straining at the bit. Thinking of a great new ship, to even consider a seaport at Antwerp, Belgium, and the wagon and train journey to get there, filled him with wonder and awe.

Wasn't it a miracle, the way the Board of Guardians in America had loaned their people so much money and all the other arrangements for the trip? Those fellow-believers, the Americans, Funk, and Warkentine surely must be faithful followers of Christ.

What had Father said? Yes. At least half of the 700 of them leaving Antanofka Village did not have money to pay for the ocean passage to America.

Andrias's mind couldn't comprehend such a generous loan to aid their people. But, in a land like America, according to Elder Tobias, everyone would be paying it back in no time at all. No time at all.

Andrias thought briefly of what was ahead, the partings, good-byes, the embraces, tears, and hand shakings with the few that were left behind. He recognized that some of their people who owned land and had achieved a modest success might not find it within themselves to give up what they had worked so hard to gain. Some were simply too old to endure such a journey.

Then too, Andrias felt unsettled, knowing that a few families with young men had decided that they could agree with the Russian government's plan of allowing them to enter forestry and sanitation work, instead of the regular military.

Andrias also remembered his father's words: *Never trust the Russian government.*

Jacob Wedel had decided to emigrate, too, hadn't he? Didn't he joined the crowd of young men at the church where Elder Tobias prayed for yielded and committed hearts? Did the Wedels sign their certificates, endorsed by Elder Tobias? *No one* was allowed on the ship without the certificate.

Andrias counted the days until December when the long trek and sea journey would begin. He knew he would not be allowed to take the 150 pounds, or even a trunk as he was not yet an adult. He grinned to himself, thinking of his belongings: his pocket knife, the blousy shirt, homespun breeches, a worn woolen coat, the boots he wore, a baptismal certificate, and Bible. *What else did he own, anyway?*

He decided to focus his mind on their journey overland in wagons to Ostrog, where they would all board carriages behind a locomotive, something Andrias had never seen, nor ridden. His heart thumped at the excitement the thought brought to him. The railroad journey would then take them to Antwerp and the great vessel awaiting them there.

Wouldn't it be a marvel? Rumors had it that it was both a sailing vessel with two giant masts, and powered by a steam engine that turned propellers, pushing the great ship through the waves when the wind wasn't blowing. *Oh, the marvels of modern civilization. They say that life in America is a hundred times better than here. Surely our people will have reached the country they sing about at church, Beulah Land, "we've reached the land of corn and wine."*

Andrias began to smile as he picked up his hammer. Mother Catherine had called his name.

***

Inside the house, Catherine and Lusanna sorted and stacked. "Stuff this bolt of wool inside my old dowry chest, Lusanna, and here, these too." She handed Lusanna a satin shawl, a folded piece of hand-woven linen. "A hundred and fifty pounds of packed belongings isn't much, Lusanna. That will be three hundred, Father's and mine."

"How is it that you are packing your dowry chest, Mother?" Lusanna studied the faded red and green painted flowers and leaves on its front boards.

"Well, Lusanna, it's about the size required. Elder Tobias said that these German dowry chests would suffice, that is if we can secure them tightly. Father is making our other trunk."

Lusanna knew that her mother, at least, was pleased that she could take the heirloom. *How much would it hold? And what?*

She looked at the piles about her feet and against the wall, the tumbled bedding.

When they had completed their task, they had gathered together the bolt of wool, the piece of linen, a feather quilt, the satin shawl, a large black woolen shawl, felt shoes called *schlorre* for wearing inside the house, two Bibles. *What else from the piles around their feet?*

Catherine handed Lusanna two small bundles that felt squishy and soft. "What are these, Mother?"

"Flower seeds in one, peas and beans in the other one. Drop them into the chest. According to the reports, things will be easy to grow in Kansas. It's a balmy country. Probably no need for extra-heavy winter clothing, which will only take up unnecessary room, anyway."

Lusanna was surprised at her mother's energy and she, at least for now, looked like she was anticipating the journey ahead. She reached out to clasp the Dresden china bowl with painted roses her mother had just wrapped in a piece of old cloth.

"A few heirlooms, Lusanna. Only a few. Father said he's going to try to stuff my clock inside bags of oats and wheat, but I don't know." She smiled, even though Lusanna realized the task seemed almost futile.

What to do with all the rest? The bedstead, the trundle bed, the chest of drawers, the table that held their Bible and lamp? Mother's kitchen utensils, kettles and pans? The looms, the spinning wheel?

Though the clothes hanging in their wardrobes were sparse, hadn't mother clarified that she and Lusanna would wear two sets of undergarments and an extra skirt or dress over them, instead of packing them? Of course, Andrias and Benjamin, Father, too, would be doing the same. She smiled to herself, thinking about how they might stumble around at the wharf, awkward and bulky. But Mother had said, "That's the way folks travel to America, Lusanna."

She picked up a worn hymnal, then an ink pen and a small tablet.

The chest was filling quickly.

***

Lusanna's mother couldn't get over the shock of it as she peered at the crowds of people in the village streets, going from house to house, yard to yard. Her heart plummeted as she watched a young Russian man with a

33

black, bushy beard pick up a rocking chair and head toward a wagon.

She glanced southward and saw Elise Becker with feather pillows in her arms, walking with one of their sisters from Waldheim who'd ridden down with her husband in their wagon for the sale. *It's here. I can't stop it. Time doesn't seem real. Oh, Joseph, where are you? Who will be living in my house? Whose tools will hang along the walls in the shed? What cattle in the barn? The great oven-stove. Whose and what kind of meats will hang in the chimney?*

Will their pair of faithful storks, whom Lusanna named Ichabod and Ketura, return to the chimney when strangers roamed through their rooms?

She looked for a place to sit, but then realized that on a day like this there was no time to sit and rest. A woman, obviously Bohemian Catholic, from the way she was dressed and the cross around her neck, held up an enamel dishpan, asking the price in broken dialect.

"Twenty kopeks," replied Catherine, trying to smile.

The large woman smiled back, swung the dishpan under a stout arm and picked up the matching water bucket and dipper. The woman lumbered close to the table where Catherine stood, set down her purchases, and reached into a leather pouch for the kopeks.

"How much?" She pointed to all three items.

Catherine looked at the dipper and bucket. She had a flashback, her little boy, Benjamin, lifting the dipper, placing it to his lips, greedily sipping the cold water.

She cleared her throat and tried to smile. "That will be one ruble for all."

Catherine was grateful that Lusanna had now entered the yard and was heading toward her. *One person cannot bear this alone.*

"Mama, Fraulein Koehn from over by Feuerstendorf wants to buy these feather comforters and this wicker basket."

Catherine greeted Helena with as steady a smile as possible, under the conditions. *Why is she buying my things? Aren't they going to be emigrating to, to...I do not want to say that name. Not today.* Catherine lifted her head, batting her eyelids to hold back the tears. More kopeks and rubles were exchanged. A cacophony of voices rose in the air, German, Polish, Russian, Yiddish, and Plattdeutsch.

Lusanna's great poplar tree, off to the side, shook its top leaves, which were gilded by sunlight as if say, "take courage, Lusanna, the trees and good earth are always there to support you."

"It's almost over, Lusanna," Catherine said as Lusanna gathered together a few left over odds and ends which they would leave behind, or yet sell to a belated searcher. Weary and with aching feet, she knew that most of the painful tasks were finished. *Except for tomorrow. The loading of the trunks and bundles. Who would be there? Who would stay behind?*

Lusanna looked up as she heard the yard gate squeak. Through the gate stepped schoolmaster Heinrich Schmidt and his hobbling mother, Gerda.

"Greetings, greetings." Heinrich's voice echoed like caw from a grackle.

"Why, your yard, your house, too, is mighty near empty, Catherine." Gerda smiled broadly.

Lusanna and Catherine both tugged at their aprons.

"Good evening, Frau Gerda, and Herr Heinrich. Good evening." Catherine nodded her head. *When I am so weary, now this?*

"Herr Heinrich." Lusanna nodded. "And Frau Schmidt." She nodded again in respect.

"What brings you to our place on such an evening?" Catherine asked.

"Why, Frau Catherine," Heinrich spoke up, "we came over to give you encouragement. Yes, encouragement on such an evening as this." His eyes lifted to Lusanna's gray-green ones, a slip of her chestnut hair peeking out from underneath her headscarf. The thatched-roofed house, the trees in the back, the garden fence were all softened by the light of the setting sun.

"Yes, greetings," continued Heinrich. "According to St. Paul, greeting one another, carrying one another's burdens." His spindly frame half-turned as he stepped closer.

Catherine smelled the garlic on his breath. "Well, yes, we do need encouragement at such a time as this, but..." her voice faded.

"And, ah, our Fraulein Lusanna." Heinrich's eyes opened widely, his mouth half open. "What a *scholar* we have in Lusanna. Isn't that right, Frau Catherine? Top of my class last year. Yes, indeed, she advanced to the head of the table next to *my* chair."

Catherine saw Lusanna blush deeply, her eyes focusing down at her boot tops. "Why, is that so? Why, Herr Heinrich, Lusanna never told me..." Suddenly she felt foolish. She looked at Lusanna again, bewildered.

Energized, Heinrich continued. "And, my dear Fraulein Lusanna, when we get to America, to Kansas, I mean, I'm going to take you on as *my assistant*. Our people will surely open a school there, first thing. Yes, first thing." He almost leaped as he said the words, reminding Catherine of a snowbird with fresh salt on its tail.

But Lusanna found her tongue. Her words flew out, swallows darting at a swarm of mosquitoes. "Schoolmaster Schmidt, I will be *far too busy* in our new home in Kansas. Besides," she inserted as if even she was surprised at how the words leaped out, "I believe that I will be setting up *my own* school."

Her eyes flashed, *so there!*

Catherine turned to Frau Gerda, whose mouth fell open at the testy girl, who seemed to be lacking proper Mennonite modesty.

Gerda's eyes burned as she turned them on Catherine's face. "Catherine Becker, I thought you would have brought up a daughter to be more respectful of her elders..."

"I am in perfect agreement with Lusanna. Yes, when we get to Kansas, I will help her make the bricks for the school if I have to." *O God, guard my tongue. Surely it must be my fatigue, my...* Catherine's hand flew to her mouth.

"Well," harrumphed Gerda, "Heinrich and I just came to inquire," she licked at her lips, "as to whether or not you folks *gained enough* from the sale of your goods to *pay your way* on the great vessel to America." She stood, batting her eyes as if she had not been nosy. No, not at all.

"Wouldn't it be a blessing, Fraulein Lusanna and Frau Catherine, if you folks and Mother and I would be on the same deck on the great ship, *The Vaderland?*" Heinrich hadn't given up.

Catherine felt a shiver slide down her back. *On the same deck? Hadn't the committee in their congregation handling all these matters said that they would mostly be traveling in steerage? That would surely be below deck, wouldn't it?*

Catherine recognized that the gaunt and nosy Heinrich was trying to impress them. With his paltry salary, his mother, poor as she was, knew that steerage passage surely awaited them both.

But let it be at opposite ends of the vessel. Catherine's lips puckered as if she had just bitten into a green plum.

Catherine saw Lusanna lift a hand to her brow and her body shift. Her tongue felt tied. *All the painful hours of the day, and now this. God, help me. Help Lusanna. But brother Tobias has called all of us to unity.*

"I don't know, Frau Gerda. I simply don't know. The journey will be very expensive. I'm going to wait until Andrias and Joseph come back before I answer. Joseph is delivering our horses to the Jewish village over north."

No, Catherine decided not to reveal to her nosey neighbors, schoolmaster and his mother or not, the situation of their finances. But Joseph's words from last night had weighted her heart like a stone crock of sauerkraut all the livelong day.

"Catherine, I've been able to sell the Crown lease on our land, but at only at one-third of what we paid for it. That, plus what we received from the sale of our cattle, the horses, our home furnishings, and tools will be it. I doubt if we will have enough for the journey across. I'm counting on meeting all of our expenses to the seaport of Antwerp, at least."

She had turned her head so that Joseph could not see her weeping. *No wonder those Americans speak of us as the helpless, poor Poles.*

By evening, a lonely wind swept over empty yards in the village of Antanofka, moaning through the bruised goldenrod and broken sunflower stalks. The green tops of the left-over turnips in the gardens were pulverized by tromping feet.

Inside the houses barren rooms echoed the lonely footsteps. From the barns came sounds of boards cracking, hinges squeaking. No lowing of cattle, bleats of sheep, or friendly neighs of horses awaited their evening scoop of oats.

In the morning the great Russian wagons would arrive, six teams of oxen hooked to each wagon, drawing them onward, onward.

6

MY FEET FORWARD IN HOPE

Lusanna, sitting alongside her mother, gripped the bundle on her lap as she clung to her perch high on her mother's dowry chest, bound securely by the blacksmith's iron bands. To her left sat Joseph, Benjamin, and Andrias, their shoulders rocking with the sway of the great wagon. She turned to catch a last glimpse of their village as the wagon train made the turn in the wide bend in the road leading to Ostrog, horses snorting, oxen straining, pulling the burdens behind them.

Could she bear it? Her mother's tears. The silence. Even the breeze stopped momentarily as if to allow time for the sobs from aching throats.

She lifted a pale hand to wave to her poplar tree.

Good-bye, dear, dear and faithful tree. I loved you all my sixteen years. I'll think of you in Kansas. Why, how beautiful our village looks from this rise in the road. It's like one of those pictures on the calendar in the schoolroom, softened by the light from the early morning sun..

Doves called plaintively somewhere in the hedge to the left. Lusanna joined her mother, whispering, "Good-bye, dear village. Farewell forever. Farewell forever." She couldn't help herself as she buried her face in the cloth-covered bundle on her lap to hide her weeping.

Never had she dreamed that beginning such a journey would so wring her heart. Last evening, they'd held their final service at church, the dear, dear, church, built by the hands of grandfathers before them. Faithful brethren, seeking peace, love, community and the blessings of Christ. Their own minister, Samuel Koehn, his eyes glistening with tears, read: "Let us go forth therefore unto him without the camp, bearing his reproach. For here we have no continuing city, but we seek one to come." *We seek a home. We seek one to come." Yes, Yes, surely, yes. But where? Across that wild, unknown ocean? Traversing endless miles of a foreign landscape to - where? Kansas?*

It seemed as if, when she thought of *that* word, the place itself began to slide off the very world.

She focused her eyes to the dozen wagons lumbering ahead. She shifted them backwards to the two dozen behind her. *Oh, dear God above, we are now without a home.*

Brother Eck was right, wasn't he? We are like the blessed Jesus who had no home, no lair, no nest, no place to lay his head. Like him, we go forth in hope. Hope, trust in our hearts that the dear Saviour meant it when he told his sorrowing disciples, "I will never leave you, nor forsake you."

Her heart felt like it had been grated by that old kitchen utensil, the cheese grater, when she finally faced the terrible truth: *Elise and Jacob Wedel and their parents, left behind. Left behind.*

"We will stay in this land. This is our home," their father, Amos, had announced as they, the Beckers, were loading their bundles, trunk, and chest into the waiting wagon. Their feet shifting, their eyes lowered, then raised, the Wedel's own sorrow evident upon their faces.

Lusanna tried not to focus upon her last embrace with Elise. Her words to her, "I won't forget you."

Oh, Elise, Elise and Jacob, how could your father make such a decision to stay behind? How could he trust the Russian government when Father says the times are so unsteady and the rulers are corrupt?

Her mind refused to focus any longer upon such painful episodes. She forced herself to look ahead across the rumps of the powerful Clydesdales with the feathered hoofs, faithfully drawing the overloaded wagon. Half-consciously, Lusanna decided to distance herself from such awful tearing. *For now. For now she must focus upon this journey. Step by step. Even if our hearts are bleeding buckets of sorrow.* But brother Eck did say, didn't he, "Let us go forth…" *Yes, that's what we will do. I resolve to do it. I'll put my feet forward in hope.*

***

Andrias crowded in alongside his father and Benjamin on the wooden bench in the third-class carriage rolling onward towards Antwerp, Belgium, pulled by the ponderous black steam engine. He glanced up, admiring his father's steadiness, after all they had left behind; his bright, dark eyes focused out the window at the passing landscape. They both wore their cloth caps, their waist-length woolen coats Mother had made, two long-sleeved blousy shirts underneath. Yes, each wearing two shirts and two pairs of wide trousers. How would they have had room otherwise? *And, look at the women? Padded and clothed as they were.*

Was Father thinking of an oat field? Was he pondering how he would plow those great plains of Kansas, preparing them for sowing wheat?

Andrias recognized that only a very few of the men in their group were successful farmers in the poor soil near Ostrog. *What would they do on the plains of Kansas?*

He looked down at the thick, yellow calluses on his palm. Relief flooded over him. No more backache from drawing the cross-cut saw. No more half-frozen feet from the days and nights spent in the woods in winter.

Andrias knew, however, that Joseph Becker suffered the same uprootedness, the frayed edge of tornness borne by them all. He realized that his father held himself within, trying not to show his worry over the fact that they would have to rely on relief for the ship passage to America. *Then what?*

What had it cost? $35.00 to $37.00 per person on the Red Star Line? A yearly salary, in their village. Only a few in their congregation had been able to fully afford the passage fees.

He, too, remembered the brethren in the churchyard speaking about some kind of disagreement between the American Mennonite leaders who were working so hard in their behalf. Brother Funk scheduled them on the Pennsylvania Railroad, but changed his mind, passing the responsibility over to a brother C. B. Schmidt, who represented a railroad company called the Santa Fe. *That was Spanish, wasn't it? What kind of country is this America?*

Then, too, hadn't Father said that when they arrived in Pennsylvania that they would be staying with the Mennonites there during the winter months?

On farms in the countryside? In the great city of Philadelphia? With whom would they live? Who would pay for this lodging?

But then his father had shaken his head, saying, "Our tickets are for transporting us all the way to Kansas. There's no provision for us to stay the winter in Pennsylvania."

Besides, hadn't Elder Tobias given the strong impression that they wouldn't be needing much in the way of coats and gloves in balmy Kansas?

Then what? What would they do in America? Would the Santa Fe Railroad be giving out free land?

There had been so many confusing stories.

Didn't the land really belong to the Indians?

And the locomotive. Never had Andrias and other of his teenage pals expected to ride in carriages drawn by such a contraption. The ponderous black engine squatted on the tracks, black smoke billowing from its stack. Its powerful wheels screeched and clanked. Spellbinding, too, how that mighty piston, like a giant arm thrusting forward and back, turned the wheels.

Andrias thought of how his father had to call him out of a semi-trance, fixed as he was upon those wheels and that everlasting piston, pumping, shoving, thrusting the engine

42

forward. He realized that if his father hadn't called his name, he might have become unable to move. What do they call it? *Spellbound?* The smell of the burning coal was exciting, invigorating in its own way. Even the stink of it. He knew power derived from it pulled them onward down the shiny tracks, edged by elder trees and overgrown bushes, past cattle grazing in pastures, past cottages with plots of fall garden plants, now wilted by frost.

He glanced across the aisle to his right and caught a glimpse of schoolmaster Heinrich Schmidt and his mother, Frau Gerda. Heinrich's eyes glowed with the light of his fascination. His thin knees were pressed together, his mouth, half-open, as he absorbed the marvels of the trip. If Herr Heinrich's purse was as empty as his, he gave no such notice.

He turned to his left and focused upon his mother. Her face looked weary, but calm. The terrible pain of the parting, now behind. He knew she struggled not to show anxiety. *"My peace I give unto you."* That was Mother's verse, her attitude, her prayer. Yes, she would be praying for the peace of Christ in the face of the great unknown ahead.

How many children were on this journey? Three hundred, Father had said.

He surveyed the dozen or so in the carriage car. Their heads rocked, many asleep, at least the little ones, cheeks against their mother's gray or brown-clothed bosoms. He glanced at brother Benjamin, his eyes wide-open in amazement.

Teenagers? Persons like Lusanna and himself? Surely must be about a hundred, maybe more.

No. They weren't classified as children, even as they were not of age, yet. They were in no-man's-land on this trip. Neither adult nor child. He was sure, however, of one fact. Both he and Lusanna would be considered adults when it came to carrying on the duties that awaited them in America.

And what would those duties be? What work? Was the soil as easy to till as Elder Tobias had mentioned? Was it true that out on the plains that if you wanted it to rain, just open up a furrow? The rains follow the furrow, Elder Tobias had said. How could he believe it?

Then a startling remembrance. Brother Nachtigal from church had clarified to a small group in the churchyard the night of their last meeting.

"You do know, don't you, that Elder Tobias Unruh *never visited* Kansas on his trip with those eleven other brethren? He decided to visit the Dakotas, whatever they are."

With perplexed expressions, the brethren stared at each other as Nachtigal continued. "The only two out of the twelve to actually visit Kansas were William Ewert, and Ben Buller. Of course, they did give promising reports on the land, its climate and the crops the land would raise. "

A bone-chilling howl split the air as the rocking iron machine drew the cars into the arched glass canopy as they rolled into the Antwerp Station, a cloud of black smoke settling around them.

7

THE S. S. VADERLAND

The three hundred-twenty foot long vessel with the towering black smokestack seemed suspended in time and place, almost completely shrouded by the early morning fog. By a quick glimpse, one could see the name of the ship painted along its broad side: *The S. S. Vaderland.* A dampness clung to Lusanna's clothes, causing her heavy skirts to cling to her legs.

"I heard some of the crew back there say that this ship weighs almost 3,000 tons," Andrias said, flashing a smile toward Lusanna.

"Well, I guess that's heavy enough to sink rather quickly," Lusanna added, thinking she would be humorous. However, she regretted having said the words. "How fast does it go, Andrias?"

"Well, something like a speed of 13 knots per mile, that'd be somewhere between 14 and 15 miles per hour, I think..."

Lusanna concluded to herself that that would be sufficient enough for her.

"This way," a navy-clothed steward called, huskily. His arm beckoned.

Lusanna's heart picked up its beat. "Where, when, how...?" she found herself whispering, trying to cling tightly to little brother Benjamin's hand, lest they be separated in the confusion.

She kept her eye focused upon her father's broad back and nodding head, Andrias beside him, thrust now and then to the side. Whenever had she seen such a turmoil, so many people?

"Third class this way," yelled another steward, taller than the first, his forehead furrowed, cheeks flushed.

She saw him grab stout old Anna Ratzlaff, her bags clasped tightly in each hand, and turn her toward the stairs. "This way. Don't you understand?"

It was obvious to her that this ship's crew, at least some of them, were already weary of loading confused and puzzled passengers.

Passenger? Was that what she was? And those words from the steward's lips, *third class.*

She who had been "first class" at school now had to reckon with herself that her feet would be turned to the shadowy hole where black-and grey-clothed backs were now disappearing. Never had she dreamed that the bundles they carried would weigh like this, arm tendons straining. She saw her mother faltering. "Keep your eye on Father's back, Mother." Benjamin clung to her skirt in his attempt not to lose his family or be tromped.

Andrias stepped back, "Here, Lusanna, I can carry one of your bundles in addition to my own. We must follow the orders.

At these words, *follow orders,* Lusanna realized that, yes indeed, she was a passenger, a sojourner, headed for a strange land, subject to the orders and commands of those in charge of their destiny.

She looked to the side and up on deck above her where stevadores were tossing baggage, trunks, chests. *Will Mother's chest and the one Father built be stored safely, wherever they put baggage in the hold? Who could manage a trunk in this confusion?*

Her mother had worried about it though. "My chest, Lusanna. I lost sight of it in the loading and unloading. I trust...." Her voice faded.

Lusanna realized that this was another situation wherein one relied on faith that the stevadores and ship mates had done their duty.

But those words, *third class.*
The gaping staircase was illuminated by dim gas lights.
Sounds became muffled.
How many steps down to third class? Is it the same as steerage?

Lusanna caught glimpses of well-known acquaintances, church members, brothers and sisters, heading toward the same dark recess. Yes, it helped to see their friendly but sober faces: Berent Jantz and his wife Elske, Carl's parents. She glanced at the familiar faces of Martia and Cornelius Wedel as well as those of Maria and Tobias Ratzlaff. Then the tall, thin man, grinning like he had just given an entire ruble, none other than the schoolmaster Heinrich Schmidt. His mother, Gerda, clutched a brownish bundle, which bumped his side.

She turned her eyes away. *We'll have a berth, won't we? Isn't that the way folks travel on ships like this? Third class was not a humiliation, was it? Almost all of them were in third class.*

She remembered that the captain or someone had announced that there were 710 passengers to be loaded and that 682 were her own Plattduetch people, almost the entire passenger list.

She recalled, also, that their kindly elder Tobias was not on this ship, overseeing the situation, giving calming words of assurance and even his exhortations. *Didn't Father say he was with another group from the Waldheim area, traveling on The Abbotsford and that Elder Tobias intended to go directly to that place called South Dakota?*

Well, she concluded to herself, he will surely visit us soon after we land in Kansas. Probably only a few miles distance between.

When she saw her mother's scarved head lower to begin the steps, the thought hit her like a wadded dishrag thrown into her face. Something she had tried not to think about. *All passengers are ordered to bring a burial shroud.*

Shroud? What a weird ugly-sounding word. Like a tough spider web clinging to one in the cold morning dew.

No, they hadn't talked much about that, had they? The words were too chilling.

Her mother had said, her eyes shifting straight ahead, that if one of them was to die on the journey, to pass on into the blessed arms of the Savior, that in their family, at least, they would simply be born to the watery grave in the Sunday garment, packed in the trunk or chest. It was rumored, though, that the captain's aides, the stevedores, or someone stuffed the corpse into some kind of bag before they placed it upon a flat board and tipped it over the rail.

Ahead, she saw a cluster of people on the dimly lighted landing hesitate. Another steward's voice called out, "Fraulein, just step down. The ladder leads to *third class* below.

"Merciful Heavenly Father," breathed Lusanna. "How will Mother manage that, weary as..."

She didn't have to worry long, the steward with the bushy beard extended a broad hand, nudging a shoulder, steadying an elderly man. "Only about a dozen steps. You'll find your numbers for your lodging space at the bottom of the ladder."

Numbers for lodging? Lodging space? No berth? Lusanna realized that she should have known it. "Poor people have poor ways," her aunt Heidi used to say.

Back in the village Lusanna hadn't thought of her family as poor. *Hadn't they always had plenty to eat?* They were simple people with simple needs and ways. She knew that they were not as prosperous as those South Russian Mennonites who had trained teachers in their schools where mathematics, languages and music were taught. They had houses of brick and shiny floors. Even their teachers had training in their own special schools. She had heard about the fabulous farm machinery, some invented by their own talented members. They had grown rich with abundant crops, that everlasting wheat..

No, those people would not be traveling by third class. Well, maybe too, some of those folks giggled at their kind,

over at Antanofka near Ostrog. Snickered at them and their Polish Plattdeutsch tongue.
Someone shouted out a question to the steward. "How many people are carried on this ship?"

Lusanna turned to see that it had been Herr Heinrich Schmidt who had been bold enough to shout out the question.

"The ship is designed to carry about nine hundred people, sir," replied the steward. "Eight hundred in third class, and 20 in first class. The rest is for staff, officers and shipmates."

Hearing that, Lusanna didn't feel so tacky and peasant-like. *No. The ship was built for their kind. Definitely for their kind.*

If it only wasn't so dark in here with these flickering gas lights.

Up ahead she saw her father raise an arm among the shifting hordes. He beckoned. "Catherine, Lusanna, Benjamin, this way. Our names are on the little sign stuck to the wall of the ship here by this porthole."

Thank goodness, we'll soon have beds, berths are they called. Lusanna strained her eyes to glance through the bodies and the gloom. A sour smell hit her nose. All she could see was a tacky wooden bunk shoved against the ship's wall.

Third class? Why, third class was just plain old steerage, after all.

8

WHAT IS THIS MEAT?

"What is this gray film coating everything? And that wooden bunk thing? A bed? Five of us on that..." Catherine grabbed Joseph's arm to steady herself from the roll of the vessel. "Joseph, can't you do something about this? Surely we aren't supposed to sleep on boards covered with coal dust."

Then she saw the two mattresses, one in the upper frame, one below. Nothing but thin straw-filled pads.

"I guess this is it. They're all the same. Everywhere." Joseph's hoarse voice faltered.

"Mama, we can't all crowd into this space, can we? It's so grimy and dirty."

Thuds, scrapings, querulous voices rose up into the heavy air. Somewhere a child began to cry. Little Benjamin stood, clinging to Andrias's hand. His eyes strained to take it all in. People poured in, filling the spaces, their lungs inhaling the stale air.

A woman's voice called out, "Why, husband, there's no way the seven of us can crowd into this little pen they've allowed us."

That was it. The little pen with its two-tiered bunk of wooden planks. Two people above, two below, and the rest of the family spread on the floor.

"Why this space is no more than ten-by-eight feet. And that, er, *bed* takes up most of the space." Joseph bent over to see if he could scoot some of Catherine's boxes and bundles to the side, making some room, at least, for them to sit down.

"Father," said Andrias, "why, it's hard to see *anything* down here. And the smell..."

But it was Lusanna's voice that gave Catherine caution. "Mama, Mama, *look* who shares the space just opposite us."

Catherine turned her face away from their meager earthly possessions and stared at a heavy woman's broad bottom, bent over as she was, shoving bundles under their berth.

Who was the tall, hunched man sitting on the pad of straw on the wooden planks?

Then Catherine saw that it was none other than the schoolmaster Heinrich himself, and his widowed mother. She had not time to turn, before Heinrich's face lit up, even in the gloom.

"Why, Frau Becker, could you imagine our good fortune to be neighbors as we experience the passage together?" He beamed.

Catherine didn't know how to respond. Her mind whirled. *Experience the passage together? Me with a teen-aged daughter, no privacy, no divider between the berths? Even myself, should I decide to strip off one of the dresses I'm wearing, or lower a petticoat? Our personal business? It's true. We'll not change our clothes until the entire journey's ended.*

She saw that Lusanna was staring at her with a wide-opened mouth. She knew the Christian thing to do was to acknowledge his greeting.

"Yes, uh, yes, why, Frau Gerda, and Herr Heinrich, we'll be neighbors crowded together like this, won't we?" *What else could she say?*

Catherine heard loud scraping and the clanging of heavy iron.

"It's the engine room ahead, Catherine. Yes, the steward told me that it takes about 180 men to shovel the coal into the mouth of the great furnaces which heat the boilers."

"Boilers? Joseph, don't those things blow up? Why, I've heard..."

She felt the strong hand of her husband creep around her waist. "No, Catherine, you mustn't worry. Not at all. This ship is not more than two years old. It's a modern ship. The latest. We'll be in Philadelphia in no time at all. No time at all."

Catherine turned to look him in the face. She realized that he was trying hard to reassure her. She'd have to be patient. She would discipline herself to be a good model for Lusanna, Benjamin, and Andrias in this new situation, fraught with change and unknowing. Perhaps they would only sleep down here, frolic and stroll on the decks above in the morning. *Yes, the ocean will be beautiful in the sunlight, won't it?*

The rumble of voices around them mingled with the clangs sounding from the engine room. Protests, coughs, voices echoed as housewives, with whatever bits of cloth they could find, brushed away coal dust. A child cried, "Mama, I'm hungry. When do we have supper?"

***

Most of them did, however, trudge up for "supper." Lusanna, at least, was relieved that her father had found out that they would have three meals a day in the mess hall on the deck above. She wished that she had a cloth so that she could wash her face with a bit of cool water, but they had been instructed that they would have a bucket of water delivered for a quick scrub-up in the morning. A bucket, also, for those *other* functions. She shuddered, thinking about it. Mother would have to hold up a blanket, *something*.

Surprising how silent they were, these pilgrims who still had tendrils reaching back to Antanofka. They, she thought, all had handled their sorrow as Christians should, not in self pity or burdening others with their pain and fears.

They clustered around the long tables and sat on the bent-wood chairs. There must have been about 200 at their special shift. The servers, young men who spoke differing languages, their aprons greasy, plunked down the ironstone plates before them, tin cups of water at the side.

Preacher Eck stood to offer the prayer of thanks for her group. His reverent voice with its slight wobble, comforted her.

At his "amen," there was the rustle and clink as tin forks were lifted, the aproned boys forked chunks of meat, plopping them onto the plates.

A bowl of boiled potatoes dropped onto the table. Silas Koehn picked it up, passing it to the left with his big, woodsman's hand. She looked at the far end of the table to see Heinrich and Gerda, Heinrich's fist clutching a fork. She looked down, quickly.

Manners. Mother said that we should remember our manners.

Lusanna awaited her turn. She dipped only a small portion of potatoes, picked up her fork to test the strange-looking meat that lay on her plate, red-brownish in color. Still, she was thankful. When had she had a portion so large? *Especially beef?*

Most of them were used to broth, soups, vegetables, grains. Meat or any kind of beef was only for weddings and special occasions. Lusanna's mouth watered as she caught the smell of the browned meat.

But this was a *special occasion*, if ever there was one, wasn't it? Being a sojourner to a strange new land? Crowded into a dark hole a little larger than a pantry? *But didn't Aunt Elise always say that it is always darkest just before sunrise? Yes. Sunrise in America awaited them. Sunrise on the Kansas plains.*

She forked the portion of meat into her mouth and began to grind with her teeth. *Surprisingly tasty.* Next she forked a slice of potato, dipping it into some of the broth surrounding the meat.

Why, this is right tasty. Father hadn't said anything to us about good meals like this. She dug for another portion and for the first time, realized that she had relaxed, and that her apprehensions had fallen aside.

Three good meals a day! Think of it.

Folks pushed back their chairs, scraping the floor as they adjusted themselves, getting ready for brother Eck to lead the evening worship service.

It was just then that Lusanna caught Helena Jantz's startling words echoing from across the room.

"Why, Frau Sarah, did you hear the steward say that was *horse meat* we just ate for our supper?

She saw Elske Jantz and Maria Wedel flash their mothers one of *those looks* with raised eyebrows. She heard someone gasp.

Brother Eck's words drew their minds away from their focus upon strange announcements and foreign news, the surprising and unfamiliar. After all, how many people actually do get to make an ocean voyage?

To Lusanna, in spite of the announcement about the supper, the excitement about the ever-new and unexplored, the shock and the wonder, reigned uppermost in her thoughts.

She glanced at schoolmate Agnes staring at preacher Eck, her tongue giving her lower lip one more lick. She folded her arms across her bosom, settling in for the food for her spirit.

Lusanna opened her spirit, too. No, this room where she would sing and hear the brother's message was not the picturesque Antanofka Church left far, far behind. *For Christians, any space, any room, shade under any tree or grove, could become a holy place. couldn't it?*

Brother Eck called on Benjamin Voth to lead a hymn from memory. He struck his tuning fork and hummed. They began to sing in earnest. Rich, full-bodied singing.

She looked around her and realized that it was, indeed, true worship, such singing together. All around Lusanna, faces reflected the awareness that they were suspended in a fragile world between land and sea, past and future, - headed for the great unknown.

Holy God, we praise Thy name,

Lord of all, we bow before Thee;
All on earth Thy scepter claim,
All in heav'n above adore Thee.
Infinite Thy vast domain,
Everlasting is Thy reign.

Lusanna took Benjamin's hand as she descended the stairs. Then each of them turned to back down the ladder to the steerage floor below, where the faint gas lights flickered. Here in the must and dust among fellow believers, men, women, grandparents, babes, teenagers and children, they searched for their stalls where they now faced the great conundrum of just where and how they would lay down their weary heads.

9

IN THE BELLY OF THE WHALE

Here it was, ten o'clock on a sunny morning, and already they were at sea. Fifteen or twenty Antanofka young folk clustered on the front deck, braving the December air nearing the English Channel. The rounded white officers' quarters and captain's quarters towered behind them. A salt breeze stung their faces. Their laughter caught in the wind and bounced back. Their eyes opened wider as the worries about where to store their baggage and find corners in which to rest their weary bodies.

Young-folk laughter, merry, hip-slapping laughter encircled them as they staggered in their efforts to gain sea legs. Snickers and giggles hid other worries and apprehensions about what might yet come.

"Whoeee," Andrias's voice drifted in the wind. "Would you believe this giant of a thing actually wallowed out of the port?"

"We were pushed. Shoved, Andrias, by tiny tug boats," yellow-headed Carl Jantz replied.

Lusanna could hear and feel rumble and vibrations from the coal-powered engines powering the ship. She looked up at the tall masts, wondering when they would be out in the high seas so the captain could command the crew to unfurl the sails.

Anna Jantz staggered, her brown-clothed shoulder nudging Lusanna's. Lusanna shifted her feet quickly. Her body leaned and tilted until she bumped into tall, curly headed Jake Unruh, his cloth cap tipped back.

"So sorry, Jake." Her cheeks flushed.

"Captain says we have a fine day for sailing, fine day." Jake looked skyward in the bright, hazy sky, sea gulls squeaked and dove, circling as the skyline of Antwerp faded behind them.

Lusanna glanced around, scanning the faces of her friends and Andrias's friends clustered about her. People of faith, young faith - maybe in some ways untested faith, she thought to herself. Surveying their faces, she couldn't help but recognize that they all had various ways of hiding their fears.

What better place to put faith into action than when one leaves one's homeland behind, journeying like this towards new horizons?

Of course they had trust that they were headed for better times, better places. Less of government sending out new proclamations, new taxes. No military noose encircling Andrias's, Jake's, and Carl's necks. No more high land fees burdening their parents.

Agnes Unruh, catching Lusanna's eye, hollered, "Lusanna, you roll out of your bunk last night?" She giggled.

"No, Agnes, I didn't. As a matter of fact, Benjamin, who slept in the wonderful bed beside me, was exhausted. Both he and I snored away." Lusanna guessed that the others, too, had been forced to make awkward and strange "sleeping arrangements."

In their own case, their mother and father slept on the bunk a foot off the floor, she and little brother Benjamin high up on the upper bunk. And *bunk* it had been, at least at first until Benjamin quit his turning and the sand man carried him away.

"That left me plastered on the floor," Andrias chimed in, grinning. "Stretched out on a blanket Mother dug out of her chest."

"Sorta like in our stall," Carl Jantz added. "Brother David and I picked out the choice spot, too, on the floor. Good thing we were still in port."

Lusanna was aware that she was staring at Carl, his cap tipped back rakishly. *The crocheted bookmark he gave me. I hope it isn't lost.*

"But you got your rest," Jake chimed in. He lifted a boot to place it upon a brace on the rail.

"Not at all, Carl. Not at all. How could we sleep? Our village schoolmaster kept us awake most of the night." He glanced over, eyes surveying Lusanna.

"How's that?" voices inquired.

"Why, you know Heinrich, I mean Herr Heinrich and his loud voice? Well, his daytime voice only prepares him for his night time snoring."

Their howls rose in the air to join the cries of the sea gulls circling their heads.

Then Aga Foth, who had broken her engagement to Heinrich Schmidt, months ago, mentioned the Wedels. In particular, Jacob and his sister, Elise.

A hush spread over the crowd. Water lapped and swished at the prow of the ship. A bit of a sail, loose from its mast, flapped in the wind.

Lusanna believed she knew what they all were thinking. Same as she.

Where were these dear friends? Jacob with his dark archangel eyes? Elise, laughing, good-hearted Elise, who would give away her last kopeck? And, the thirty-five or forty others who stayed behind in Antanofka.

Grandmothers with white, silky hair; grandfathers, leaning as they walked with their hand-made willow canes, knowing they had neither resources nor the strength to emigrate.

Did they grieve, too? Were their hearts breaking that the community that had been together for so many years was now shattered? Or did they understand that, like Abraham of old, in this world, one hears calls. People step forth, away from land familiar to one's feet because of conscience. Conscience where the words of the blessed Jesus echo: "Peter, put away your sword."

Tobias Ratzlaff was the first to speak. "It was a real struggle for Jacob. I saw him weeping on the last day of school. At his age, how could he come with us without his parents, or their approval?"

"Elise, too," Tobias's sister," Eva added. "Elise's eyes were red and swollen the entire last week when we all had our sales."

"But the Crown prince promises good things ahead for those in Russia. Good things. Why, I don't believe it will be long before even the peasants gain their freedom, have land of their own. There were many good things about our homeland," added Ratzlaff.

"I grieve for them," Eva said. "I wish their parents had decided to sell and join us. How can they live there now? All those Polish Bohemians moving in. All those people who settled into our homes for practically nothing?"

Andrias spoke up. "We mustn't judge them. Sure, the Wedels were prosperous, maybe even more so now. It's our duty to pray for them that they will be able to maintain the faith. Surely there are enough for worship, still."

"You're right," Jake Unruh added. "You're right, Andrias. They can still worship, though they will rattle around in our church building, empty, now as it is. Jesus said, didn't he, 'where two or three are gathered together, there am I in the midst of them.'"

"But," asked Carl, "they can still join us. Some of our other colonies will be coming to America. Soon, very soon." His eyes searched Lusanna's face again.

Lusanna, glancing up at him, knew that Carl was trying to reassure them. She recalled Elder Tobias's words before they signed their certificates to emigrate. "We don't know just when the door will close. We must take advantage of this opportunity now while the Russian government still allows us this concession."

A shroud of heaviness fell over Lusanna as she comprehended her brother's words. And on the others too.

Just when would the Russian borders close forever. Then what?

***

Below in steerage the older women, too, struggled with the challenge of adjusting to the strange new world that ship steerage provided. Catherine Becker couldn't help but think of Jonah and the big fish. *In the belly of a whale, that's where we are. Jonah was disobedient to the Lord. We are trying to be obedient to the Son's blessed commands.*

She then thought of the apostle Paul's words that Joseph had read to them all last night before they lay weary bodies down upon strange beds, if they could even be called that. *"...in perils of waters, in perils of my own countrymen...in perils of the sea...My grace is sufficient for thee: for my strength is made perfect in weakness...*

In spite of her aching back from the night on the thin straw pad and boards, not even thinking of sleeping in one's clothes, she tugged at the blanket on the bunk, folding in the corner, smoothing it with her red chapped hand. She tried not to stumble against the chest or entangle a foot in a bundle.

To her side Benjamin, still filled with amazement at all the newness about him, rolled a string ball back and forth to a boy his age, Wilhelm Jantz. They laughed at the way the ball zigzagged almost out of their control.

Catherine was relieved that at least her youngest was focused for awhile with his play, but her mind kept pitching up the questions. *How many days for this crossing? Elder Tobias said that it would be in no time at all, fifteen or sixteen days to Philadelphia. Wasn't that the city of brotherly love? Would the Quakers and Mennonites be on the wharves to welcome them? What do emigrants do when they have empty purses and no land under their feet to claim as their own?*

Her reverie was interrupted by a voice. "Do you think we will be able to endure over two weeks stuffed in this hold, Catherine?"

Anna Jantz, putting the lid back on a chamber pot she had just emptied, had asked the question.

Catherine didn't need to answer as Gerda Schmidt in the space opposite theirs chimed in. "Endure? Why, this is nothing. Heinrich says it will make wonderful material for a book he will be writing when we get to America." Gerda smoothed her grayish skirt, brushing away wisps of straw, and smiled broadly at Catherine and Anna.

Now this, thought Catherine, looking at the school-teacher, hunched on the top bunk with his back against the wall, pencil and notebook in hand. *Spare us from his nosy spying and notetaking.*

But then she realized she needed to be charitable. They were all exposed, one to another. Folks turning their backs, eyes lowering as, last evening, it was necessary for her husband and Lusanna to hold a blanket over that crowded corner so that she could hunch over the chamber pot to relieve herself.

Over six hundred down here? Lids clanging, groans, snickers and shuffling feet. Muffled voices. Babies squalling while their mothers made attempts to change their diapers. Then what? What to do with the soiled diapers, or the clothing on their very bodies that hourly bore the soil and wear of the trip?

Catherine looked northward across the length of the hold called steerage. Through the gloom and haze, amidst the odors of bodily sweats, coal smoke, soiled bedding and clothing, folks tried not to stagger into each other as the ship began to pitch in the ever larger waves of the high seas.

When would Lusanna come back down from her stroll on the deck with the other young folks? When would Joseph return from the group of worried-faced men who had clustered in the dining room to discuss the doors that might open to folks in their predicament. Then how to pass the time?

Faith. Yes, faith was required for this hour, for this journey.

Catherine looked down as Benjamin, smiling in eagerness, spoke. "Mama, don't you have a cookie for Wilhelm and me?"

10

GROANS AND WALLOWING

The sea had been balmy almost the entire day as *The S. S. Vaderland* ploughed eastward through the cold Atlantic Ocean. Lusanna, along with her friends, took pride that now they had gained sea legs. *Why, actually there was nothing to it. This little rocking? This little tilting from a swell?* When the December wind permitted, those who braved a walk on deck rejoiced over the friendly dolphins breaking the surface, ushering them onward to their goal. *Sunshine, new land, no more oppression, freedom to follow the commands of the blessed Jesus.*

Lusanna's worries had decreased, seeing how her mother had adjusted to the cramped quarters and noise, in spite of the soot and bad air. She took delight in the fact that Benjamin found new ways to amuse himself. He and little Wilhelm toured the steerage area, visiting with the scores of families holed up in their "bunk berths," with miserly spaces between.

She smiled as she thought of the coal stokers who walked through the steerage on their way upward to the deck, how they took pleasure in both of the little boys, giving each of them a shiny penny.

She thought of how little brother Benjamin, gaining sea legs almost automatically, stepped along in his wide pants to ask his mother, "are those men the *black men* from Africa, Mother?"

"No, son. No. They are from Belgium, not all that far from where we lived. No, they have white skins like the rest of us."

Lusanna tried hard to wash her face in the small enameled pan with cold water and a small cloth. However, she couldn't help but ponder: *Does my face look like the faces of the coal stokers?*

She concluded also, that the food continued to be agreeable. *Turtle soup today, the captain had announced.*

Lusanna had never tasted turtle soup, but she, along with Agnes Unruh, agreed that it would be one more special event to write about in their diaries, once they reached flat land, a steady place, positioning themselves at a table in an actual room. A place where they could look out a window and see the trees blowing in the wind, fluffy clouds drifting across fields of ripening wheat. *Certainly Father said that in Kansas, all of them would be wheat farmers for sure.*

She knew, though, that her father, being a woodsman along with many others in Antanofka, would be faced with scores of new challenges. *Where would he get money for horses? Oxen? Plows, harrows? Would there be a town where he could sell the grain? What would be its name?*

She had no doubts either about her father's religious faith. He was of the quiet type, one who did not talk about sensitive aspects of his inner life to others. He was among those who walked humbly, circumspectly.

She knew that he would be among those, who upon being asked "Are you a Christian?" would reply in modesty, "Why, for the answer to that question, I guess you'll have to ask my neighbors."

No, Father was not at all like the pharisee who stood on the street corner beating his chest and loudly proclaiming his prayers. And if worry tempted to crease his brow, he gave no notice. His kindly eyes surveyed each of them at evening Bible reading and prayer time. Of course she knew he struggled with the same anxieties facing them all, being almost penniless, facing a strange American seaport, and the responsibility of leading his family westward. She admired him for his efforts to stay calm in face of such obstacles, and to encourage the others.

She smiled as awareness of her love for her parents surfaced. Right now, she concluded, her hope and faith were secure enough. She trusted that *all these things and events* would fall in place at their proper times. "Seek ye first the kingdom of God and all these things shall be added unto you," the Savior had said.

The Antanofka folks crowded into the gloomy dining hall at lunchtime, hunger gnawing their stomachs. Though the ship's prow seemed to rise a bit more than usual, the green turtle soup only slopped a little in the ironstone bowls.

Lusanna sipped from the spoon, holding back her giggles as she watched Agnes Unruh across from her. Agnes, like her, had worked her head scarf forward a bit more than usual to hide hair, which she hadn't combed for several days. How could she? No mirror. No time. Someone always watching. The ever-present eye of Heinrich Schmidt, with his tablet and pencil.

She wiped the thought out of her mind of Heinrich encouraging her to write down her experiences on the trip, then letting him survey them with his own eyes. "It would be a fine lesson in composition, Lusanna, telling the story of our voyage together."

It had been his last two words, *voyage together*, that had caused her to close her mouth, lift her head to see if Mother needed any help at that moment. *Voyage together?*

Though she hadn't even told Agnes, it was that smile on blond Carl Jantz's face that caused her to turn her head for a second look. And, too, it was so easy to talk with Carl Jantz, once his sister Anna stopped her endless gripes about the long trip. But, in this crowd, she discovered it was almost impossible to be alone with anyone.

Lusanna glanced out the windows eastward, noting how dark the sky had become. *Was that thunder above the engine rumbles?*

Suddenly, she felt the ship shift to the right. A quick shift. Next, an unsteadying heave that caused some of her soup to slop out on the table.

'Why, Lusanna, I think this turtle soup is simply del...."

But Agnes Unruh didn't get to finish her sentence. Lusanna, too, and six or seven of the folks around them, dropped their spoons, raising hands to their mouths. She glanced back at Agnes and saw that her face was a deathly pallor.

What is wrong?

Before Lusanna could search for an answer it seemed as if the vessel dropped from underneath them, sending their stomachs soaring to their throats.

Cries rose up, chairs overturned. Soup tureens careened across broad and tilting tables.

"Oh, Lusanna, Oh, I have to get to my berth, oh...."

Before Agnes could finish the sentence, there was a gurgling sound as a streak of the green soup gushed out of her agonized, open mouth.

Seasick? Seasickness? Is this what it is, why...?

Lusanna grabbed Agnes's shoulder as she bumped into the sharp edge of a table, knowing that she had given herself a dreadful bruise. "Agnes, hold on. The ship is rocking. We've hit a storm. I'll help you below."

Pandemonium. Wails. Pallor on cheeks even paler than red-headed Agnes Unruh's.

"I told you take a walk on the deck, Cletus," a female voice called.

Down the staircase, now facing the ladder, Agnes said, "I'm dying., Lusanna. Just let me pitch through the hole. I have no strength to..." Another torrent of vomit gushed from the gap in her face.

"Get out of the way, Lusanna, Agnes," yelled curly-headed Carl. "If you don't get out of the way, I'm going to...."

He didn't get to finish, either.

"My God, my God," prayed Lusanna, "help me get this stricken girl to her pallet below." She realized the back of her dress was saturated with Carl's vomit.

"You shouldn't have partaken of that draught of schnapps last night, Ezra," called Elizabeth Dirks, holding up her prostrate husband.

Lusanna, hearing the pops, wrenching, and creaks coming from decks above, the rattle, squeaks and screeches of the metal beams and braces that held the ship together below, dragged Agnes toward her bunk bed.

Where to put her?

All about them bundles shoved into any available space above came crashing down. Boxes bounced, broke open and spilled their contents across the floor. Chamber pots rolled.

Folks raced to find pallets and places where they could quickly flop upon a straw mattress or a spot on the grimy floor. *Who could stand with the ship heaving as it did in what must now be twenty-foot waves? Who had time to focus upon an Atlantic gale with the violent agony within their stomachs?*

Lusanna lost her footing, her bottom hitting the grease slick that drained from the engine room.

Everywhere folks were crawling miserably onto straw pallets, clutching for their beds. Eyes in their pallid, off-colored faces, searched for their family members. Cries and yells echoed in the frenzied din as bundles, boxes, and stacked bedding tumbled and tangled. Everything pitched upward with the increasing rotary motion of the wallowing ship.

Lusanna clung to her space in the upper bunk. *Where was little Benjamin?* Then she saw him tottering toward their space. She reached an unsteady arm downward to grab him before he hit his head on some hard post or iron partition.

Staggering, falling, getting up again, her father managed to creep to their stall, squashing a box with his boot. She watched him drag Catherine into the lower bunk. "Hold on, Catherine, hold on."

Then Lusanna saw something which she never dreamed in this life to see, her father turning green, groaning and vomiting over the back of her mother.

She realized that her bed with Benjamin was heaven only for a moment. Then little Benjamin leaned over and added the contents of his stomach upon the slimy, trash-strewn steerage floor.

She heard a voice; *was it Anna Jantz?* "Carl, I told you to take a walk upon the deck. If you had listened to me, you wouldn't be gagging now." Her voice was lost in groans and the sounds of the ship's wrenchings.

A man's voice rose up in the din. *Was it preacher Eck, who had so far been unusually silent on the trip?* "Brethren, sisters, listen to me, it's all in your imaginations."

No one seemed to respond to the preacher. If they had a flash of rejection of his words or of anger, Lusanna didn't hear it with the pressure and din in her ears.

Then her own stomach shoved up like a glove turned inside out, the fingers extended to push out one more tiny particle. She gagged and heaved, head hanging with her slobbers dangling over the edge of the bunk. When her stomach was thoroughly emptied, the hand behind her stomach kept turning it inside out. Now, nothing but gall, strange secretions, then just dry heaves.

After a half-hour, the groans were too weak to be heard above the creaking of the ship's braces and the everlasting rattling of the rudder chains overhead.

Outside in the violent storm, the great, dark iron ship crawled, trembling down a long briny slope until it met another rolling, smothering crest that seemed to overwhelm the struggling ship.

For two-and-a-half days the Antanofka folks, along with the other few passengers and crew, endured the storm's rolling, worming, and tossing. Almost three days of unending sensations of dissolution, all the hours of groans and wallowing.

Even Lusanna found herself nursing an almost unend-ing regret that the next moment was not her last.

Only brother Andrias in their family was spared the violence done to their stomachs. *How did he do it? All that tossing and wallowing?*

He had found a piece of rope and had tied himself to the frame off the bunk bed, but he was not spared the sour stink, the smear of vileness that covered the floor, people's bosoms and chests, heads and chins.

The floor? However would the floor be cleaned?

As the *S. S. Vaderland* righted itself in the calmer seas and ploughed on, the shipmates and cleaning crew descended. Passengers, who still had modest muscle support left in their legs, hunched themselves and climbed the ladder, then the steps that led to the deck above, gasping the fresh air into their lungs.

Below, the ship's third class shipmates began the messy, unwelcome task of scraping the floors. They shoved barrels ahead of them, trying not to inhale as they held on to the handles of floor scrapers, raking up the muck, shoveling it into the barrels. *And they tell us that on a journey like this they scrape the steerage floor at least twice.*

Lusanna, one of the last to ascend the ladder, wished that they weren't Mennonite people: otherwise, she would surely dig out a perfume bottle like the worldly ladies do and douse herself thoroughly.

Will the revolting smell endure until I reach Kansas?

11

FOR THOSE IN PERIL ON THE SEA

Joseph Becker leaned over the deck rail alongside Andrias, both of them grateful for the southeasterly wind caressing their faces, invigorating them. He was thankful, too, that the dancing, light-touched waves that rose and fell were only happy, normal waves, waves that the dolphins took delight in. He stared at the ever-lapping sea, pondering: *How obedient to the hand of God, eternally folding each upon another. Trust and obey. Trust and obey.* But now there was a hitch in the way the ship meandered on through the water. In the storm it had lost one of the blades of the giant iron propeller that thrust the vessel through the waves, causing it to wallow more to the right, surely a matter greatly distracting to the captain.

Joseph didn't want to repeat the words the deck crew had used in mentioning the sorry situation and how it slowed their journey to Philadelphia harbor, the women and the seashore taverns awaiting them.

However, all of the Antanofka folk were saddened that the oldest among them, Madgdalena Foth, a woman in her seventies from the southern edge of their village, on her straw pallet, had passed on to her eternal home just as the ferocious seas had calmed.

Joseph swallowed the lump in his throat, thinking about the recent burial. Old Magdalena's stiff body (was it in a shroud she'd prepared?) was placed upon a board as pallbearers from their own congregation, three on each side,

69

assumed the duty of easing the burden to the rail with quite, solemn steps.

All eyes were focused upon the bearers lifting the plank to such an angle that Sister Foth's cold body went sliding into the dark, swirling waters.

There had been weeping and gasps, but Joseph believed that the solemn occasion had reminded them each of their own mortality, that one should always be ready when the Savior calls.

Preacher Eck, permitted by the captain himself, held the short service as they clustered on deck in their gray, brown, and black clothing, the women's scarves whipping behind them in the December breeze.

"That was the saddest song I ever heard," Andrias said, looking into his father's dark brown eyes.

"You mean, "Eternal Father?" "Yes, son, it is a sad song, but it is also a song of faith. Joseph realized that the service and the burial had been a shock to the young folk. He had watched them, clustered together as if seeking added security and safety by their closeness to each other.

"Father, I think I'd like to sing that hymn more often. It's not just for funerals, is it?"

"No. Perhaps we can sing it more often. It's a fine song of faith: 'Eternal Father, strong to save, Whose arm hath bound the restless wave...'

"Well," added Andrias, a faint smile tracing his lips, "After our ordeal, most of you seasick, I'm glad that the those restless waves were finally bound." He grinned.

Joseph noticed, though, that Andrias's face suddenly sobered as he stared pensively into the green-gray sea. He could not stop his thoughts:

Oh, hear us when we cry to thee,
For those in peril on the sea.

Joseph turned to look as Carl Jantz, cap thrust back, blond hair poking out in front, stepped up aside Andrias. The teenagers visited together, their comments a mixture of discussing old times in Antanofka, mingling with the thrust of the new that ever invaded their young lives. The boys soon moseyed back toward the stern of the ship where the stricken propeller growled, thrusting them forward. The boat's sidewise lurching reminded Joseph of a dog limping down the dusty street of Antanofka, hind quarters shifting to the left.

Helena Kohn's husband, David, his coat collar turned up against the December wind, joined him at the rail where Andrias had stood.

Joseph was glad for his presence - a little visit to help pass the days. *They had fallen behind, hadn't they? Pennsylvania still a long, long, way ahead. Late December. Why, back home, folks began preparations for Christmas celebrations, didn't they? The first, second, and third feast days. Celebrating the birth of Christ on the first and second day, and on the third day, the births of John and Stephen, the first martyr.*

Joseph felt his mouth fill with saliva. "Surely would be a restful thing to be settled for the feast days, David, but I know it won't be possible."

David Kohn, taller than Joseph, lifted a chapped hand and adjusted his coat collar. "You're right, Joseph. And our women, too. Helena's been sorrowing over it, not being able to have us all around the table. Not being able to make the wheat verenika, the pluma moos, and borscht for the table. Slice the smoked ham." David sighed.

Joseph was aware that sighing was an appropriate behavior. He sighed, too. Often, in fact. Sighed when Catherine or Lusanna weren't looking as his mind caught on just how a person like himself would pay back the loan for the journey.

What had been his share? Nine hundred dollars? And they had written out pledges for each other, he pledging to pay David Kohn's debt, if an unforeseen tragedy took place. David pledging to pay back his, should he....

Joseph almost spoke the next thought aloud: *Let us have no more funerals.*

However, who is in charge of thoughts? Who can keep them from bursting from outside, from inside - thrusting themselves at one's innermost core, digging and excoriating, burning, healing.

It had happened. *Another funeral*

It had been two nights after Frau Magdalena's funeral and the ship had ceased its pitching. It seemed as if everybody waited, afraid to move, lift a head, extend a leg and foot to see if there was any floor beneath that would sustain the weight of a body.

They crawled out like goblins emerging from a hole in the earth. Staggering, rubbing stubbly faces, they stared, trying to focus their eyes.

Babes began to cry. A woman's voice rose across the growing din: "Eli, oh, Eli, the baby, the baby." Then, a startling, chilling wail.

In the haze of the smoke and coal dust from the engine room, Joseph squinted his eyes and saw that it was Eve Nachtigal, clutching a small form to her breast. "The child isn't breathing. Eli, the baby died in the night."

His own wife, Catherine, had tightened her clothes around her and found foot purchase between the boxes and bundles to slip to the stricken woman's side.

"Catherine," screamed Eva. "little Jonathan died in the night." She buried the still little form in her bosom.

Another funeral. Another shroud and board, tiny as it had been. Joseph swallowed as the memory flooded his mind. The silence of that burial. Captain had sought out Preacher Eck to say the words, to pray the prayers at this service. But it had been the songs, the hymns at both Frau Magdalena's and the baby's service that still found their way through Joseph's soul. *Eternal Father, strong to save…*

And as the tiny form had dropped into the dark endless ocean, they were led in song: "The Mag auch die Liebe winen."

Though love may weep with breaking heart,
There comes, O Christ, a day of thine!

There is a Morning Star must shine,
And all these shadows shall depart.

Joseph felt a touch at the sleeve of his coat. There stood Catherine, his tall Catherine. She took his hand in hers, rubbing it to bring warmth to the surface. He looked into her face, lined with the same weariness that lined his own. *She is beautiful, my Catherine.*

He took her by the hand as a bell rang, announcing that the cooks now allowed steerage travelers to enter the mess hall. "Let's go, my love," he whispered, not even bothering to look over his shoulder to see if anyone overheard.

"Why, of course, Joseph. What if we find *verenika* on our plates today?

"That would be a pleasant surprise, indeed, Catherine, but not as pleasant as your company."

"Well, then," added Catherine, faint smile at her chapped lips, "may I ask you to come on in for *dinner?*"

12

ONE BLOOMING CONFUSION

Andrias pondered the words from Isaiah his father had read last night before their bedtime prayers. *I have called you by name, your are mine. When you walk through the waters, I will be with you: and through the rivers, they shall not overwhelm you.*

He recognized that for the last two weeks they had without doubt been "through the waters." A cloud like the heavy gray ones that swept the tops of the waves, descended over spirit. A part of him recognized his uprootedness. He was aware that Lusanna, too, grieved over leaving her home and Jacob and Elise behind. *How could it be that Father believes that God knows us so well that it is written "I have called you by name...you are mine"?*

Are my thoughts sinful? How come I don't feel the hand of God as this stupendous ship meanders and wallows to a land that will be strange to me?

Right now I don't even know the significance of my own name, my own person and where I am going.

In spite of the wet coldness of the wind, he clustered along with Carl Jantz and Jake Unruh, facing away from the salty spray. They had decided to endure the dampness and cold at the rail in order to escape the hordes of people, hanging blankets, crying babies, snores, vomiting of the sick, and the foul air below.

Andrias was disappointed, too, by the snail-like progress of *The Vaderland,* losing a propeller blade in high waves of the English Channel and now, yesterday, the

Captain announcing the sad misfortune. "We have lost
another propeller blade in the last squall."

"I thought this was a modern ship, one of the best,"
Carl said, looking up at his friends. "Look how we limp
along, now. How can the pilot steer the ship?"

"Well, after fourteen days of this wallowing and what
I've seen on my inspections, I've concluded that this is a
hastily built boat," Jake added. "We should have been in that
Philadelphia port by now."

"You're right," Andrias said. "I agree. This is a utility
ship designed to crowd people together. Of course, this isn't
a slave ship, but you can see it was thrown together just for
human cargo - almost a thousand of us stuffed into what is
nothing but a dark hold. *Twenty* first class? Who would want
to travel first class on this bloated monstrosity? What a
laugh."

"Our folks are weary enough, without this last calamity.
Can you imagine, losing *two* of three propeller blades? And,"
Carl added, "we have such stormy seas that the Captain
refuses to use the sails. We'd travel much faster with the
sails." Carl hunched his shoulders, shivering in a sudden icy
blast.

Jake turned to Carl. "I worry about the weather when
we finally get to Kansas. After all, it is winter time. Look at
what we've been told. I read some of those railroad
pamphlets describing Kansas land, how fertile it is, how
warm the weather, the rain, and the pictures..."

Andrias interrupted Jake. "Yeah, the pictures of farmers
wearing broad smiles and wide-brimmed straw hats, and
those sentences about the *Great Arkansas Valley*, the rivers
and such stuff. My parents brought that up, too, Jake. Won't
it be bitter winter when we actually arrive there? Then
what?" He sighed, his red, chapped hands struggling to draw
his jacket collar closer to his neck. *Am I getting a sore
throat?*

"Well, nobody wants to talk about that *other situation*,"
added Carl, 'but folks can only stay in the *same clothes* so
long, *without, without...*" his voice faltered.

"Yeah, I was going to bring it up," Andrias said. "Everybody scratching under their arms. Frauleins jerking off their head scarves and searching for a fine tooth comb. Nobody wants to say the word, *lice.*"

"I saw Wilhelm Becker tear off his outer shirt down at the south end of the steerage. I tried not to pay too much attention, but look at all we've gotten used to, losing our privacy like this?" Carl shuffled his scarred boots. "I know. I know what it is. I saw Eli Schmidt. He didn't think I saw him. He found a porthole and pitched his louse-ridden undershirt right out the porthole. Now he has only his one shirt and his thin coat to protect him from the cold."

Neither Andrias, nor his friends chuckled. No time for chuckling, making fun, dirty and chilled as they were. Minds fogged with unanswered questions, which layered hourly in their brains. *When? Why? How? What then? When will we be able to have a bath?*

Another thing, Elder Tobias Unruh, leaving with another group on a ship called The Abbotsford. How will our ministers know how to function without his guidance? It seems like everything is falling apart. Don't we need the steady voice of Elder Tobias?

Pity rose up in Andrias's heart as he thought of his mother and how she liked to keep everything immaculate, her cooking pans polished, her own person, hair combed properly, her apron ironed in the mangle. He saw the discomfort in her eyes, and in Lusanna's as their appearances grew more disheveled daily.

Andrias thought of how Lusanna spent extra moments when brother Benjamin lay seasick so often on this journey. How she took on the distasteful tasks of emptying slop jars, vomit pans. How she always searched for fresh water and a clean cloth to wipe his face and hands.

Why, Lusanna would make a good nurse, wouldn't she? Look how she works down there ignoring the bad air. I know she doesn't like to be crowded in with so many others. I remember how she resisted moving up next to Schoolmaster

Heinrich back in Antanofka. In spite of her discomfort, she buries it, leaning in to help others.

Andrias pondered the facts: Lusanna, refusing to sit and complain about the slow trip or to break down in anxiety at being at the mercy of others' eyes every daylight hour, except when she was asleep.

He saw how she leaped over to help Frau Gerda Schmidt when one of her carry-on bundles burst open, spilling out old patched undergarments, a few turnips, a chunk of moldy smoked ham, a bottle of herbal cure. *What else?*

Heinrich, sitting there on his-- Eye like the eye of a troll searching from under his bridge. If only Heinrich wouldn't grin so much.

His own flesh recoiled when he saw Heinrich leap to every opportunity to engage Lusanna in conversation.

"Lusanna, have you started your writing? I've written a dozen pages about our people on this noble journey. Lusanna, if you'd allow me to peruse your sentences, it would give you a forward push, yes, forward push."

I'd like to push Heinrich off his bunk and up the ladder, shove him up the steps to air him out on this deck. Let this December air chill his overheated desire. Why doesn't he associate more with the men of his own age? I feel like telling the Chief Steward to put him to work polishing the brass or scrubbing the deck.

***

Below deck, Lusanna held the tiny red-faced baby, wrapped in a piece of flannel blanket, while Catherine attempted to minister to the needs of Frau Kohn who had, after an agonizing night of labor, at last given birth. Catherine shoved aside the basin of water the Chief Steward had supplied. Fortunately, the Captain had sent the ship's physician, a tired-looking old Romanian, to check on Frau Kohn's labor and progress. She lay on her thin straw mattress, beaded in sweat.

Catherine swayed, maintaining her footing as she headed for the ladder for fresh water to bathe Helena's face.

Lusanna smiled as she gently rocked the baby in her arms, humming a lullaby to the newborn, who had ceased its crying. "We'll soon be in the port at Philadelphia, Helena." *Why had she said that? Well, of course, to encourage the woman. Hadn't their progress been at snail's pace since Andrias told her they had lost the second propeller blade?*

Lusanna had long since ceased pinching her nostrils half shut. *One did have to breathe, didn't she?* She ignored the grimy coal dust on every surface, ignored the greasy, gritty floor, now slick and straw-strewn. *When would those lower class shipmates tackle that scraping job again? Supposed to be at least twice on this journey, wasn't it?*

She ignored her itching scalp.

Frau Helena, exhausted from her ordeal, turned to face Lusanna and reached out for her newborn son. "His name is Hanz, Lusanna. *Hanz*, which means a gift from God. He'll be the new one in our church in Kansas. Maybe he'll become a preacher."

After Lusanna had placed the infant Hanz into Frau Kohn's arms, she followed her mother's encouragement to go up on deck for air and fellowship with some of the young folks. They clustered by the wide, black smokestack, bracing themselves against the roll of the ship and chill of the air.

Standing by Aga Foth, Lusanna brought her friends the news from below, how Helena's ordeal was now over. "She named her newborn Hanz," Lusanna said.

"Well," Anna Jantz replied, adjusting herself to avoid a sudden cold blast. "That sure is better than *Heinrich!*"

In spite of the winter cold and heavy salt air, they laughed together. For Lusanna, and maybe for the others, too, the birth of the baby on this journey had given them hope.

"You mean our schoolmaster in Antanofka?" Anna Jantz asked. "I'd never, *ever* name my son such a name. What does it mean, anyway, *Heinrich?*

"I know what that name means, Anna. My mother's uncle was named *Heinrich*. She always said it means 'he rules at home'." Eva Unruh smiled at Lusanna and Anna, hand raised to brush back a strand of straying hair.

"Well," red-headed Agnes said, "I'll never have a Heirnrich ruling over me!"

"What of the Bible, Agnes? Didn't Paul say that wives should submit themselves to their own husbands?" Anna's eyes peered.

"Well, I'll tell you what, Anna. I'm going to be working on understanding that word *submit*. That's for sure. And," she added in seeming afterthought, "who says I'll be married, anyway?"

Before their laughter could mount and soar, they were startled by the tromp of hard leather boots. Footsteps toward their group, not at all aimed toward the gaggle of young men on the other side of the smokestack.

"Why, my good fortune, indeed." Heinrich Schmidt, who had launched himself from his roost in steerage, leaned against the roll of the ship and sidled beside Lusanna at the edge of the cluster of young women. "We have the good fortune, now, to share our travel experiences. Lusanna," he grinned, "why don't you begin first?"

13

GIVE, FOR WILD CONFUSION, PEACE

The captain says that we will arrive in the new Phila-
delphia port on a river called the Schuylkill today. How that
is possible I don't yet know as the pilot nor the shipmen can
see anything at all in the cold thick fog that blankets
everything. Even I cannot stay long on this deck, my jacket
and trousers growing soggy with dampness and cold. And
that announcement an hour ago from the captain's own
mouth to the pilot and chief engineer:
  "Unfortunately, we have just lost our third propeller
blade. The ship now drifts at the mouth of the harbor."
  Is this a foretaste of what is to come? Will our further
journey be replete with misfortune? Carriage wheels falling
off, train wrecks on twisting and lonesome westward tracks?
Our land settled by strangers when we arrive? Blustering
winter winds instead of balmy breezes? Perhaps the Wedels
were right, after all, anchoring their feet into the soil of
Antanofka.
  Joseph Becker allowed himself a break from his family
and the horde below. On deck he could see the oilskin-
clothed second class deck mates, half hidden by fog, pulling
at chains, tightening ropes, bending into the wind at their
duties.
  What are we to do? I have about nine dollars left from
the sale of our properties back home. I'm indebted to that
Aid Committee for their loan for this trip and also for the
loan to David Kohn should something happen to him. Of
course, his to me, in case....

His mind wandered as the wind changed direction. He yanked up his coat collar.

He thought of their morning prayers, crowded as they were around their bunks, Lusanna and Andrias leaning in, Benjamin upon his mother's lap.

Those startling words of Jesus in the Sermon on the Mount.

...Take no thought for your life, what ye shall wear, or what ye shall drink; nor yet for your body, what ye shall put on. Is not the life more than meat. and the body more than rainment?

How foolish the words had sounded. His tongue almost tangled reading the verses when he knew their poverty and that they faced so much unknown. Yet, he had read as a father should, hadn't he? Read in spite of what seemed like a great chasm of emptiness ahead of them all. *What a gulf between sounding the words and living them.*

Joseph vowed upon the cold deck that at least he would try. He would not give in to despair.

Despair disarms a man. Keeps him from fulfilling his duty.

He realized in his depths that he faced the heaviest duty of his entire life, to walk by faith when he could not see or know the answers to his questions.

Then, too, who wanted to be indebted to this aid board and that aid group, whether or not they were Mennonites from a variety of funny-sounding states across America?

Joseph reckoned that his faith was small, minuscule, like the mustard seed Jesus spoke about. *Yet it grew into a bush which gave shelter and rest, didn't it? Faith so small?*

He vowed to himself that he was a man of faith and that the Lord Jesus knew what he was about and how his chosen should walk. *I'll demonstrate this faith to Catherine, dear Catherine, who has suffered from our uprooting, all she left behind. So much sorrow and discomfort on this ship.*

***

When Joseph stepped off the last rung of the ladder leading to steerage he was met with cries of anticipation: "We're almost there. Praise God. We shall celebrate the birth of Jesus on land at last."

Children rushed by, bumping into his legs. Mothers dug for string and rope to retie their bundles. To his left Catherine, who had smoothed back her hair as respectfully as possible and replaced her head scarf, bent over a bundle, her hands busy folding a blanket that had covered their "bed."

"Can it be true, Joseph, arriving at last? What was the name of that river and the port at Philadelphia?

"It's called the *Schuylkill River*, Catherine. My tongue tangles when I attempt to say it." Joseph was aware that suddenly he felt lighthearted.

Is it the Christ of Christmas illuminating my heart?

Can it be the lightness of hope surfacing - lifting my despair?

"Who will be meeting us at the port, Father?" Lusanna asked. She shook straw off her skirt, fixing her eyes upon his face.

Joseph noted the new brightness in her eyes. "Well, Lusanna, I've been told that we will be met by members of our own faith. Yes, it will certainly be some brothers from the Pennsylvania Aid Committee. That's the information Elder Tobias gave us back in Antanofka."

"Well, thank God. Praise be!" Catherine's face reflected both a lightness and new hope. Benjamin tugged at her skirt.

"Will we be eating pearl barley cooked with sweet milk and honey for Christmas Day, Mother?" Benjamin's face, too, reflected his new happiness.

"No, my son. No, we won't have those treats. But I just feel it that when we set our feet upon the boards of that dock, there will be people there who will help us celebrate. Yes, indeed, celebrate Christmas Day."

Then Andrias, who had been unusually quiet the last week and now during the din of straightening, stuffing, and packing asked: "How can we celebrate with our feet on the boards of the deck when we sit here? Father, this ship isn't moving at all. We're bouncing about in these oily waves. Has our captain given up?"

***

While *The Vaderland* wallowed in the mouth of the *Schuylkill,* Preacher Eck corralled his congregation to gather for worship in the mess hall, graciously allowed by the captain under their unfortunate circumstance.

Lusanna clustered with a group of girls her age. She noted how Agnes Unruh beamed, a hank of red hair thrusting up from her head scarf. She noticed, too, that since it was Christmas Day, some of the sisters of the congregation, including her mother, had unpacked their black *haubes,* carefully tying the wide strings below their chins. She realized that they had made a special effort to honor the day.

Brother Andrew Eck began the service, his face reflecting a weariness from the trials of the sea journey thus far.

"It is the day when we celebrate the birth of our blessed Savior. It is a special day as we remember, too, the poverty of Mary, Joseph, and the babe, who lay only in a manger upon a bed of straw."

Agnes nudged Lusanna with an elbow. Lusanna was aware that her friend meant, *and we, too, we have been sleeping on near-rotten straw upon hard boards.*

Good old Agnes. She with the red hair and big feet. Make a young farmer a good wife. Yes, indeed. Lusanna felt her face relax into a smile. She resisted from scratching at her rib.

"Like Joseph and Mary, we go forth with faith in our hearts. We trust that God answers our prayers as he so faithfully has done thus far on a passage that has been perilous at times."

Perilous, indeed, thought Lusanna. She swallowed trying to forget how many times they had sung the saddest song that Andrias and she had ever sung, that song, "Eternal Father." Five times, crowded on the windswept deck, they'd

sung it in quavering voices. Voices sometimes drowned by
the howling wind.

> *Most Holy Spirit! Who didst brood*
> *Upon the chaos dark and rude*
> *And bid its angry tumult cease,*
> *And give, for wild confusion, peace;*
> *O hear us, when we cry to Thee,*
> *For those in peril on the sea!*

"Though we have left the bodies of a babe, sisters, and
a brother behind in the cold deep, we have given our minds,
our hearts, and our faith to the Christ of Bethlehem. Perhaps
it is fitting now, that we be among the faithful who come to
Bethlehem, "O Come All Ye Faithful." Let us lift up our
voices and sing it. Brother Heinrich Schmidt, please lead
us."

And so Lusanna sang *"O come ye to Bethlehem, Come
and behold Him..."*

Startled, at first, that preacher Eck would call on the
schoolmaster, still, hadn't he been the one overseeing and
leading hymn singing back in school at Antanofka? Lusanna
concluded that it was time to be charitable and forgiving on
Christmas Day. She, along with Agnes, raised her voice to
sing words that echoed their hopes and aspirations. In
addition, she broke down and allowed herself to scratch
under her arm.

The ship seemed to momentarily cease rocking in the
waves and tides of the mouth of the Schuylkill. She heard the
distant throbbing of engines. *Tug boats? Tugs coming to
push us into shore?*

Then Schoolmaster Heinrich announced: "And, now
brothers and sisters,: for a moment his eye rested upon her,
"let us join our voices in singing, *"Stille Nacht, helige
Nacht!"*

It was Christmas Day. Again they raised their voices
just as the sun lifted the gloom from the Pennsylvania shore,
and sunlight from the east cast wide beams upon them.

Silent night, Holy night,
All is calm, all is bright.

In the quiet following the carol, they noted a slight bump and heard stevedores calling to one another. Deck hands yelled to the boatswain. The tug boats had arrived. Soon they would find out whether or not they had land legs as they planted their feet upon the planks in Port Philadelphia. One thought coursed through their minds: *What manner of folk will be waiting for us?*

14

AT LAST IN PHILADELPHIA

Joseph stood to the side by the wall while his family members attended to personal matters. He surveyed the flux of people coming and going. inside the cavernous new building at the Philadelphia Port. Words crowded in his mind. Glad, indeed, he was to leave behind the misery experienced on The S. S. Vaderland. *God help the souls who fall victim to the wiles of such a journey.*

Such a great bumbling confusion, here. Agents from many railroads, land agents, and agents with placards, hawking jobs to folks they assume to be ignorant peasants.

Our people have had schooling. We have kept our traditions. When Elder Tobias came to our community to baptize new members, he never conducted the baptism unless he was assured that the candidates could read and write.

Our young people, too, know the Bible as it was their main course of study their last years of study in Antanofka. Though many of the young people resisted Schoolmaster Heinrich at times, still, he encouraged them to enlighten their minds and spirits. Give him credit for that.

Lest we wander around on the outer deck, or within this monstrous building, which still smells of new wood, we must regroup and organize. What lies ahead? We surely do need Elder Tobias. Preachers Unruh and Eck seem confused and faltering.

My family? Little Benjamin is almost bursting with the newness of all of this, asking continuously about the train that will take us further west. Lusanna and Catherine, along with a whole crowd of girls and women, headed for the washrooms provided in this port. There is a great line of women by the door. I'm sorry to report that our girls and women do look weary, some even sick, yet their eyes burn brightly with the joy and expectations of what lies ahead.

I wish I could say that they look better in their clothing, but I cannot. Being unable to change their garments during such a long sea passage is something not to be discussed.

Looking out these massive windows, I note the heavy snow on the ground and streets, yet the sky is bright with sunlight. Kansas is in a southern clime, isn't it? That's what the way the railroad pamphlets described it.

Nevertheless, I know all of us are thankful for any woolens, jackets, cloaks, and coats. If only we had cash in our pockets. It is a sad, sad thing to say to each other, "We are poor, indeed."

We men and boys? I guess I can say we endure our stink and our rumpled clothes. The fact is that we scratch when we think nobody is looking. We will, at the times when we can get into the men's washroom, tidy up as best as we can. I'm remaining here with Andrias, making certain our chest and trunk are properly transferred from The Vaderland. I could not endure looking at Catherine's face if somehow her old hope chest was lost.

I look at Andrias proudly as he returns. Though I think he has grown thinner on the passage here, I see how manly he steps, feet securely on the planks as if he never used sea legs at all. After twenty-one days at sea, Andrias could benefit from a trimming of his hair. I see him calling out to the young blond, Carl, the one to whom Lusanna's eye seems to turn. I know she still is sad over Jacob and Elise, left so far behind in our old homeland.

Since there are other ships in port, I hear many tongues, German, Polish, Russian, French, and English. My ear is tuned to our own Plattduetsch and the voices of our own people.

Carl Jantz and his sister Anna drag bundles, Carl with a package in his other arm. He asks the same questions that I ask. "Where is the greeting committee from the Mennonites? Or since we were shipped on a Quaker line, who from their group will greet us?"

I'm looking about, here, there. I've gone to the desk of Port Authority and Immigration. With great difficulty, I finally was able to have the clerk there understand my question. "Where are those who are to meet the immigrants from The Vaderland?"

The almost 700 of us have been waiting here, some of us on benches, many of the men and boys sitting on the floor, backs against the boarded wainscotting.

Others milling around, staring out the windows, one way at the sea, through the opposite windows, the snowy streets that lead into the city of Philadelphia.

Surely we will need horse-drawn carriages or wagons to transfer so many of us to a train station.

My stomach growls and I realize that I'm hungry. Mothers dig in knapsacks, searching for a piece of bread or a slice of sausage left over from the trip. One hears voices of children saying, "Mama, I'm hungry."

Who, what? Where? When?

Now that it is almost two o'clock in the afternoon, according to the great round clock on the west wall opposite me, two men advance toward us. Their faces seem to register a serious concern.

One of our brothers, Berent Jantz, steps forward. I'm guessing he assumes that they are representatives of one of the Mennonite greeting boards.

Joseph watched as Berent, a man with red cheeks, perhaps from the recent scrapings from his razor, extended a hand and calls out in Plattdeutsch: "Brethren, are you the Mennonite committee? We are newly arrivals from The Vaderland."

The attention of the tallest of the two seemed caught when he heard Berent's words and turned toward him. He responded in words not unlike their Plattdeutsch.

"You are the brethren from Antanofka?"

A number of the brethren rose to their feet and clustered around the two wearing such well-cut suits, brushed felt hats with uncreased crowns, clothing surely in sharp contrast to their baggy, rumpled wear. Joseph lowered his eyes to check his staring at their splendid overcoats with shoulder capes. Obviously they were of a fine wool. *We wouldn't see anyone in our old country with such coats, unless, of course, it would be Elder Tobias.*

Both preachers, Andrew Eck, and Samuel Kohn, stepped forward. Joseph concluded that their smiles hid their weariness. They extended their hands. There were handshakes, then embraces as the American brethren gave our ministers the kiss of peace.

I hear names: The taller one is a brother C. B. Schmidt, and I gather, is a railroad agent. The shorter one evidently is from the community here. He announces his name as Gabriel Baer. I hear him mention Pennsylvania Mennonites, and I gather he is a local representative from the churches sent to greet us. Thank God! We've made proper connections at last.

***

The great iron engine rolled down the Pennsylvania Railroad tracks drawing the packed cars containing the Mennonite settlers from Polish Russia. Lusanna, sitting alongside her mother and little brother Benjamin, allowed herself a sigh, which expressed her thought; *at last.*

Her mind wandered in review of their recent experience. *Two whole days in that seaport. Of course when the Mennonites and the Quakers heard of our arrival, they quickly made up baskets of freshly baked bread and some of their home-made sausages stuffed in casings. How our mouths watered. Those kindly folk also insisted we take extra loaves for our journey to Chicago, which, they say, rests on the shores of a large fresh water lake.*

According to Father, the Pennsylvania Aid Committee did not give us any more money but a brother Funk arranged for our railroad expenses to Atchison, Kansas. From there, I understand he made plans for us to travel on that Atchison, Topeka, and Santa Fe line. It sounds so foreign.
The train rocked. A long wail pierced the air as they approached a crossing. A trail of black coal smoke descended, dirtying the snow outside. Horse-drawn carriages halted at the grade. *Never in my life have I seen such spider-like carriages, thought Lusanna. Why, back in Ostrog all the carriages and buggies are bulky, heavy things.*

Lusanna, more than happy that at last she could relax, turned toward her father sitting alongside Andrias on the bench opposite her. She felt a smile slide over her face, "Father, we finally got out of the port. What was the mix-up?"

"It surely was a tie-up, Lusanna. It seems that there was confusion between the two Mennonite boards over who would take charge of our journey from Philadelphia."

"Well, at last, we shall be in Kansas in another day or so?"

"I'm not sure, Lusanna. That Brother Schmidt seemed hesitant, himself. I'm not even certain that Bernard Warkentine, the Kansas brother who has done so much for our people, even knows we are on the way."

Lusanna felt muscles in her neck tighten. *Father tries to keep a smile on his face even when we face so many unknowns. He has to be strong for Andrias, for mother, and for me. What went on in those discussions back in Philadelphia?*

Lusanna noticed how the smile slid off her father's face, and how Andrias's shoulders slumped. *Were her people as really as desperate, now, and poor as Father had said? How does one have hope if that is the situation?*

"Didn't that Brother Baer," Lusanna asked, "insist that we stay in Pennsylvania from January through March, and then make the rest of the journey?"

"He did indeed, Lusanna, and others of the Pennsylvania Aid Committee. They probably would have transported us out into their communities where we would have lodged with their people until spring comes." "Wouldn't that have been a great burden to them, Father? So many of us dumped into their homes." Lusanna shifted in her seat.

"Yes, indeed. It would have cost our people an extra two thousand dollars, at least. That's why we met and decided that since our tickets were for passage all the way to Kansas, and already paid for, we should follow through and not be such a trouble."

"Maybe we needed Elder Tobias to give us direction," added Lusanna.

"Well, yes, but our ministers seemed eager for us to continue as we already had our tickets."

"Sounds to me like it was a good decision." Andrias shifted his legs.

"Anyway, we can be encouraged. We will be given further directions, I'm sure, when we reach the French city of St. Louis, by a river that has a name I cannot begin to pronounce," Joseph added.

"I think that's the Mississippi River, Father. Yes, it would have been a big expense for the Pennsylvania folk. I'm glad, Father, that we decided to continue. I'm anxious to get to Kansas," Andrias replied.

"The aid committees have already done so much for us. I thank God, indeed I do." Joseph shifted his shoulders as the long train leaned, chugging around a long bend of the track.

Lusanna looked over the heads of the Voth family in front of her, noting how the women ahead had tried to tidy themselves back in the Philadelphia Port. At least their head kerchiefs were neatly tied, though faded and even wrinkled.

Up front a baby cried. Its mother bent to dig into a bag on the floor. Thank goodness, thought Lusanna, we have heat in the carriage. *Thirteen carriages for our people and every one of them has a stove up front. A coal-burning stove.*

Oh, the luxury of it. Coal was something we certainly couldn't afford back in Antanofka, for sure.

Of course, from time to time, there was a belch from the gases of the burning coal, which emitted a stench that worked its way backwards through the carriage.

We take the bitter with the sweet, Aunt Caroline Buller used to say.

By now, with the passage of at least an hour. Lusanna looked outside the carriage window, surveying the countryside. *My tree. My poplar tree in Antanofka. I shall search for one like it.* She felt a smile creep to her lips.

She lifted her eyes to see giant red barns in the distance with houses, two stories, three stories, even. Houses which would have been called mansions in Antanofka. *Were these the homes of farmers? Or were they the residences of great land owners and barons?*

But already, back in the Philadelphia port, she had heard it. Mennonites had been here in Pennsylvania for more than 100 years. *Surely, by now, they would have prosperous farms. Yes, big houses, wide gardens, and splendid orchards.*

To her left, her eyes lingered upon the cattle in the fields. *Were those Guernseys? What kind of cattle were the big black ones?*

The engine wailed as they rattled across another country road crossing. After a few miles, the train eased into a dark woods, tall trees on both sides of the carriages. The cars swayed as they passed through. *Limbs lifting up toward me. Winter trees without friendly leaves. Are they reaching out in welcome, or are they snatching at us in some unfriendly manner?*

Then Lusanna fixed her eyes upon a cluster of tall conifers. *Were they spruce? Cedars, firs?*

She smiled to herself. *Yes. This is like Antanofka. But I'll have to keep looking for my lone tree.*

15

BERNARD WARKENTINE

When Bernard Warkentine arrived from Russia, he settled in the town of Summerfield, Illinois, headquarters of The Mennonite Board of Guardians. In 1874 he and his new wife, Mina Eisenmeyer, left Illinois for Halstead, Kansas, where they built a large house and a mill on the Little Arkansas River. Warkentine, from a prosperous family of millers in Altona, Russia, near Odessa, brought his milling skills and introduced the Red Turkey winter wheat to Kansans. With his boundless energy, he had labored for hours in behalf of The Mennonite Board of Guardians, advancing loans for travel, cash, and making land arrangements for newly arrived Mennonite settlers.

With his organizational and business skills, Warkentine had already shepherded a large colony of his people from Russia to the Kansas plains.

Unlike the Antanofka pilgrims, these settlers had been well-to-do. Some of them carried as much as $50,000 with them. Already they had, with his aid, purchased 100,000 acres of rich land in south central Kansas. With such prosperous settlers, town merchants all the way from Topeka to Newton, Kansas, eagerly extended themselves to market their wares to people such as these, with real hard cash.

Now, with his wife, Mina, Warkentine was visiting her family in Summerfield, Illinois, and reviewing the Mennonite Board's work with emigrants.

He had just received a telegram. Opening it, he scanned the words. With raised eyebrows his eyes cut to his wife's face.

"Mina, listen to this. I simply cannot believe this!" He read the telegram from railroad agent A.S. Johnson. *Schmidt left Philadelphia yesterday with seven hundred Mennonites via St. Louis. Wants you to meet him in St. Louis.*"

"What is Schmidt thinking? There's no way I can get to St. Louis in time for that train. What has he done?

"Why would these people be coming on to Kansas in the middle of winter, Bernard? Mina placed a hand on her husband's shoulder.

"I have to get involved, Mina. These are the people from Ostrog, Polish Russia. The poor ones. Why didn't Schmidt and Funk arrange for their stay in Pennsylvania until spring? It was their responsibility. God help those immigrants. By now they must be hungry and destitute."

Bernard rose to go to his desk to compose a letter to The Mennonite Board, while Mina raced to the bedroom to pack his valise.

Dear Brethren: I have just heard from agent A. S. Johnson and found out that at about two or three this afternoon C. B. Schmidt with over 600 Mennonites will arrive in East St. Louis via the Vandalia Route and that they will continue tonight with the Missouri Pacific... as he states, the Vandalia R. R. Company is negotiating with the Bridge Company in Topeka, regarding the rates to bring their trains to St. Louis.... How I wish it would be warmer....If only you were here - there will be a lot of work involved. How things will work out in Kansas with all these people, God knows.

Hearty Greetings, B. Warkentine[1]

---

[1] Letters from Bernard Warkentine are printed in Allison, Leslie B. "Russian Mennonites in Florence in 1870's," Kanhistique. Nov., 1993, p. 7-9

***

Bernard's mind focused upon the hordes which would soon arrive. *Schmidt and I alone to shepherd all these people. God, give us strength. What kind of condition will these people be in after traveling for twenty-four to twenty-six days?* He was well aware of what faced the immigrants. Upon reaching St. Louis they would have to be loaded on horse-drawn busses to cross the Mississippi River. Horse-drawn cars, too, for their baggage. Then, after loading themselves onto the Missouri Pacific, they faced the long miles to Atchison, Kansas. *Surely, then, they would be the responsibility of the Santa Fe Railroad.*

Warkentine reviewed in his mind how the recent group of several hundred had landed in Topeka, housed at the King Bridge building until they had purchased necessary equipment, foodstuffs, oxen and horses for their journey further west. Each adult among them possessed at least a thousand dollars.

Voices from established Topeka citizens, which he had overheard, raced through his mind.

"Have you seen them? These strange, strange people? Women with handkerchiefs tied over their heads? Have you ever seen such things as they bring with them? Their own funny-looking bedding? Crocks for sausages and sauerkraut, and kitchen utensils. One would think that they thought they were going into a land without civilization at all.

"Those of us who dared enter the King Bridge Company, where they were temporarily housed, stepped carefully, indeed. What manner of vermin clung to them?"

Bernard smiled to himself thinking of how the dialogue changed just as soon as *the Topeka establishment* discovered how padded were the emigrant's pockets.

Even how within a few days the attention came to the mayor's office regarding their fat billfolds and purses, in spite of their plain and odd clothing.

And adding to the bewilderment, when the Kansas governor found out about the money about to be spent, he invited them immediately for a reception in the state capitol. *Well, of course the settlers had to open their trunks, pour some water into basins and wash themselves. No jewelry at all upon the women. Who cared? The coffers in the stores and businesses would soon be bulging.*

Yes, grinned Warkentine to himself, *that group of Mennonites established themselves on that occasion.*

A Colonel Terry of the omnibus company in Topeka extended himself to bring the settlers and the Topeka citizens together. He arranged for a dozen omnibusses and prancing horses for a city tour. But not without inviting the citizens of Topeka to join them in the excursions, helping to point out the points of interest.

Before the settlers moved into central Kansas to set up farming, they had gone to the state fair grounds, where sellers brought their farm machinery, oxen, horses, wagons, and equipment needed for breaking the prairie sod.

By the time the great Santa Fe train rolled out of Topeka for Harvey, Sedgwick, and Reno Counties, the engines groaned, pulling the monstrous loads. Five hundred head of work horses, 400 fresh milk cows, and 50 yoke of oxen. And the merchants and cattle raisers around Topeka congratulated themselves, saying, "And there will be more coming."

Warkentine hurried through the Missouri Pacific Station vowing to fulfill the seemingly impossible task that God had assigned to him.

Thank God he'd taken time to wire Hutchinson, Kansas, and had received a reply from Mayor Hutchins. *Surely a good man. Baptist preacher, wasn't he? Yes. The town of Hutchinson, Kansas, would welcome the Polish-Russian Mennonites. Land available all around. God be praised! What a relief.*

16

WHERE ARE THE ROSES?

Four days of travel and we've still not reached our destination. Bone chilling cold outside. What's happening to us?

Lusanna and her family members, packed into a carriage of the Santa Fe train, had just rolled out of the station at Atchison, Kansas. She was almost too weary even to say her name. She struggled to lift her shoulders. Her coat collar made her neck itch, reminding her of her need for a bath. She reached out to place her arm around her little brother Benjamin, who had fallen asleep against her side.

I have to be strong for my family. Look at us. All of us. Mother, exhausted, her head hanging. She needs to lie down. I'm beginning to wonder if any of us will ever have a home again. Who would have thought that our journey would lead us to such a situation? Did our elders give the whole matter their best deliberations?

Our belongings, chests, trunks, pots, crocks, cloth bolts, garden tools - all the other things we brought with us. Where are they now?

Lusanna wondered, after the transfer of stations in Chicago, then St. Louis, and the crossing of that wide, frightful Mississippi River, what had happened to her mother's hope chest. But she was so tired she could hardly lift herself from the bench, let alone step down from the train carriage in Atchison to face another transfer.

She did admit to herself, however, after seeing that Brother Bernard Warkentine that she did have a bit of renewed hope. *Tall. Handsome. Wearing one of those fine American felt hats. A coat that seemed immaculate. Such fine wool. The way he strode across the tiles to greet them, speaking their language. Yes. A German-Russian, himself. One who had visited Antanofka, who knew their situation and what they faced. Surely the answers lay with a man like Bernard Warkentine. Thank God he lived in Kansas. He would be their neighbor.*

The farther they traveled, the lonelier the countryside appeared. She had long given up searching for her tree. They rolled and rattled through isolated plains, through great rolling hills, and those everlasting waving brown grasses. Here and there, large hawks soared and swooped, some resting themselves on lonely telegraph poles along the forlorn tracks.

What are we going to eat? Father spent all of his left-over money for loaves of bread back in St. Louis. Sure, it was a Christian thing to do, sharing the bread with the others. How did a whole congregation of people end up in this predicament?

The wheels clackety-clacked on the frigid rails that seemed to lead to infinity. Snowflakes zoomed straight across the land toward a desolate horizon. The engine wailed like a lonely banshee seeking a house of death. The carriages rattled over another of the loneliest crossings Lusanna had ever seen. *Reminds me of the railroads on the Russian steppes. Why didn't we stay home with the friendly sheltering of the forests of Antanofka?*

She glanced across the aisle and noticed that Andrias had awakened from a sleep. Father's head still nodded, his shoulders rocking.

How old Father looks. His clothing so soiled, his collar torn. This bitter weather and none of us have gloves. Some of our people have only cloth wrappings instead of stockings. Father, Father, your poor hands.

"Well, Lusanna," Andrias said, leaning forward. "Where is the balmy wind, the wonderful green of Kansas? Where are the roses Elder Tobias spoke about? The strawberries, the fruit?"

"I guess it's truly winter here, Andrias. Winter and no trees and hedges to shelter us from the fierce wind. I'm beginning to wonder if I were outside this carriage if I could actually stand up against it."

Lusanna and Andrias surveyed the travelers stuffed into the benches ahead of them. A fetid smoke from the pot-bellied stove in front drifted, mixing with the sour odor of bodies in need of baths and changes of clothing. In more need, though, of hot bowls of soup and slices of freshly-baked bread.

She noticed how quiet they were, those who were not sleeping.

Are we all recognizing that our fate is in other peoples' hands?

She braced her back at that thought.

No. Not me. Not Lusanna Becker. I have my faith in God, in the blessed Christ. In the church which has nurtured me. I'm weary but I still have my energy and my will that God gave me.

Her eyes focused upon the backs of the young folks seated with their family members, here and there, throughout the carriage. Agnes Unruh, her red head still covered with a dirty scarf, stared out the window as if she defied the elements. *Surely these winds won't subdue good old Agnes.* Lusanna found herself actually smiling at her thoughts.

Yellow-headed Carl, his cloth cap tipped awkwardly, was exchanging words with a bewhiskered father. And, yes, even Schoolmaster Heinrich, sitting with his mother, still wore his grin.

I guess, indeed, he will have plenty to write about.

Outside, the snow had stopped, but the wind whipped at straggly, tough-looking bushes along the side of the track.

"It will be dark, Lusanna. Nighttime when we arrive in Hutchinson," Andrew said. "At least, that's what brother Bernard Warkentine said."

"We can be encouraged, Andrias, members of the Mennonite Aid Committee will surely be there. Our brothers and sisters. They will have food already prepared. Beds for us so we can finally lay down our heads."

"I wish it were so. I'm not certain that I believe it." Andrias shifted on the bench. "There have been too many mix-ups on this trip. Maybe we needed the strong voice of Elder Tobias, after all."

"Well, by now he's probably snug in that place called Dakota, wherever it is. Nestled in with his chubby wife and his plate of potato noodles." Susanna drew in a long breath of air.

"Lusanna," added Andrias, "don't even mention food."

By ten o'clock the train of emigrants pulled into the Topeka Station by the Kansas River. Lusanna scraped frost from her window to look out at the town of Topeka, the capitol of the state. Six hundred forty-two of them, waiting, waiting. *Maybe they will let us get off this train and stretch our legs awhile.*

She heard coughing from the rows behind. Someone said in a voice conveying worry: "Why, Henry, this child is burning with a fever."

Billows of smoke drifted back, settling upon the cars.

***

The tall, slightly stoop-shouldered Colonel A. S. Johnson, agent for the Santa Fe Railroad, stepped out of the station to greet Mr. Warkentine, whom he knew, and with whom he had corresponded. Together they had worked out land deals for newly arrived Russian settlers. He gripped Warkentine's hand.

"Well, at last, Warkentine. At last."

Warkentine, still unsettled by the whole arrangement, or lack of it, extended his hand. "Yes, Colonel Johnson. Yes, well - we've got a desperate situation on our hands. I've spent all of my cash, over seventy dollars, for bread for these people. They're more than exhausted. Can't we arrange to house them here in Topeka for now?"

"Well, my brother Warkentine, that's not what your board member C. B. Schmidt wants. No. Not at all."

"But we must negotiate with Schmidt. This all seems outlandish. Look into the windows of the cars. Don't you see the crying children? The destitute mothers? Surely we can let them step down from the train here in Topeka."

"Schmidt sticks to his plan. He told me you have also contacted Mayor Hutchins of his city and that they are ready to receive this train," Johnson replied.

"That surely can be changed. Plans can be changed, Colonel Johnson. It's still a long ways to Hutchinson. People can only endure so much. Bread, milk, and clothing, things they need can be negotiated cheaper here than in Hutchinson, I know." Bernard Warkentine pleaded.

"We'll find homes for them until spring comes, Bernard. Then, I'll work with you to get land to settle these folks."

Bernard, his face stern, took leave of the Colonel and entered the station to send a letter to the Mennonite Board back east.

...I cannot grasp with my understanding how the Pennsylvanians could have sent these poor families to Kansas without giving them a cent for the trip...it cries to heaven when you think about it!...Do not leave me in this predicament for too long...Nothing remains for me but to supply the families with bread until help arrives, which I shall do in the name and on the account of the Board.

A happy and heartfelt New Year from,
Your Brother, B. Warkentine[2]

***

---

[2] Ibid, p. 8

Lusanna was thankful that the darkness was illuminated by bright stars. Like back in Antanofka, maybe even more so, the stars twinkled with brilliance.

She noticed, too, that the wind had declined in its winter rage across the prairie lands. *Mother, look at Mother, how she sags against the window, clutching Benjamin's hand as if he might slip away. Is she thinking of the little graves in Antanofka? O Blessed Jesus, our church. Will we be a congregation out here in this wild loneliness? Where will we settle? Where will we sing together and kneel for prayer? Who will bring the basins for footwashing?*

She could hear numerous children crying for a piece of bread, some crying because their toes and hands were cold. They had stopped at another Kansas town on another river. *The Cottonwood, wasn't it? The town, Florence...beautiful name. Florence, flower of Italy. Florence...only a beautiful lady should have a name so lovely. What would it be like to be able to say: "I live in Florence?" Wasn't that the city of fountains, statues, marvelous churches, a cathedral?*

But the train had only stopped to pick up baggage. *Cream cans from a frontier farm family? Maybe it was sacks of potatoes. Do they make potato pancakes out here? Do they even know about potato noodles?*

C. B. Schmidt meandered through the aisles of all the cars to announce that they would soon arrive in the town of Hutchinson, named after the mayor. They could also take heart, for the mayor was also a Baptist preacher. "Yes, they want settlers in their town and in their countryside. Yes, indeed." Schmidt had been certain. "Good wheat land all around Hutchinson," Schmidt added.

"But most of us were woodsmen, weavers, a few millers and day laborers," Andrias said, leaning ahead to look at Lusanna.

Perhaps it was Schmidt's words alone that sustained the travelers, who by now, were like mountain climbers clinging to the edge of the Matterhorn with their fingertips, their energies fading fast. *Could they rally to the occasion, here in the night? Just how cold was it outside, anyway? Was that more coughing from the rear of the car?* Lusanna saw that Andrias was wide awake, straightening his shoulders. He nudged Father in the ribs to awaken him. Ahead she could see flickering lights. *The town, the town. Home, we have arrived at our new home.* She had a fleeting image of a hot bowl of beef stew and a chunk of freshly made bread. She could feel her heart quicken. Saliva flooded her mouth.

Folks around her were murmuring, waking their babes and children for the momentous event ahead. *Here in America. In Kansas at last. Home. Everyone should have wide-open eyes. Legends are built upon such events.*

17

HUTCHINSON, KANSAS

Joseph and Catherine yanked their coat collars up to their necks as they found their footing on the platform of the Santa Fe Railroad Station in the spanking new town of Hutchinson, Kansas. Baggage they had stowed above their heads in the carriage clustered around their feet. Benjamin shivered as he reached for his papa's hand. Flames from gas lights illuminated, though dimly, in a night registering twelve degrees below zero. A portion of a pearl moon shone against the purple sky punctured with bright stars. Small clouds of frozen vapor escaped from noses and mouths as they disembarked, their bodies cramped, legs stiff from prolonged travel.

Murmurs, coughing, excited voices, cries of awakened babes, all mingled with the hissing of steam escaping from the hunched black engine, which had done its faithful duty. Rich land, resting frozen and snow-covered, stretched beyond the town boundaries, which had been recently laid out with buffalo bones.

Hadn't Schmidt kept saying, "Folks in Hutchinson are eager to welcome new settlers? Surely they knew we were coming."

Catherine's words broke through the din of voices as she stared into her husband's face: "Joseph, we're all milling around here. Where is the welcoming committee?" Her thin body shivered. Her chapped hand drew her scarf down tighter and closer under her chin. She reached with her other hand to place it around Benjamin and draw him out of the frigid wind.

"Why, Catherine, why, why…" Joseph's words drifted. He strained his eyes surveying the growing pandemonium. Hundreds of people staggering into the raw air, gathering in groups. Eyes searched wide-opened in attempts to understand this unexpected situation, giving evidence that in every mind the same thoughts coursed: *We've had only bread for five days. Where do we get food? Who will lead us to our beds? What is going on? How can this be?*

Joseph looked southward, his eyes following the flickering gas lights outlining the frozen street ruts. He looked northward. Buildings. Stone and brick buildings. *At least this isn't some forsaken outpost on the prairie.*

Lusanna grabbed her father's sleeve; "Papa, we can't just stand here, we'll freeze in this air. Look at us? Why aren't Brother Warkentine and Brother Schmidt telling us what to do next?"

Then Jospeh saw them both entering the depot. A solemn-faced Warkentine beckoned the crowd to follow him inside out of the ghastly cold. Joseph knew, however, that it would be impossible for the entire group to crowd into the depot. He noticed that the people began to scatter. Agnes Unruh with her parents, Jake and Eva, had started walking northward, baggage in their hands, toward the tallest brick building. *Maybe there was appropriate shelter opening down that way.*

"Come on, Catherine. Let's try to get into a building of some sort." Joseph, hand behind Catherine, ushered her toward the people pushing into the station door. However, with at least a couple of hundred who had already entered, it was obvious that they would have to wait for the directions here on the platform by the green door beneath the overhang.

The station master's freight workers cursed and grunted, their cries mixing with the bewildering Plattdeutsch phrases drifting in the wind. Joseph could hear the thud as chests, trunks and baggage hit the ground or were heaved upon waiting baggage carts. *Catherine's chest. Has it arrived? How shall I retrieve it? Where on earth are we going?*

Lusanna crept as close to her parents as she could. Joseph knew that his daughter was trying to protect her mother from the terrible chill.

"Father," Andrias said, a determination in his voice. "Why don't we head toward those buildings with the others? He pointed with a bare, chapped hand.

"For now, son, let's stay together. Perhaps Warkentine..."

Before Joseph Becker could say another word, Andrias's short coat was already ballooning out at the back from the wind as he tromped over ruts hard as cast iron toward a board sidewalk to join Carl and Jake, who were proceeding uptown.

Joseph stared after Andrias as words of bewilderment of his own people pummeled his ears.

***

Pity still reigned in some peoples' hearts. A lone merchant on the sidewalk saw the clustered groups of settlers, heads bent against the wind as they struggled uptown. Hurrying over to the lead group, he began to wave both arms.

"This way, this way." He beckoned to the shifting mass of people, pointing to his store. Though he spoke in English, the wanderers seemed to know what he was trying to convey. *Get in out of this sub-zero wind.*

Warkentine was indeed grateful for this generosity. He was aware than no real help would be available until after sunrise to untangle this diplomatic mess and failure. He knew that the settlers were forced to, if they could find a space, lie down on the rough boards of the station and on the cold bricks, or cement of the building that had been opened for the others.

***

Fatigued as he was, Bernard took his pen and paper and began to write to the Mennonite Board of Guardians.

I arrived here in Hutchinson with all these people...about two hours ago...where Col. A. S. Johnson had ordered houses for the 90 families who are without provisions; must report, however with anxiety and concern, that the people of this town do not want to receive the families in their present conditions under any circumstances. I don't know what to do. Have paid $70 for bread since we left St. Louis and have offered $400-$500 to pay for ovens and the groceries needed immediately until our relief committee will take over, if only the town would let us use its buildings. However, this seems to be out of the question because they claim that they have enough people in their town already that need to be supported and they will therefore accept no responsibilities for these people. Hutchinson has sent a telegram to Topeka and expects the railroad company to take the people back to Topeka and put them up there.[3]

***

Next morning, Mayer C. C Hutchins opened his office before sun up, air outside so cold and crisp it hurt to breathe it. Around his desk clustered five of the Hutchinson council members, plus Colonel Johnson of the Santa Fe Railroad.

Hutchins leaned forward, his face drawn in a serious determination.

"How has this happened? Didn't we send messages to Johnson that we would welcome another Mennonite group?"

McGinn, the leading town merchant, who had even taken time to dress in a starched white shirt and a spanking navy suit, cleared his throat and began.

"Sir. I don't want to appear unchristian or rude, but we have a real problem with these people. A number of us have

---

[3] Ibid, p.8

been out mingling with these settlers. Not the kind of people we expected. Not at all." McGinn sat back, gold fob on his watch chain quivering.

"I'm with McGinn," piped another supporting voice, a thin man in a worn overcoat, buttoned tightly. He stared at Hutchins. "Not at all like them settlers what come through Topeka we read about in the paper. Why them settlers put the Topeka merchants on the map with their spending. These people..."

His voice was drowned out by the others, all speaking at once to affirm the sentiment expressed.

"But," interjected Hutchins, "we gave our word. Let's get them in some kind of shelters. Aren't there any vacant houses? God above, we can't let seven hundred immigrants starve or freeze to death. Where is your pity?"

"Well," replied the tallest man, rubbing his ham-sized hands together, "these are hard times, Reverend Hutchins, and we got enough paupers in this town right now. Seven hundred hungry people, ain't had a change of clothes or washed up for a months, besides their empty pocketbooks, you want them for neighbors?"

"My wife Matilda said," another member piped, "these people got diseases and they stink to high heaven. Pass them back to Florence. They got low land there on the Cottonwood where they can settle." His words were spoken with finality.

In spite of his pleading and appeals to Christian charity, all the mayor was able to accomplish was to bring the disgruntled group around to agreeing to shove the Polish-Russian people into some abandoned houses and try to provide water, heat, and food for a couple of days.

Let the Santa Fe Railroad worry about 'em, was the expressed sentiment.

They brung 'em here. Let 'em haul 'em off somewheres.

***

Astonished at the cold rejection of the immigrants by the citizens of Hutchinson, Bernard Warkentine groaned, yet went on working deep into the night hours, wrestling with the tasks ahead. *God help us all.*

His words to the Mennonite Board of Guardians at Summerfield, Illinois, flowed from his pen.

Dear Brethren!

I have already sent two telegrams and a letter to the Board concerning the 90 families of needy fellow-believers. I also contacted the Aid Committee in Philadelphia, but as yet I have received no answer, which puts me in a difficult situation.

Since the railroad company started yesterday to mediate in behalf of the families, the Huthchinson citizens soon decided to let the people move into the empty houses. I had 16 or 17 ovens set up, so that the living conditions during the present quite cold weather would be more comfortable. Due to urgent personal business I sent Brother C. Schmutz to deliver the 700 loaves of bread, which I had ordered. At the same time he is to buy and butcher an ox to provide the families with meat, since they had eaten nothing but dry bread for the last five days. This evening I also sent 6,000 lbs. of flour, so that tomorrow each family may bake its own bread. To my satisfaction I just received a telegram which reads as follows:

"People are all comfortable, warm and enough to eat."

With the help of God we have come this far, but where from here? We need you for advice and action. Therefore I like to invite you, Brother Krehbiel, and anybody who can to come and see what needs to be done. Right now is the time to demonstrate willingness for sacrifice and show Christian charity.

You can imagine how one feels when an old mother with gray hair and tears in her eyes tells of her sorrows and that she will probably have to die of hunger.[4]

---

[4] Ibid, p. 8

James D. Yoder

Bernard Warkentine lay down his pen and wept.

***

Next evening at home in Halstead, Kansas, with Mina, Warkentine looked out the spacious window of his office. His eye fixed upon the frosty glaze on the bare branches of a hackberry tree sweeping over the banks of the Little Arkansas River. Mina had just entered his walnut wainscoted room with a hot cup of coffee.

"Bernard, I'm worried about you. You have this new cough and you haven't been getting enough rest." She set the cup and saucer on the edge of his desk close to the letter he was writing to the Mennonite Board.

"I rested, Mina. I rested, but I could not help dreaming of those poor rejected people from Russia. Surely their faith sustains them. Think of it, this bitter cold, Mina, and almost three hundred of them are children."

Bernard saw the tears in Mina's eyes as she placed a warm hand on his shoulder. "I'll be fine, Mina. Pray for the emigrants. I guess the Santa Fe Railroad will pick up some kind of responsibility for their next move. The poor abandoned people."

"I would have hoped that you would have heard from the Summerfield group by now, Bernard. What is keeping them from responding? Surely someone will have to notify all the churches and conferences about this overwhelming need we have on our hands here in Kansas."

"That's what I'm about to do, Mina. That is the task apportioned to me."

He dipped his stick pen into the ink bottle to compose his letter.

My Dear Brethren:
I will again go to Hutchinson to relieve Brother Schmutz, but in the meantime await encouraging news from

you. In any case, you already have written Brother Funk and the member in Pennsylvania.

Greetings to all the dear brethren and tell them that I am not able to describe the situation of these poor people, and that every one should do what his heart tells him.

The weather seems to be getting colder. The coal is shipped by the railroad company. Last night I went with Johnson by special train to Hutchinson, and he assured me that the company would do its best to provide the people with shelter.

Your faithful,
B. Warkentine[5]

Bernard rose from his desk after folding his letter and placing it into the addressed envelope. "I must get this in the morning mail, Mina." Mina stepped quickly to the hall closet for his coat and hat. He coughed, feeling a chill race over his shoulders, then donned the coat and hat.

"I have to leave for Hutchinson, as soon as the morning train comes through. Maybe I'll have to stay for two or three days until we find a way through this situation. There's no time for delay, Mina. The last thing we need is an outbreak of some disease."

Bernard kissed Mina on the cheek and headed out the door, coattails flailing behind him.

---

[5] Ibid.

18

REJECTED

Lusanna lost count of the number of people who were crowded into the decrepit house by the railroad, where she and her family were temporarily sheltered from the bitter cold.

"Well, at least we have to give credit to Colonel Johnson and his Santa Fe Railroad," Lusanna said, turning to Agnes Unruh, who was stirring the bubbling ox tail soup in the cast iron pot. A fire glowed in the kitchen range, one leg propped up by a block of wood.

"Look at this," Gerda Schmidt said, pointing to the shovel of coal she pitched into the side door of the range. "Why, back home this would be same as gold."

Indeed it would have been, thought Lusanna. *Think of it, Gerda actually joining in like this. And also, we would never have tried to bake bread in an oven like this little thing, let alone the kerosene one that brother Warkentine ordered and had delivered to the back porch.*

To their left, a group of women gathered around a bare-topped old table, her mother among them. They dipped flour from the large sacks with their hands, pitching it into an old dishpan they had found hanging on a nail on the back porch. They added water, then yeast from a little jar they discovered in the staples that brother Schmutz had brought by each of the seven houses. Next, they mixed, rolled, and kneaded the dough in their improvisations and hurry to get the bread baked for the drooling Anatofkins, who were already hovering over their shoulders, having returned from their surveys out in the frigid air.

She heard her mother's voice. "That brother Warkentine, what a fine, fine, man. He's the one who arranged for us to have this wonderful wheat flour."

"And," added Agnes's mother, Eva, "to think of it, back in Antanofka we only had *wheat bread* for weddings and maybe, once in a while, funerals."

Lusanna noticed that Eva, in her blackish-gray skirt dusted by flour, actually smiled.

There were at least ninety persons crowded into this abandoned dwelling. The Santa Fe Railroad, under Colonel Johnson's direction, had found six other empty houses for their people. Though scattered, Lusanna knew that with the encouragement of bread and, at last, hot and wonderful ox tail soup, most of them could look beyond the uncertainties of the present hour.

How could I forget sleeping on the hard floor in that train station - and the bitter cold? It's a wonder we didn't catch pneumonia.

"This is only temporary, Lusanna," Agnes said, brushing back a dislodged wisp of her red hair with the back of her hand. "We're going to be shipped to another Kansas town." Lusanna noted that Agnes scratched at her waist when she thought nobody was looking. *Poor thing, I scratch too. When will this journey be over?*

What would be the name of such a town? Already she had heard preacher Eck speak of one of their Polish-Russian groups landing in a place called Pawnee Rock. *Pawnee Rock? What a name. Wouldn't there be ferocious Indians behind the rock? Who would want to live there?*

Other towns were named, too: Moundridge, Newton, Buhler, a place called Hofnungsthal, another named Gnadenau, and still another with the name, of all things, New Alexanderwohl. *What about that town we came through on our way here, named Florence?*

Lusanna tried not to let her spirits sag, but she felt more uncertainty gnaw. She could hear Benjamin's voice call out, then his laugh as he attempted to play with other boys in the crowded upstairs room. *Bedroom?* Well, she guessed one could call it that. *All of us, at least fifty women and girls plopping down in our clothes on the floors in three of the rooms. The men and boys? Well, they had to make do with the other spaces left. We are like the blessed Jesus, rejected, He, a man of sorrows and acquainted with grief.*

Her eye shifted for a glance out the east window. No blind, no curtain to soften the searing glare of the morning sun. She noted that there was still a line of people, even in the frigid wind, at the privy door out by frozen stalks outlining a garden.

As far as she knew, faith and a forward look hadn't completely vanished. Andrias and Jake Unruh, along with Carl, bent their heads into the wind and hiked down to the Santa Fe Station to see if they could gather any news from the station master, or that Mr. Warkentine. She knew they would be back when the soup was done and the bread baked, then the everlasting waiting for the next scene Brother Warkentine or Colonel Johnson plotted for them.

How are our preachers, Brothers Eck and Unruh, handling this? No doubt, worried and sick at heart for their people. Who is working to untangle this mess? The Mennonite Board? That Pennsylvania group? Did Colonel Johnson have the most to do with it? None of us have any money to buy their land. Merciful Jesus, what next? What are we to do? Don't we need the presence of Elder Tobias?

Lusanna found it near impossible to reflect on her many questions, stuffed together here with the wind rattling the windows. She concluded that they were just like chickens in crates, waiting on a railroad platform for shipment into the great unknown.

I need space. Time to be alone. Oh, my Antanofka tree. My beautiful poplar. My storks, Ichabod and Ketura. Are they lonely without me? Our thatched-roofed house. Why, on this entire journey I haven't seen one single house with a straw or grass roof. Why didn't I realize how warm and comfy the sight of our village roofs made me feel?

Again Lusanna glanced out the frost-glazed east window, noting there were still tinges of orange and pink in the cloud layers from the morning sunrise. *The light. The light here in Kansas. Why, it would make an artist crazy.*

She noticed that more and more of the people clustered around the ovens as the baking bread gave off the most heavenly odor, mixing with the savory smell of the soup bubbling in the kettles.

It had been quite surprising, though, when a small group of church women from the town knocked on the door and offered carrots, cabbages, and the church's whole crate of tin cups so that they could eat the soup like civilized folks. They had to exchange greetings and information in their own Plattdeutsch. *Oh, the mercies and kindness of strangers.* And, she supposed, they weren't Mennonites at all.

Lusanna reckoned, her parents always had taught them that God was in every person and that religion had a lot to do with the community in which you were born. *Our religion? Well, of course, about the love of God and the Christ who is all and in all.*

Lusanna agreed with Agnes's mother that by the confused looks on the women's faces, they must have thought their own women sounded like old hens clucking together. Anyway, the Mennonite women gave them loving looks of appreciation. Surely looks and gestures communicated their gratefulness. Lusanna was certain that their women tried not to scratch in their presence.

She noted, though, that the town women didn't tarry long. No, not at all. *How can I blame them? What more could they do? And I have to admit, I don't want anyone looking at me. Not for long, anyway.*

Lusanna tried to straighten her disheveled skirt.

***

Joseph, along with Gerhard Jantz, and Eli Unruh, waited on the shoddy little porch facing the railroad station a few blocks away. He made an attempt to lift his shoulders and face the bare realities before them. He vowed not to appear to be a burden, cast down and sorrowful among his people.

He thought of Preacher Eck's words. Preacher Eck, knocking on the stairwell rail to get the attention of the wall-to-wall people, more like refugees, who turned their eyes upon him. Then he'd read:

> "By faith, Abraham...went out, not knowing whether he went. By faith, he sojourned in the land of promise, as in a strange country...For he looked for a city which hath foundations, whose builder and maker is God."

Strong words. But are they foolish words? Was it a response of faith to God's call that put us in this predicament? Are we dangling, like Abraham?

Gerhard Jantz lifted his eyes to Joseph's. "We may have made the biggest mistake we could possibly have made, Joseph. Look at us, I hardly have courage to look Maria in the face."

"Same with me, Joseph. Same with me. When Eva looks at me with those eyes of hers, it's all I can do to try not to flinch. God help us. What foundations are we laying, freezing here, a few hours away from starving, completely dependent upon strangers?" Eli's head dropped.

"I think," Joseph said, "we have to keep in mind that we uprooted our families, braved this journey here *for our faith. Yes, our faith.* Our principles were worthy, following the example of Jesus. We could not in good conscience give our families over to godless Russia."

The wind whipped and howled as it soared around the corner of the unpainted boards of the house. Joseph cast his eyes southward, fixing them upon a flat field that stretched to a seemingly endless horizon.

He shivered. Then he realized that the barren prairies threatened him. *This land goes on forever. No boundaries beyond the railroad tracks. If I started walking, which way would I go for a place to call home? If we are ever settled, God help that may be soon so, how will a common old woodsman from Antanofka dig in to make a home upon such lonely prairies?*

"I can hardly stand it," Eli broke in, "having to depend upon the handouts and benefits of boards and aid groups." He, like Joseph, stared at the land beyond as if he shared Joseph's thoughts.

Then Eli added. "We're forgetting something, brothers. Forgetting something." He shifted his boots on an icy patch of leftover snow on the porch. We're forgetting that though we're tempted to be despondent, someone is leading us. Yes. I believe it."

"Explain that, Eli," Gerhard said.

"Well, the latter part of the verses Preacher Eck read: *'whose builder and maker is God.'*"

Joseph, seeing Andrias and his friends trudging back from the station, lifted a stubbled chin. "Eli, keep on reminding me. I guess we're discovering what Abraham found out. Faith is just keeping on stepping out, even though the answers aren't there yet, and there don't seem to be any boundaries to the land."

***

The hours of waiting were taking their toll. Though they had the nourishment of soup and bread the last two days, a sense of lostness nudged at Catherine's mind and heart. She hardly had the strength to say to Lusanna and Andrias, "Grab our hand luggage, they've instructed us to return to the train station."

Joseph, struggling with the largest bundle, led little Benjamin who was hanging on to his coat sleeve.

Catherine had bound his thin shoes with strips torn from a blanket she'd dug from her bundle. The questions stirred. *Will my hope chest be shipped with us? Where is it, and the other trunk Joseph made? Why does all this moving and traveling have to be done so late at night. It's so hard on*

117

Benjamin. Oh, Lusanna, Benjamin, and Andrias.... Joseph, what have we done to our family?
Indeed it was late at night, 11:30 PM, to be exact. The bitter cold had not lessened. To Catherine, it seemed even colder. *How is it that the Lord seems to stir everything up for us at night?*
She had a flashing thought of Moses leading the children of Israel through the wilderness. *At night. A pillar of fire by night.*
All the light we'll have after we leave the dimness of the station will be what light we have in our hearts. Dear Jesus. The prairies are so dark and lonely here.
"Mother, they're saying we'll soon be going to a place where we will be welcomed. At least where we will be warm and can cook our own meals," Lusanna said, tromping along, leaning sideways with the heavy bundle in her right hand.
"I wish we were back in Antanofka. Jacob and Elise made the right decision, staying behind. Look at us." Andrias shifted his focus toward the squatting black engine puffing smoke into the sub-zero air.
Then Catherine stopped as her people shoved passed her shoulder. "Why, Joseph, would you look at that? Up ahead they're loading into *boxcars.* How can this be?"
Joseph, who had stopped with his wife momentarily, stared, eyes fixed, mouth wide open. He, like Catherine, was wordless. When he found his tongue, his words faltered. "Well, Catherine, we have to hope that Brother Warkentine and Colonel Johnson know what they're doing. Maybe it's only a short trip. Yes, that could be it, only a short journey."
Catherine and her family trudged onward toward the line of people, Colonel Johnson and his aides, helping the people up the platform stools into the waiting boxcars. The engine let out a lonesome wail, steam hissed and blasted horizontally, mixing with the skin-numbing air. A fetid stink of coal smoke filled their nostrils.
"This way, folks," called Colonel Johnson.
Catherine's family took their turns stepping up the stool into the darkness where at least ninety people would be

loaded. She saw, mercifully, that straw covered the floor. She couldn't help the thought: *Is this what the Mennonite Aid Committee arranged for us? Where is Brother Warkentine? Maybe this is what rejected people deserve. The babe, Jesus, lay upon straw. I guess it is our time, indeed, to emulate the blessed Jesus.*

But he has done so much, Brother Warkentine. Yes, it is the railroad providing this shipping to another town. Florence, Kansas, did they say? Didn't we travel through there on our way to this Hutchinson? This end-of-the-trail disaster?

Catherine was certain that it was preacher Eck speaking as he helped his wife, Cornelia, up the stepstool into the car. "Oh, the bad air. Don't breathe too hard, Cornelia, the night air will do us in."

Then Catherine realized that all of it, the passage, rough and troublesome as it was over the winter Atlantic, the lonesome rail travel across America to Kansas, even the miserable experience of Hutchinson, was financed by other people. People who must surely care about them.

We must not forget it. Someone cares for us. How will we ever be able to pay them back? So, Florence, Kansas, here we come, all thirteen boxcars of us. At least, Lusanna thinks the town has a beautiful name.

19

WEEPING ENDURES FOR THE NIGHT

At first Lusanna, with Benjamin squeezed against her thigh, stood stuffed along the wall of the thirty-foot wooden boxcar with her other family members. She couldn't see her mother's form in the darkness. She felt the unease and fear creep up her throat. A flashback of the night when their cow, Basha, was stolen in the frightful village raid, and how they had sunken to the floor in the darkness, flooded her mind. *Mother - she's growing frailer. Now this? Stuffed in here where it is pitch black. Oh, this bitter cold. What was Colonel Johnson thinking? We're not pigs or cattle. Hadn't he said that it was fourteen degrees below zero? I'd like to tell you, Elder Tobias, about your balmy Kansas.*

The wheels screeched as the boxcar groaned and rattled eastward toward Florence, sixty miles away, but the people were largely silent. Mothers rocked babies in their arms in attempts to lull them back to the forgetfulness of sleep.

"So late in the night, Mother, and here we're traveling again." Lusanna reached for her mother's hand.

"We must remember, Lusanna, they have a plan. Surely, they have rooms for us ahead. We hope…" But her words were lost as the car shifted and the train wailed and wobbled around a bend. They braced themselves, trying not to plant their feet upon the ones huddling on the floor before them.

Lusanna heard another voice. *Was it Eva Nachtigal's voice?*

"Lusanna, we must keep in mind 'weeping may endure for the night, but joy cometh in the morning, Psalm 30: 5.'"

Then her father's voice broke through the mingling of creaks of the car and murmurs of the bewildered people. "We didn't all make it on this train, Catherine. There were just too many. Colonel Johnson said that the rest of our group will have to follow us in the morning."

"You mean," Andrias questioned, "that we have no real leader, that brother Warkentine, nor even the Colonel, are on this train? What happened to Schmidt?

"Maybe we're the kind of people it's best to walk away from." The voice came from the back of the car, thirty feet away.

Abandoned? Are we abandoned?

Lusanna recognized the voice. *Carl. Carl, his sapphire-blue eyes, his tousled yellow hair.* She wished she could see his friendly face.

Maybe Carl was right. Maybe we are the forgotten ones.

Then Lusanna thought of the words of the blessed Jesus: *Blessed are ye. when men shall revile you, and persecute you, and shall say all manner of evil against you falsly, for my sake...Blessed are the poor in spirit: for theirs is the kingdom of heaven.*

The words circled in her brain. Then other words assailed her like thrown stones. Words the young people were forced to listen to, not only here on these frontiers, but back in Antanofka, too. Words they tried to overlook or ignore.

"They are the ignorant ones."

"Aren't they morally deficient?"

"Their education isn't as fine as ours."

"They are the *Ostrogers*," All the words were said with a disdaining emphasis.

She had heard, even on this trip, the descriptions of their defeat and weaknesses, how they now were referred to as "the helpless Poles."

Well, Andrias and I are not helpless, and we are not Poles. Dutch. We are really Dutch. Didn't our forefathers come from Holland? Yes. Just look at our forms, tall, big noses, big hands and feet. Look at the blond ones among us, like Carl. Fix your eyes upon our tall women. Though we speak the German language, and have adopted German ways, we have never considered ourselves as Russians, and never POLISH.

Then she heard the voice of Preacher Unruh, who had said few words on the entire journey thus far. "They've done all this for us. We can't expect them to hold our hands every moment, to take over completely. Surely, they'll be on the morning train with our other brethren. We must wait and see."

Wait and see. Wait and see.

Lusanna covered her mouth with her hand to stuff back her words.

That's what this whole trip has been, Brother Unruh. Wait and see. I've had enough of waiting. And, brother Unruh, right now, I can't see a blame thing.

An hour passed. The engine had stopped at some crossing to take on water.

Wouldn't the water be frozen in this temperature?

Lusanna heard Andrias groan; she knew his muscles were tired, his legs must be aching like hers. *Couldn't someone open a door to get some fresh air?*

Her cold back against the boards reminded her of the reason why the doors remained closed. And then she remembered; some busybody was always cautioning against the *bad night air.*

In the back of the car she heard shuffling. Someone groaned between attacks of coughing. Her ears picked up murmurs of concern from caretakers.

Heavenly Father, don't let a plague break out among us.

Hadn't the Schoolmaster told us about the frightful plagues in the Middle Ages? How long ago? Rats spread that dreadful plight of death didn't they? Well, indeed, a rat would scurry from this bitter cold. The Vaderland, a better home.

***

Joseph Becker feared for his family. If their feet and hands were as cold as his, they were in danger of serious frostbite. *We need shelter now.*

Joseph and Gerhard Jantz forced open the car door when the train chugged to a stop at the Florence station. Both men stared into the darkness.

Gerhard turned to Joseph. "Joseph, the streets are empty. There seems to be nobody here to greet us."

Joseph shoved forward, his breath rising from his nose in a vapor cloud. Indeed, the station squatted empty, lonely by the tracks. A bewildered-looking stationmaster looked out a dimly lit window.

Joseph could see brethren from the other cramped cars crawl out and head toward their boxcar. Murmurs and mumbling circled. The bitter northeast wind blasted them as they tried to huddle against it, burying their hands in their sleeves or pockets. They shook their unbelieving heads in recognition of the stark reality. *There is nobody here, either from the town or from the Santa Fe Station to welcome us. Where is the mayor? Are there any Mennonites?*

My God, my God. Joseph Becker thought to himself. *We have reached the end of the line in more ways than one. I thought the experience in Hutchinson was rugged, but this?* He felt anger crawl from his chest to his throat.

Joseph and his comrades' feet quickly found purchase on the floor of the boxcars as they heaved their cold-riddled bodies back into the shelter of the car.

"We'll have to spend the rest of the night in the box-cars, folks. It shouldn't be long until morning."

Joseph realized how futile and empty his words sounded when the people were so near to being seriously frostbitten. By now, he knew that there were sick people on board. Cries and murmurs encircled his head as he closed the door.

Then Joseph heard Lusanna's voice. "Say it again, Frau Nightingale. Say it again. Maybe we can even clear our throats and sing it: 'Weeping may endure for the night, but joy cometh in the morning.'"

***

After three hours of waiting, the wails of another train drifted toward them. Lusanna shook her head to clear her brains. "Mother, the others are arriving." She nudged Catherine, who had fallen asleep. She grabbed Benjamin's shoulder and shook him.

Bodies shifted. People tried to heave themselves upward, groping for their belongings in the dark. She heard one child crying, another pleading, "Mama, I'm hungry, and I'm so cold."

The boxcar door slid open, and mercifully, there was morning light spreading across the bricks in front of the station. She saw her father scoot to the door and drop out, Cornelius Wedel behind him. Andrias, mouth open, eyes staring, heaved himself out to join them.

Then they all began to pour out of the opening toward the morning light. Hope fluttered in Lusanna's heart. *We'll have warmth. Porridge and milk. Oh, mercifully, maybe soon real beds to lie upon.*

Florence. Oh, a lovely name for a town. Florence! Joy cometh in the morning.

***

Joseph Becker stared ahead down the tracks at the second trainload, Antanofkans slowly sliding out of the boxcars into the frigid morning air. *What had they said last night? Fourteen degrees below zero? Oh, Brother Tobias, you have deceived us.* His joints ached, he shook with cold, as Andrias shoved himself to his side. "Father, I see Colonel Johnson heading toward us. Surely he will guide us to our shelter." Another man, maybe from the town, dressed in a suit and topcoat, joined Johnson.

Colonel Johnson, wide grin spreading as if he were about to open a treasury to let the golden coins spill out, waved. "This way, folks. This way. We have arranged shelter. Mayor Crawford has just joined us."

People stopped and stared as if in disbelief. A few straggled behind him, dragging their bundles, weariness beyond belief registering on their faces.

They stumbled and tottered, sore from the transport, hands and feet chilblained, and minds fogged in another seeming confusion.

Joseph shook his head to clear his brains. *What have I done to my family? The Wedels were correct to stay back in Antanofka. God, help us.*

Catherine nudged his shoulder. "Joseph, get us into some shelter. Our family can't endure much more of this." Benjamin reached for his hand with a small purple one.

Like Antarctic penguins, they staggered along after Colonel Johnson's fluttering hand. His words drifting in air so cold one could scarcely breathe it. "This way, folks. This building right across the street..." Their meager clothing flapped in the wind.

Joseph looked ahead to see someone opening the door of a brick storage building. *A new town, a new building. Thank God. Oh, merciful Jesus, let there be some heat.*

20

ELDER TOBIAS

Elder Tobias bent over his six-year-old grandson, Hans, as the *S. S. Abbotsford* rocked in the waters off of Queensland, England. The child, suffering from the outbreak of smallpox, soon after they had arrived back at the harbor, grabbed the cup, gulping the water.

Tobias reviewed the events of the third migration of his people, the Karlswalders. He had a fleeting thought of another migration, the Antanofkans, all under his parish care. Though those folks were poor in worldly goods, surely, by now the *Vaderland* had brought them safely across, and they had reached their destination. *Good old Vaderland.*

As *The Abbotsford* struggled through the stormy waters of the North Sea on the first day of the journey, they collided in the gloom and fog with a vessel named *The Indus.*

Since the collision was in the middle of the night, great confusion broke out among the emigrants, stranded, rocking, tilting in the unmerciful waves.

Tobias recalled his thankfulness when, after drifting in the violence of the waves and storm, the crew discovered that the ship would not sink after all.

His head ached from reviewing the events. The threatening waves, the endless fog, the drifting *Abbotsford.* Mercifully, another ship, the *S. S. Philadelphia* soon chugged to their aid, *I couldn't believe it! Colliding again?*

But it was the truth. Another delay, another collision in the unforgettable waters of the North Sea.

The Abbotsford, damaged and with broken machinery, was towed back to the docks at Queensland, England. Here he remained on the vessel with a grievously ill grandson. He had sent his wife, Helena, ahead with those able to proceed on to America on *The Illinois,* volunteering to stay here among the eight families who had been stricken with the dreaded disease. The very name of smallpox sent shudders down his back.

It's my duty to stay with these unfortunately ill people, including little Hans, who, God willing, may still reach America.

Within days, those laid low by the disease were lifted on their pallets and transported to a hospital ship, then towed and anchored five miles outside the port. Here they were quarantined. Tobias felt it his duty to be at the bedside of these members of his churches.

Though discouraged, he was reassured that many of the Karlswalders were able to board *The Kennilworth* and continue their journey to Philadelphia. *Surely the Antanofka group paved the way for them. Yes, that Joseph Becker, his wife, Catherine, and, oh, how could I forget that girl, Lusanna. Spunky girl!*

He couldn't help the overwhelming sense of loss he felt. So quickly his communities in Polish-Russia, now almost vanished. Those remaining might struggle to maintain the faith for a few years, then the clouds and political storms of Great Russia would overshadow them. There would be no compromises. No church operated schools. Church buildings? Turned into places of business or storage granaries.

He thought of the people of Karlsberg, the Mennonite villages of Furestenthal, Waldheim, and last of all, the Antanofka folks.

We've suffered a great break in our communion, once so near to one another, once so united, now scattered. His heart was lonely for a pulpit, his identity as Kirchenspiel, now so threatened.

I feel like Jonah being asked by God to go to Nineveh. America? Kansas, the Dakotas? A foreign land, plains as lonely as the steppes of Russia. What will it be like, starting anew? Will I have to preach standing outside on a stump? Who will open the prairie soil? Who will build the houses for the people? Oh, Lord, I need the help of the blessed Jesus.

Next, his mind focused upon the people from the church at Antanofka. How will those folks remember me? As their kindly bishop, nurturing their spirits, baptizing their children after their catechism?

He could not even bring to full consciousness the thought that pricked at his mind: *Will they believe that I have abandoned them when they know I'm settling with Helena in South Dakota?*

The child was asleep, now. Thank God. The pustules ravaged the fair skin of the little boy, making it difficult and painful for him to lie in any position for any length of time. Tears flowed down Tobias's cheeks as he sat, praying for the child's recovery.

I suppose I could sit here and endlessly ask, why? Why? I have lived long enough to know that upon this earth pestilence can draw nigh. Without warning. Striking the innocent before there is even time to sprinkle blood upon the lintel, allowing the death angel to pass over.

The Lord is my rock and my fortress, and my deliverer; my God, my strength, in whom I will trust!

In my distress, I called upon the Lord and cried unto my God: He heard my voice out of his temple, and my cry came before him, even unto his ears.

The words of Psalm 18 comforted his spirit.

He next began to think of his wife, Helena. How she would progress on the journey without his support. He could envision that, upon the arrival of her ship in the port of Philadelphia, the many Mennonites would shelter the new arrivals in their homes. Yes, that would be the Christian way. Perhaps part of the Polish-Russian group might even sink their roots right there in that abundant and fertile land. Join the established churches. Thank the Lord for their redemption from the Great Russian Bear.

Well, I am now delayed. I won't get to Kansas at all. Surely those folks have already found succor for their wounds and their aching hearts, brought about from leaving their homeland. I placed them in good hands. Hands that were extended, and trustworthy: That American Board, brothers Baer, Christian Krehbiel, the Funk brothers. Surely their aid would continue to flow for the work among the newly established Kansas churches.

His heart felt eased, thinking of how he would spend his time, once he himself reached American shores, after this trial. *Pennsylvania? In that land of milk and honey? Perhaps I will stay awhile. Even preach in their churches. Gather money for the emigrants in the Dakotas and in Kansas.*

His stomach growled. He had tightened his belt a couple of notches, quite aware that he was losing some of his corpulence. His mouth watered.

Oh, for some pearl barley cooked with oatmeal. Those Mennonite women, how they fixed it. Then, the beef and beer soup. Not to think of the buttered wheat bread fresh from the great oven.

He was brought out of his reverie by a sudden shifting of the hospital ship. He heard crying children. Eight of them? Several adults. Three had already passed on to their heavenly award. His head lowered. He raked a hand through his gray hair. "How long, Oh, Lord, how long?"

Elder Tobias sat, weary, but faithful to his duty, sitting by and praying for members of his congregations and his grandson, all who lay with only the barest of care. Once they were overtaken by the disease, it was too late for any vaccination, which had been available since the early 1870s.

Thou shalt not be afraid for the terror by night; nor for the arrow that flieth by day; nor for the pestilence that walketh in darkness...For he shall give his angels charge over thee....

The elder, sustained by the words, keep whispering them over the stricken body of little Hans.

21

BREAD OF HEAVEN

They had been in the building, approximately thirty feet wide and eighty feet long for five days now. Although Lusanna did find a space on the straw-covered floor to sleep, she had to wedge tightly in beside her mother and Benjamin. Andrias and her father had tried sleeping sitting with their backs against the wall to save space, but they finally gave up and slid in wherever they could on the floor with the wall-to-wall people. Not even to mention the bundles, bags, trunks, chests and scattered paraphernalia.

She thought of the American, Mayor Crawford, and the few minutes he took greeting them the morning of their arrival. How he had cleared his throat several times before speaking, looking right and left. His eyes then opened wide in what she had concluded was disbelief at their bedraggled condition and near impossible situation.

"Why, uh, yes. Uh, good morning, folks. I mean..." How he had stammered as he took in their plight. His nose twitched as if he'd caught a fetid smell. He reached up and lifted a smart hat, which he had forgotten to remove in his unease.

"Why, we citizens of the fair town of Florence greet you." He cleared his throat again, hand groping at his mouth as if searching for more words. "Why, we hope your stay in our town will be, uh, uh, satisfactory. Yes, we've tried to accommodate you. Colonel Johnson here tells me that the Santa Fe Railroad has provided an abundance of coal for your fires and ovens. You can be assured that you will stay warm. The Railroad is paying for your lodging until spring arrives and you folks can get out into the country where you will settle."

Lusanna braced a right elbow in her left hand, waiting for clarification from someone. Mayor Crawford had forgotten that none of the emigrants spoke English and thus, did not immediately comprehend their blank stares. He looked at Colonel Johnson with pleading eyes. Johnson, in halting German, tried to communicate the gist of Crawford's words as best as he could.

"What about something to eat?" A man's voice called out from the back. "My God, sir, we haven't had a good meal for two days, now."

Unable to understand the plea or question, Crawford plowed on.

"Your own Mennonite brother, a Mr. Warkentine, promises me that you will have plenty of flour and other provisions. Yes. He should be arriving to take over that part of it."

Then with a hasty *good-bye,* he had turned, coat tails wagging from his lively swagger, and stepped out into the bitter cold.

Mercifully, there was a big potbellied stove at the back of the building, burning coal that had been provided by the railroad. *Thank God. Thank God for all the help. When will that blessed Brother Warkentine come again with good news for us?*

People were stirring, a mother was breastfeeding her baby to the left. *Thank God the child is still alive after suffering these trials.*

Looking back through the smoky gloom, Lusanna saw her mother near the rear of the building. With a bowl in her hand, she reached to dip hot water from the open bucket on top of the stove. *Careful, Mother, Freida Koehn scalded her hands yesterday morning, attempting the same thing.*

Though it was a pitiful amount of water, she and her mother used a piece of torn cloth to wash their faces and wipe their hands. Though Lusanna knew that outside against the back wall of the building, the men had placed long benches, basins and tubs aligned on top, providing for a more serious clean-up if one could brave the cold. For now, the face scrubbing would do.

Soon there was a greater bustling, rustling, and shifting of bodies. Men pulling at their trousers, drawing them up tightly, shaking their heads, raking straw from hair and beards. Cries of hungry children mixed with the constant murmurs roiling through the fetid air. She heard the coughs and groans of the sick. Here and there rose the words of murmured prayers.

Lusanna looked upwards toward the gables at the small grimy windows. *Oh, that we could open those windows. We need fresh air. This is worse than The Vaderland.*

But wasn't that the problem?

The air. Always the air. What was it with Antanofka folk and their superstitions? Even her mother when they were back home. "*No, Lusanna, don't go out into the night air. Remember when...*"

She saw Andrias hunching his shoulders and rubbing his chapped hands together as he, along with Carl and Jake, stepped through the rear door.

No use waiting. Her mother joined her, wending their way through the maze toward the door, trying not to step on a hand, a leg or a foot. *Oh, the lines at the privies.*

Lusanna stared ahead at the four little shacks, which had been hastily thrown up for their arrival. Someone had the good sense to place them at least seventy feet back against an alley wall, outlined by stalks of dead weeds.

She looked up at the sky. Maybe she would learn to love the Kansas sky. Streaks of gold and rose stretched like giant fingers into the deep blue.

Perhaps the bitter cold has broken. She glanced to the south toward the Cottonwood River and saw bare trees, their giant limbs reaching skyward. *Cottonwood trees, father had said. Maybe it will warm up, and if it is safe, Agnes and I can stroll down there soon. And if the river is frozen, who would restrain us from the delights of skating?*

Of course, we left our skates behind in the village, but who would stop a couple of Dutch girls from frolicking on the ice, anyway?

She glanced to the left and saw Carl Jantz and Jake Unruh shivering and shifting their feet in a line of men, privy ahead. She quickly turned her head, knowing that she was blushing.

Agnes Unruh, standing in a near line, blew on her hands in an attempt to warm them. She shifted from foot to foot in urgency. "Hey, Lusanna Becker," she yelled out, "can't you see that *that* privy is occupied?"

Then she slapped her thigh and howled as the cold morning wind flapped her skirt against her thighs.

Lusanna couldn't help herself as she broke into giggles. *Why does Agnes have to make schputt right now?*

Poor Agnes. *Look how thin she's becoming, yet she never despairs.*

She, too, needed to shift her feet.

How long? How long?

"It's Gerda Schmidt, Lusanna, holding up the works. She's been in there for over five minutes, I'm sure," called Agnes. "It's from the bitter tea she gulps. She's ever swilling tea."

Lusanna wanted to say, "Oh, stop it, Agnes. For heaven's sake, stop it."

Then Agnes hollered toward her: "Why, Lusanna, if I had my father's watch, I could make sure you think of the others and don't take more than your share of the time."

Lusanna shifted her body, holding her hands tightly. *Agnes Unruh, shut your mouth.* Her lower belly ached.

She looked to the left and saw a thin, hunch-shouldered man in line not ten feet from where she was standing. She felt the heat rise to her cheeks, which she knew were as red as a morning sun rising through a haze. *Heinrich Schmidt? No, not this? Surely he won't speak. It'd be too embarrassing....*

"Why, Fraulein Becker, good morning to you. It would be unmannerly of me not to greet you." His smile spread over crooked teeth.

Should I answer? Oh, what is the Christian thing to do?

She mumbled, a *good morning*, while she stared at the back of Anna Jantz in front of her. She looked down at her worn shoes. She couldn't dig a hole with her toe to bury herself into the earth: the ground was frozen too hard. Fortunately, a flock of low-flying pigeons, their warbles and murmurs drifting, settled on the frosted, tarred roof of their warehouse lodging place.

"Oh, Mother, look up at the pretty birds," called Hans Voth, his little finger pointing in the frosty air.

The people, shifting in the lines, mouths in straight lines, lifted bleary morning eyes to the object of the child's calling. Obviously, all thankful for such diversion. Everyone thinking, *hurry, hurry*, while their shoulders shivered.

Didn't the blessed scriptures have it somewhere, "and a little child shall lead them?"

How about, "and a little child shall save them?"

Because they were refugees, sitting, waiting, time stretched ahead of them with no ordinary markers for the passing of the hours, it had been decided that morning worship would be held, everyone together. With the upheavals and disruptions, it was near impossible for fathers to lead their family devotions. No privacy, no space to settle comfortably. Constant interference.

"I will be leading the morning prayers," Preacher Eck had announced.

But, first, these morning calls. These early morning duties.

The privy door swung open, old Gerda Schmidt stepped out, staring from right to left. She made a rude attempt to throw her woolen shawl back over her shoulders. Her eyes fixed upon Anna Jantz, just in front of Lusanna.

"Why, Anna, I wouldn't recommend more than five minutes in there at all. No, not at all. And, it would have helped had these Americans who put up these buildings had taken the time to cut the weeds beneath."

Lusanna snickered. Redhead Agnes howled, tears were running down her cheeks. "Oh, Lusanna," she hollered. It's true, in life we have to take the bitter with the sweet."

***

Berent Jantz and his wife, Elske, had fired up one of the ovens, placed near the back of the brick building. Joseph and Catherine were busy stoking another one. Joseph wondered, as he held a split log of wood, what kind of wood it was. It had an orange, papery inner bark, and an orange, hard center. As he watched it burn, he turned to Catherine.

"Look at how it burns, Catherine. I've never seen wood that heats up so quickly." He smiled.

Catherine was glad to see her husband smile, to see his face change, if only momentarily. She had begun to worry. She knew that his eyes registered what he was trying to conceal: anxiety over their future, his worry over the unknown. Everyone in the brick building knew the prevailing questions: *What next? How long will we be here? When will we settle on the land.*

Catherine tried to envision it in her mind, the prairie land. *Of course, the grass, tall grass waving, blowing, sweeping everywhere. How do they plow it? Just where do we get bricks or stones to build a house? With such few trees, surely there won't be lumber, will there?*

Joseph's voice brought her back. "Go back inside, Catherine," Joseph said, "it's too cold out here. You can be more help with the other women as they get ready to bake the bread."

She had obeyed. Yes, her hands were stiff with cold.

She stepped back into the gloomy haze of the interior. Evidently the big stove at the rear, which was burning soft coal, had belched again, blowing open the door, allowing sulfuric fumes to drift across the room. The people coughed. Children rubbed their eyes.

Eva Nightingale's voice called; "Close that back door.
We have to keep that air out." She clutched her baby, for
she'd just changed a diaper.
*Another problem. How do we wash clothes? Let alone
our bodies.*

So Catherine joined the women, among them, Helena
Kohn, Elisabeth Dirks, and Maria Ratzlaff, who had laid
loose boards they had found in back over a couple of up-
ended trunks, to make a space for mixing and rolling dough.
They were thankful that only yesterday, a wagon had drawn
up in front with provisions.

Thankfully, there had been a jar of yeast provided by a
warm-hearted Mennonite woman from a town called
Peabody. There were sacks of potatoes which had been
shared from the winter supply of those Mennonites who had
settled near a place called Marion. *A beautiful name, Marion.*

Catherine began to smile as the rhythms of mixing and
kneading and rolling dough took over. The women shifted
their feet, arms and hands busy following the familiar
patterns needed for baking bread.. Odors of fresh wheat flour
mixing with the sour smell of yeast spread. Here and there
Catherine saw faces widen into smiles. She felt her own lips
relax, her cheeks warm. Here at least was one luxury, *wheat
flour.*

*Yes, bread. Bread - more than for nurturance of the
body. Bread of life. The blessed bread of the Savior, broken
for us. Bread of heaven. The blessed invitation, "Come and
eat."*

Catherine felt more of her old Antanofkan self as she
broke off a lump of dough, shaping it into a loaf. She
recognized that the lump felt like a living thing, its surface
warm, smooth. It even obeyed the movements of her fingers
as she laid it into a baking pan someone had dug from
transported belongings.

She began to hum an old hymn. *Bread of Heaven, feed
me 'till I want no more.*

22

THE PIED PIPER

"We have to do more, Mina. God, help those people over in Florence."

Bernard, sitting at his desk in his home in Halstead, raked a hand through his graying hair.

"But you were just out to Florence a few days ago, Bernard. You're working overtime. Your thoughts are consumed with their welfare. Don't you need a break from all of this?" Mina stepped toward his desk, placing a hand on his shoulder.

"You just don't know the need, Mina. I've notified John Funk who publishes *The Herald of Truth*. He's printing my letter calling for aid. That paper will reach most established Mennonite communities east of here, all the way to Pennsylvania. We've asked all the churches to send money, to send food, dried beans and peas, but most of all, money."

Mina listened, shaking her head from side to side.

"Also, I know that board member David Goerz made the same announcements in his paper, *Zur Heimat*. Donations are slowly trickling in."

"Thank God," Mina said.

"The Pennsylvanians pledged over a thousand dollars. Our own Board of Guardians gave five hundred from our depleted treasury. We also received a check for three hundred from the church at Summerfield, Illinois. But, Mina, that is just a drop in the bucket when compared to the need.

"Well, I imagine so, Bernard. I'm sure you are correct. But you already have extended yourself, giving so much. Think of your health."

Bernard sat back in his chair, took a long look at his attractive wife, noting the comb in her auburn hair, done up in a French roll.

"This is my duty for now, Mina. Duty. A Christian responsibility. I was out in Florence for a short visit with those folks. I can't explain to you the extreme poverty of their situation. The conditions under which they must live until spring - you just couldn't imagine."

Fleeting glimpses floated through his brain of thin-faced, chilblained children. Anguished mothers. Dejected men, near to giving up in their obvious feelings of worthlessness and helplessness. Not to even mention the sick.

"Is it possible to send a few of the young people back to Summerfield? How about that little church in Missouri, the one in Iowa? Couldn't they take some of those folks for the next months? At least until the weather warms."

Bernard saw tears glistening in his wife's eyes.

"In addition to the *Herald of Truth* announcement, we've sent out a general letter to all Mennonite Churches in America, pleading for contributions. We have to see those folks through the next two months"

But then, who has money for settlement on the land? Which land? Where? Who would decide? Here in Kansas land has to be purchased. What kind of prices will the Santa Fe Railroad people offer to these people?.

Bernard recognized the need for a local relief committee, right here in these south central Kansas counties. *The spring will come. The land will warm. Seed time and harvest.*

Bernard Warkentine also recognized the utility of Mina's suggestion that if possible they send some of the young folks in the Florence warehouse back to Summerfield, if at all possible. He fortified himself and made haste to take the next train to that little town along the Cottonwood.. He had received a reply from his telegraph to Summerfield. He sighed with relief when he read their reply.

Will accept twenty-four young people through the winter months.

***

The train chugged into the fresh new town on the Cottonwood River. Bernard stepped down to the station platform. It was only a few hundred feet back and across to the storehouse where the immigrants huddled, waiting. Ever waiting. *God, keep the plagues away.*

The wind still caused him to draw his coat collar close to his neck as he, with lengthy steps, hurried over to the brick building.

When he opened the door, his face was hit with the overpowering smog, a mixture of coal gasses and sulfur, oil fumes from the burning portable ovens, and the smell one would expect from bodies not receiving the benefit of water for three months. He wanted to dig for a handkerchief to cover his nose; however, manners forbade it.

Preacher Eck, stared at Bernard as he staggered toward him. Bernard saw that he appeared distraught and weak, his voice, feeble.

"We greet you again, brother Warkentine." Eck made an attempt to smile.

"I greet all of you brethren," responded Warkentine. "All of you."

A thought raced through his mind: *Where is their Elder, Tobias Unruh?*

His eyes fell upon the masses of children, some lying sick and crying, others reaching outward with dirty upturned palms, indicating their hunger. *Their eyes. Their eyes. Oh, God, have pity.*

Joseph Becker stepped through the gaggle of people, trying not to bruise a hand, to greet Warkentine. "Mercy, Brother Warkentine, we surely are glad to see you. I'm sure you have plans or news for us?"

Bernard could see by Becker's pleading eyes that he restrained himself from asking for provisions just then.

Bernard explained to the mixture of folks who had gathered around him near the door. *I dare not venture further into this....*

He reached back to open the door. A cold brisk wind blew in.

"Close it, please," Eck called. "We can't have that air coming in here. We have enough sickness without strange air in this foreign land."

What kind of belief? Where did it come from? Why didn't the worried-eyed mothers contest him?

Amidst the din of voices cries of children, and groans of sick ones, Bernard cleared his throat. *How to begin?* He did notice, however, that mothers and fathers tried to hush the crying children. Mothers picked up babies.

"I'm praying that these weeks of winter will pass swiftly, dear ones," he began. "It doesn't take a doctor or carpenter to say that you folks are too crowded in here."

He gasped for some air. *Can I even go on?*

"I have discussed your situation here with Elder Christian Krehbiel at the church in Summerfield, Illinois, to see if they would be able to employ and house over twenty of your young people."

Some mothers stood, hands folded before their bosoms. Their looks proclaimed: *No, don't send our youth so far away. Illinois? That's beyond that great river, isn't it? Didn't we come through there once?*

He noticed that several young persons tried to wend their way forward toward him.

"Did you say they would?" Joseph Becker asked, Andrias at his side.

"The answer was *yes*. They will find employment and housing for them. This would include their daily meals."

Sounds of murmuring swept through the room.

Families made attempts to draw closer together. Heads huddled. Sounds of Plattdeutsch mixed with cries and coughs.

"Who can go? How old must these young people be?"
The voice was from Andrias Becker. "I'm already *sixteen*.
I'd like to go back to that place in Illinois, for awhile, at
least." His eyes cut down to his shoes. A thin woman,
obviously his mother, lifted an open palm to her mouth, eyes
staring ahead.

"We believe that a sixteen-year-old would qualify. That
would be the lower limit. Let us say from sixteen to twenty-
four, if they are all single."

Bernard cleared his throat. He coud do nothing about
his burning eyes.

Louder murmuring swirled throughout the building. He
saw young people waving hands toward him through the
smoke-filled room. He could see eyes that had been
moments before lifeless and dull, now glisten with
excitement.

Suddenly, he was overwhelmed with the sounds and
calls, while stricken-faced parents looked on in confusion.

"Me, me, take me!"

"I'm an ox of a fellow. I'll even shovel manure in that
Summerfield."

"I'm the best milkmaid," called a red-haired girl whose
head scarf was awry.

"If they want someone to spade their gardens, choose
me," a yellow-headed youth announced.

"They'll need cooks. You ought to see how I can bake
bread. *Verenique?* why I can slap up that stuff in no time at
all. No time at all," a young lady with a very soiled pinafore
announced loudly.

Other girls began calling out. The tallest one announced. "Washwoman, washwoman. Get me at a scrub
board, you'll not be sorry. Soiled britches, dirty socks…"

"I'm Andrias Becker," called another youth in a badly
soiled jacket, a shock of black hair falling over his forehead.
"Take me for sure. I'm a woodsman, Father and I sawed the
finest boards, back in Antanofka."

Yes, thought Bernard, as he smiled. *We'll have no
trouble at all. We may have a run. I'll have to give them time*

to organize. I'll come back in the morning and start the transfer. What does that Bible passage say?
  "Thy youth is renewed like the eagles."

***

Joseph and Andrias sat with their backs against the wall. Catherine and Lusanna, who was holding Benjamin, were sitting on the floor facing them. Around them all the families with teenagers were in consultation. Voices grew louder as youth, here and there, pleaded with their parents. "Let me go, Papa, let me go. I must get out of here."

"But Mother, it'll be for only a couple of months. I'd be back in time to help Father plough."

Lusanna watched Andrias stare into his father's dark brown eyes. "Father, please, I plead, do let me go. I'm a good worker. You know that. It wouldn't be for long." His eyes lowered when he saw his mother's long face and the tears in Benjamin's eyes.

A surge of jealousy arose within her. *Carl going, now Andrias. No. No, I can't let Andrias go without me. God knows how hard I can work. Maybe those Summerfield women would like someone like me to polish their wooden floors. Shovel out the privy. Why, I can even clean out the milk barn. How about sitting at their spinning wheels?*

She started to interrupt Andrias, but when she glanced at her mother's face, she saw the fear. The hand she lifted to her mouth was frail and trembling.

She realized that she couldn't go.

And I hate this crowd, the everlasting people shoving against each other. The shifting. The unknowing. I hate the itching, the lice and fleas embedded in this straw. Maybe I've gotten used to the smell in here, but I still detest it!

She noticed how silent her mother had become as she shifted her body. Benjamin moved over to sit beside her, looking up into her face. Lusanna saw that her mother knew that words were about to hemorrhage from her daughter's mouth.

"Lusanna, though it would be a very hard thing for me to see Andrias go, I simply couldn't bear the loss of you right now." Tears streamed down her lined cheeks.

"It will be difficult for us, Andrias. You're strong. You were a good worker with me in the woods in Antanofka. Perhaps they will have lumbering in Illinois. If Brother Warkentine can promise that it is only for a short time," his words faltered in uncertainty, "until we, we, uh, get settled."

Lusanna saw his eyes shift to the floor. She recognized the thinness of his hope, the fatigue of his body and spirit.

"Oh, God, help us all," she whispered. Suddenly, she realized that she had to restrain herself to keep from screaming as the din in the room increased in volume.

***

When Bernard Warkentine returned midmorning the next day, the smog and gloom in the room was the same, if not worse. There seemed to be more weak cries from both children and a few older folks lying on their pallets. Steam boiled up from the kettles on the potbellied stove top. Sulfur fumes still permeated the room from the burning coal. Masses of people stared at him.

He did not need to call for their attention. He was almost crushed by the circle of youth shoving for a place near him. Pity overwhelmed him, but he tried not to let them see how the situation affected him. "I have good news. Tickets to Summerfield for twenty-four of you."

Hands flailed in the air. Other hands searched for a way to reach him. He felt someone patting on his shoulder. He steadied his legs which had begun to tremble. *Who? Which ones? Oh, God, how can I leave so many behind?*

When the task of selecting, sorting, and choosing was over, the fourteen teenage males and ten young women stood before him. He batted tears in his eyes as he saw how they tried to stand tall and straight. Some of them, he noted, were thin as newly split rails.

143

One youth, the yellow-haired one named Carl, kept wiping his runny nose with the back of his hand.

A young woman, named Anna, shook straw from her dingy skirt, neglecting the straw in her hair.

A redheaded girl, named Agnes, bellied forward, her big feet at the edge of his own fine shoes. "Brother Warkentine," she said, "I'm ready. Let's march like Napoleon into Russia." She beamed.

Bernard knew that the sooner they left the confusion of the storehouse for the blessed fresh air outside, the better they all would be. Besides, he hated good-byes. Their parents stood staring, their owl eyes fixed upon their youth as if they expected them to vanish into some great American unknown. His heart ached.

"This way," he said, turning. Like the Pied Piper of Hamelin, he led the line of awkward Polish-Russian-Plattdeutsch youth with their soiled bundles of meager belongings onward toward the waiting train.

23

AT LAST A CHANCE

Though the setting was one of utmost gloom, the light in Heinrich Schmidt's eyes leaped brightly. He could scarcely conceal his excitement over the fact that now Lusanna Becker was without the ever-scanning eye of that snot-nosed brother, Andrias. Her parents, like all the other parents, were mind-boggled with the unknown that lay ahead. With the worry etched upon their faces, they paid him no attention at all. Not, at least, the recognition a *schoolmaster* deserved.

He had noticed, too, that on this journey that gangling youth, Carl Jantz, kept flashing smiles at Lusanna. *Glad that that bishop had picked the awkward youth for the trip back to Illinois. Probably advance to chief manure shoveler on some backwoods farm. That's one thing she doesn't need, the bother of a undisciplined kid. Maturity. She needs the mature arm of a fully-developed man. A scholar.*

He was full up, too, of his mother's goads and ridicule. Since his poor shoemaker father had died eight years ago, her nagging increasingly stung him. Bitter gall bubbled up into his throat when he remembered the pale-faced frumps old Gerda shoved before him. *What even were their names? Knock-kneed creatures who stood simpering. Forlorn spinsters with hanging lower lips and split thumbs from years at the spinning wheel. Flat-footed, simple-minded, Nature's mistakes with not even half his height.*

But that Lusanna Becker! How she read almost two years ago this very day. Plowed right through that David and Bathsheba passage, giving it a no-never-mind. Yet, the blush on her cheek reminded me of a peach I once ate on that trip to the market in Ostrog. I would never have assigned that Bible passage to another of my female scholars.

Heinrich could feel a smile spread at the memory.

He found his long fingers twitching when his mother cornered him with her everlasting prodding.

Well, I tried. Agatha Foth agreed to marry me, didn't she?

The burn of the embarrassment when Agatha broke the engagement smoldered like a stinking clinker in the hulk-of-a-stove at the rear. He was certain that to this day his heart still bore the scars.

It could be forgiven, couldn't it, that his manners sometimes faltered? He remembered how the church women found ways to bend over and tend a baby or step aside when they noticed Gerda's approach. His, too.

Just wait until we settle out upon the land. I see a stone schoolhouse. Respect will no longer be delayed. My rule. My law. Yes, and they shall pay for it.

Oh, I know I should love my mother. The Bible commands it. Love thy neighbor as thyself. But didn't the blessed Jesus say something about hating one's mother and father?

Heinrich shook his head, raked back his hair, which felt like straw from last year's shock of wheat.

He'd had his morning porridge of ground oats and hot water. He'd had his trip to the privy. He'd sat through the worship service, led by Preacher Unruh this time.

What was wrong with those two preachers? They seemed to be sinking - lacking any necessary authority. No command to their voices at all.

He could not take pity upon superiors - leaders of the congregation. So far, there had been little leading as far as he was concerned. *Couldn't they see the congregation was dissolving right before their eyes?*

Elder Tobias? What a laugh. Probably spreading butter upon thick slices of freshly baked bread in a Pennsylvania

Amish woman's kitchen, asking for more strawberry jam. Waiting until he could push his belly up to the table and dig a fork into a serving of ham and butter beans. Fork in the thick, hand-made noodles along with a chunk of savory beef. Saliva filled his mouth. He swallowed, feeling his Adams apple bob.

But what was that strange sickness? That Jantz fellow, over in the back corner behind the stove came down with it first. Next day there were three children with high fevers, coughing, wallowing on their pallets. Mothers and wives distraught.

Heinrich, in spite of his feelings, vowed to mumble his prayers faithfully to ward off the disease-carrying spirits. *The sickness is peculiar to America, isn't it? Whatever it is. That's why old Eck keeps hollering "shut the door."*

***

Elder Christian Krehbiel, stepped onto the train in Halstead, Kansas. A gaggle of cowboys, some chewing on straw stems, watched from the saloon across the muddy street. The train chugged out. He wished his wife, Susanna, was with him, but how could she go? *How many children had she born him now? Thirteen, wasn't it?*

He wondered how it would be when he reached the Antanofkans in Florence.

Maybe God will be merciful and send an early spring. But then what? We haven't made any agreement with the railroad about payment for land for them. Shall we offer money to them as loans?

This all, he knew, would require the best of brains from brother Warkentine, and many prayers to the Lord. He checked his satchel to see if he had included his notes and his Bible. Since he was a preacher and Board member, he planned to hold services for the destitute Polish-Russians. He thought of Elder Tobias: smiling, he remembered a few years back in Summerfield when Tobias and the others came through, inspecting the land. Tobias reacting like a giddy

147

youth presented with his first horse and buggy. *Elder Tobias in charge somewhere, by now, up in South Dakota, isn't he?*

Krehbiel's eyes scanned the lay of the land and how it changed soon after the train rattled through Peabody, Kansas. He glanced out the window, noting that plowed fields had given away to almost complete grasslands. Rougher land, hills and swales. Valleys. A creek here and there. Hawks soaring in a sky with white scattered clouds. He thought that if he was involved in choosing land for the folks now housed in Florence, he'd vote for land west of Newton. *Yes, that rich flat prairie land, for sure.*

He awakened from a short nap just as the wailing whistle announced his arrival at Florence on the Cottonwood. Little town. Sunken down by the river. Striving to flourish. A few brick and stone buildings. Couple of church steeples soaring up.

He stepped down from the car, satchel in hand. His black coattails wagged as he took long steps, planting his feet securely toward the storehouse up the board sidewalk. He breathed a prayer. *Oh, God, do make me a messenger of peace.*

He could smell the place before he even knocked on the door. He had glanced up at the grimy windows in the gables, noting that they were bolted shut.

Surely they have some kind of ventilation in there.

The door opened. A man with sad black eyes stared deeply into his face. He extended a red chapped hand. "I'm Joseph Becker, you're..."

"Krehbiel. Christian Krehbiel. I'm the chair of The Mennonite Board of Guardians, and am acquainted with your situation." The air pummeled his lungs. He halted his breathing in shock, recoiling as if a pugilist had given him a blow in the gut.

What is this? How can I...

Becker turned to look through the smoky fog, searching, searching. He coughed and wiped his eyes. A woman edged her way through an impossible maze of people and crying children to Joseph's side. "He's looking for Preacher Eck and Preacher Unruh, isn't he?"

"Yes, he is, Catherine. Thank God. Can you find Brother Eck and Brother Unruh back there somewhere? They haven't taken ill, yet, have they?

There were bowings and greetings with the preachers, Unruh and Eck, along with clarifications regarding calling the horde together for the worship service.

"We are indeed blessed this day." Brother Eck's voice failed to carry more than eight feet in front of him.

Someone in the back yelled out, "Silence. A bishop is here."

More rustlings. Mothers stepped over boxes and bundles, leaning over to hush crying children.

Krehbiel heard several voices from the pallets on the floor calling out. "Oh, God has heard our prayers. Thank the blessed Heavenly Father."

He couldn't stop the thought circling in his mind: *This is a house of pestilence.*

Within minutes the preachers, Eck and Unruh, consulted with Elder Krehbiel and agreed upon the order of the service.

Christian began. "I know you brethren and sisters are weary of travel. You have suffered more than I can ever begin to know. Perhaps there will be times in the future when we can talk together of the trials of your journey from your homeland so far away."

He heard a woman break into sobs.

He began to read words from Psalm 18: "The Lord is my rock, and my fortress, and my deliverer...In my distress, I called upon the Lord...He heard my voice...my cry came before him."

A tall, hollow-chested man with a shock of wheat-colored hair and bad teeth wedged through toward the Elder. who obviously was having trouble breathing.. "I will lead us in singing," he announced. He lifted a tuning fork, striking it on the hymnal edge, then began: *Holy God, We Praise Thy Name.*

At first, the voices were feeble, almost drowned out by the cries of children, groans of the sick and coughing in the thick air. Yet, here and there, rusty and sore throats opened, lips parted for the words.

Holy God, we praise Thy name;
Lord of All we bow before Thee;
All on earth Thy scepter claim,
all in heav'n above adore Thee....

Strangely enough, the volume grew, the words spilled out of opened mouths, eyes brightened as if the singing folks had touched something truly beyond their impoverished surroundings, the foul air, the death and sickness invading their dwelling.

Even the man leading the song did so in a manner proclaiming his own immersion in the experience. Elder Krehbiel could not hold back his tears.

***

When Krehbiel returned to his home in Halstead, he was immediately surrounded by his children and Susanna. He could tell by Susanna's wide-open eyes that she saw the weight and sadness upon his face.

A daughter took his coat, a son his hat. He rested his satchel by his chair, falling into it. "Susanna, Susanna, you can't imagine. You simply can't know the suffering." He buried his head in his hands.

It was not until they were alone in their bedroom that he began to disclose the experience that almost overwhelmed his soul.

The staring eyes of the people, eyes that proclaimed little hope. Emigrants whose harps were hung upon willows in a strange land, people who had almost forgotten the songs of Zion. The pestilential stink filled the place. Surely some kind of plague has stricken the people. Pallets, fouled clothing. God have mercy.

In their transition, after months, caught between yester-day and today in a frightful unknown. Penniless, not knowing their future. Would they ever have soil beneath their feet they could call their own.? Ordinary boundaries no longer existed. Drifting, losing both faith and hope. Oh, the suffering mothers. There soon will be scores of new graves in a common burial place in that forlorn place.

"I had to stop preaching, Susanna, I could not breathe because of the awful air. I reached back and opened the door. I gulped the air blowing in.

"But they have some kind of delusion that the air here is bad. 'Shut the door,' they yelled."

"There were several who tried to move forward to get a whiff of the breeze blowing in. One brother thanked me, as he tried to struggle toward the door. We have to get them out of there and soon. Pray, Susanna, pray for warm weather.

"Before I go to sleep, Susanna, I must write to the Summerfield group about these conditions."

24

OH, PRAY TO GOD

Lusanna Becker looked back through the swirling haze to the west corner of the building. "Mother, something serious is happening. Why are so many children sick? Adults too. I'd say there are at least a dozen who have fallen ill, including the children."

Catherine glanced quickly back over Lusanna's shoulder toward the pallets laid out in a row as if they were organizing a sick bay back there. "I just don't know, Lusanna. I felt the forehead of Anna Jantz's little Wilhelm. He was feverish. Yes, it worried me."

"Well," Lusanna added, "it's no wonder people are falling ill breathing this air. Even our preachers won't stand for us opening a door, let alone a window. We're stuck here until plans change. What old-fashioned ideas they have."

Oh, how do I restrain myself from this overwhelming miserable crowd, and I one of them? Dear Lord, can't I shove open the door, and in spite of the fact I don't have proper shoes and gloves, race down to that river? Frozen or not. Perhaps there would be a tree like my tree back home. Oh, God, oh, God.

Benjamin slid through the space between Lusanna and his mother.

Lusanna realized the boy was trying to be brave without Andrias's attention and support. Yet, Benjamin did not whine. She noticed how he kept rubbing his forehead and how his cheeks were getting redder since morning.

"Benjamin, do you feel all right?" Lusanna bent to place a palm on his forehead. "Why, Mother, he has a fever." Catherine confirmed that, "Yes, indeed, the boy's forehead was too hot - the red, too, in his cheeks."
"Mama, my throat hurts." He sat down on the floor. "And I'm so thirsty."

"Unfold the blanket, Lusanna, we have to make a pallet for him. Right here by the trunk. He'll be protected a little there. At least no one will step on him while we get him settled." Her mouth drew into a solemn line.

Lusanna loosened Benjamin's clothes so that he would be more comfortable and helped him stretch out on the pallet. She covered him with an old woolen piece, woven back in Antanofka. "Benjamin, I'll go to the back and bring you a dipper of water."

"Thank you, Lusanna. Thank..." His eyes closed. The child had fallen asleep.

Lusanna stepped past Maria and Tobias Ratzlaff, who were sitting on a chest, reading from the Bible. She wedged through the space left by three women in a discussion over where to hang another clothesline. By the time she got back to the water bucket on an improvised bench, a voice startled her.

"Why, Lusanna. At last."

She looked up. Schoolmaster Heinrich leaned toward her. A moldy odor drifted from his clothes.

I might as well be cordial. No one knows if this is our last day on earth.

"Yes, why, good morning, Heinrich." *Might as well go ahead and call him by his rightful name. I'm tired of calling him Schoolmaster. I don't believe I'm up to saying "'brother Schmidt,'" or "'Herr Schmidt.'"*

A glance to the left made her aware of Gerda, sitting against her luggage, knitting needles in her hand. Lusanna nodded to her, but if the old woman saw her, she gave no notice.

"Lusanna, you and I need to share the things we've been writing. Yes, our notes and expectations, surprises, and the events of our travels." He smiled as if it was St. Valentine's Day, and he held a box of candy behind his back.

"I won't be able to do that right now, Heinrich. I need to get some water for Benjamin. We believe he's fallen ill with a fever."

"Let me. Let me, Lusanna." Before she could stop him he had inserted a thin thigh between Cornelus Wedel and Maria, knocked over some open boxes that had been poorly stacked, tromping his way to the water bucket.

"Here, Lusanna," he hollered. "I'm coming. Schoolmaster Schmidt at beck and call." He giggled as he tried not to spill the water and weave his way back to Catherine and Benjamin.

Here and there she noticed women with heads lowered, as if in sympathy with her plight. Gerda's face, though, had broken into a smile.

Lusanna followed but not without her thoughts. *I feel like heading for the back door. Maybe the privy. Wasn't it Freida Kohn who always hid in the privy when the preacher came calling? He, always questioning her about her commitments and faith?*

By mid-afternoon Helena Kohn and Anna Jantz had their heads together along with three other women. Lusanna, who sat wiping Benjamin's forehead with a damp cloth, overheard their words.

"I've never seen anything like this, Helena," Anna said, her eyes opening starkly.

"Look at those small red spots that have broken out on this child's forehead."

From the other side of the mass of people spread helter-skelter amidst the scattered belongings, straw, chests and bundles, came another voice, replete with worry. "Would you look at this, Eli? I just opened this child's mouth and it is full of sores. Oh, pray to God..." To her side, a youth was wiping his face, pleading, "Water, bring me some water."

Through the stifling air, moans drifted. Lusanna heard more weeping toward the back. Suddenly the room grew quiet. People turned with haunted eyes, staring at each other as if they'd caught a glimpse of the fourth horseman of the Apocalypse - the one on the pale horse whose name was Death.

Joseph Becker was the first to break open the door and hasten down the board walk toward downtown. He searched, eyes glancing up, looking to the opposite side of the street. *Doctor. Doctor. Where is the doctor's office?*

Seeing the sign, *Orvin Heppner, Medical Practicioner*, he raced up the stairs and barged into a small office, winded, heart pounding against his ribs.

Two waiting patients stared at him, their faces registering fear. "I must see the doctor," he announced, with a tone in his voice that amazed even him.

Dr. Heppner, who was aware of the circumstances of "the poor Poles," had kept an ear to the sidewalk to gather gleanings concerning the affairs of the town, and the bandied-about gossip concerning these settlers.

Nevertheless, after seeing his two last patients, he grabbed his black bag and hurried along the walk with the strange German, whose gestures he understood even if he did not speak Plattdeuttsch.

Within three days there must have been at least twenty-four people, adults as well as children stricken with the grisly disease. After the first appearance of the red spots on their foreheads, then came the sores in their mouths and the rash. The sores spread until bodies were covered with thick opaque boils, depressions in the center. Horrendous fevers racked the bodies of these unfortunate ones.

After the fifth day, the bumps changed into hard, sharply raised pustules, some forming crusts, then scabs.

"My God, my God! No wonder," Heppner announced as Joseph swung the door open, and the toxic fumes hit his lungs.. "This is a pestilence house. A plague... May God have mercy upon these folks."

Joseph led him to Benjamin's pallet. Benjamin was tossing on his back, his body riddled with angry pustules, his tongue hanging out of his mouth.

"Pray to Jesus." Dr. Heppner opened his bag. He looked up at Catherine's tear-stained face. He glanced at a comely girl who was attempting to stop the flow of her tears with a torn rag.

The mother. The sister.

"Oh," proclaimed the doctor. "Don't you folks know that you have an outbreak of smallpox here?

25

IN ILLINOIS

Back in Summerfield, Illinois, within the Mennonite community, the twenty-four youth from the dismal storehouse in Florence, Kansas, entered the world of work in a new land with unknown people and ways of working, foreign to them.

Andrias Becker and Carl Jantz latched onto the offered jobs at Brother Enis Hostetler's, who owned a hundred-and-sixty acres. Andrias, amazed at the size of the farm when compared to the fields and woods they leased from the Russian Crown, vowed not to disappoint farmer Hostetler, regardless of the task. Andrias had already seen the huge manure pile, reminding him of the smaller one behind their barn, heating up and composting, turning waste into black loam for garden or field.

More surprising to both youth was what they considered the opulence of the Hostetlers, Enis and his wife, Esther, situated in their two-story white frame farmhouse on a half-acre lot, their long lane running parallel to Esther's extended garden with the winter onion stalks sticking up through the snow, their bulbs buried in the black earth, awaiting spring.

"I'll need you young fellows in dairy work. If you aren't used to milk cows, you'll have that chance in no time. No time at all." Enis smiled pleasantly at the boys. A twinkle in his eye may have registered: *you don't quite know what you're getting into.*

When Carl and Andrias first saw the milk cows, huge black-and-white creatures such as they had never in their lives seen before, they stood, staring.

"What do you think, Andrias, would Lusanna want to crowd against such a monster, her bucket underneath, tugging on her tits?"

Andrias grinned. "Well, knowing Lusanna, she'd certainly try. She was the one who always milked Basha."

At the mention of the little Guernsey's name, he had a fleeting image of Lusanna and himself, walking along the road to Waldheim, searching the ditches for the lost family cow. A sadness crept through him.

"That was a world that seems long ago - a land far away." Carl's face registered his pensive mood. He swallowed, foot encased in a ragged-toed boot raised upon a rung in the wire fence at the barnyard.

Within three days, Andrias got the hang of milking by hand, the squish and squirt of it, including getting used to the tabby cat sitting near the wall awaiting a squirt of the rich warm milk from time to time.

Carl, his yellow hair falling over his eyes, had more of a challenge. On the second night his cow, named of all things, *Wilhelmena,* let him know she had a life of her own. Wham! Her foot had raised so quickly Carl wasn't able to remove the pail fast enough. Down went her sharp, heavy hoof into the bucket, spoiling the milk, at least a one-third-pail full, which would have to be poured out into a hog trough.

In time, however, he learned the rhythms, the squeezing, the pulling - just the right amount of tension, aware always of Wilhelmina's levels of comfort.

Now he and Carl shared a large bed in what for him seemed to be a huge bedroom overlooking a part of the garden and a cornfield beyond. This he already knew. Here in Illinois, there would be cornfields. Miles and miles of cornfields.

Sister Hostetler had served a bowl of her garden corn with the marvelous dishes she placed upon the supper table.

She'd told them that it was dried sweet corn. When she added water, it fluffed up as she steamed it on the kitchen range. Andrias tried to eat a spoonful, but he couldn't get over the idea, learned from back in Antanofka: *corn is food for the hogs.*

The way both he and Carl shoveled in the other delicious food Esther prepared gave notice that her cooking passed muster. The beef and gravy. Mashed potatoes, butter swimming in a pool at the top. Garden peas. Butter beans. For dessert, apple crumb pie. And if they didn't care for that, how about the sour cream raisin?

Coffee for breakfast, too. Oh, when the scent of it rose through the ceiling ventilation grill into their bedroom, his mouth started watering. He and Carl crawled down from the lofty bed, its fine quilts and sheets, pillow shams, embroidered, too. Lusanna would have a fit.

He couldn't wait to tell Lusanna, in a couple of months when they returned to Kansas, about the breakfasts here in Illinois. Nobody in Antanofka would have believed it. Thick slabs of smoked bacon, fried crisp in a big iron skillet. All kinds of iron pots, brass or copper-bottomed pans and kettles. A large steaming teakettle made of cast iron.

Besides the bacon, there was an endless supply of eggs. Think of it. One was permitted to eat *two* or *three*. Even then, Sister Hostetler always offered more.

On alternating mornings, how about thick slices of smoked ham, tender, juicy, fried gently to bring out the best flavor. Don't even mention the sausages. Pork sausage. In both casings and in patties. Sometimes with it, Esther served a platter loaded with something called corn mush. She sliced it into thick slabs and fried it in the wonderful ham grease in the iron skillet. Why, with the brown crust, egg on top. Andrias thought he'd arrived at the gates of heaven.

Then, what a surprise. She trotted out a bread made of cornmeal and flour which they called *cornbread*. When spread with butter, however, it melted in the mouth.

On days when Esther didn't make the cornbread, she came up with some biscuits, browned on top, called soda biscuits. Some quick kind of bread she made fresh in a wink of an eye, saying: "One has to work fast making biscuits. Also, never pound or wallow the dough too much.

Oh, Lusanna, I wish you were here to taste it when it is dripping with melted butter and I put gooseberry jam on it.

During the first week of their arrival, when they sat at what they considered a banquet, Andrias felt guilty. Guilty and lonely. His thoughts drifted back to the dark, stifling storehouse on that strange river. The crowded horde within. No elbow room. The straw on the floor, fleas, lice....

But knowing that he wanted to return to his family and that he also knew it would be within a few weeks, he adjusted to the seemingly endless spread of food.

Maybe it was a foretaste of what lay in store for them. Yes, the Beckers. Their new Kansas farm, although Father never was much of a farmer. Here in Illinois the soil was loamy and soft. It ploughed easily. A farm implement called a harrow raked it smoothly.

Surely, it will the same on the Kansas prairie, won't it? But how on earth do you get rid of that tall prairie grass. Wouldn't that take an extra strong team of oxen to pull some kind of special plow to turn those roots over?

He decided that there was enough to do, here at the Hostetlers. *He and Father would tackle the prairie in time. Give them time. Lusanna and Mother would soon be living in some kind of very nice house. Maybe stone? The Kansas winds, though strong, were sweet when they blew over the prairie grasses and the abundant flowers. Nothing like butterflies sailing right into one's living room.*

Carl Jantz aroused him out of his reverie. He stood grinning, staring at Andrias. "Enis has a new job for us, Andrias."

Andrias, stirred, turned to look at Carl. "Yes? What is it?" He grinned in return.

"Get your wraps on, Andrias. Gloves, too. Sock that cap right down on your head, we're going to load up."

"Load up?" *What could he mean? A trip into town? Than usually didn't happen until Saturday when they took the cream and the eggs to market.*

He shoved his feet into his boots, slipped his arms through his new lined jumper that sister Hostetler had insisted on buying at a clothing store in town. One for Carl, of course, too.

The boys headed for the barnyard, Carl leading the way, loping along over ruts that were beginning to thaw.

Enis was busy hitching his team to a strange-looking wagon. In a way it looked like a regular wagon, although the sides at the back seemed higher. *Of course these wagons in America weren't nearly as squat and heavy as the Russian wagons.* That Andrias already had noted.

Enis waved for the boys to step forward. He bent over to hook the harness to the doubletree, a black horse on each side of the wagon tongue.

"Gonna spread this manure on that twenty-acre ground yonder." He pointed southward.

Carl scratched behind his ear. Andrias stood, staring. "You mean you want us to load up that manure and haul it out to that field?"

"Sure thing. Won't raise as good a crop without this manure fertilizer. Couple of shovels over yonder." Enis pointed.

The boys got the message. *Pitch the manure.*

"I'm trusting you both to take over, whilst I start doing some pruning in the orchard." Enis turned and with long farmer's strides headed toward the tool shed.

The two youths shoveled and loaded. They perspired and wiped their brows with their coat sleeves. They laughed and hooted. Soon, they took off their coats. Ever shoveling, ever swinging the cow dung.

"Whew! This old cow manure will blow your head off." Andrias bent over in a paroxysm of laughter and gasping for fresh air at the same time.

Andrias noticed that Carl, too, was trying to drawn in some gulps of fresh air. He shook his head and grinned.

Oh, the wonders of America. Of Illinois. What would Father think of this?

And Lusanna? Why, Lusanna, if she were here, would want to climb right on board, maybe even sit down or a ride to that field. And she'd be thinking, "Why, just think of the flowers, Andrias, the flowers that will come up after we spread all this wonderful manure."

Then Andrias brought up the name of that redheaded girl, Agnes Unruh who had been hired by a Stucky family over north in the community. He remembered seeing her in the church, last Sunday, sitting there, head towering above the heads of the other girls. She flashed him a big grin as she noticed him and Carl over on the men's side.

"You ought to go over to that Stucky farm, Carl, and bring Agnes back over here. I can't think of anyone who'd have more fun heaving rotted manure than Agnes. Why, she could..." he broke down laughing.

"Agnes? Why, yes indeed," Carl inserted, howling. "She's always been good at shoveling *you-know-what*."

They had to lay down their shovels and lean against the barnyard gate. Their laughter startled a flock of crows, which had settled around them, looking for rotted morsels of corn.

"Well," Carl said, "I'm afraid that that oldest Stucky young fellow, name of Peter, the one with muscles like Samson, has taken to her. Yep. He loaded her up after church, that last snowstorm, and hauled her off in his sleigh."

Carl looked up as he wiped his eyes. "Andrias, here comes Enis. He's holding a letter or something in his hand. Must be news from Florence."

Andrias stared at Enis as he came through the barnyard gate. He noted that his head was lowered, the wind fluttering the paper in his hand.

When he stood before the two young men, he looked at one, then the other. His face twisted as if he had a toothache.

"I'm so very sorry to tell you this, Andrias, Carl. "I've just heard from Brother Warkentine from Halstead, Kansas. There's been a serious outbreak of smallpox in the storehouse in Florence."

His eyes lowered.

Andrias stared, mouth open, into Carl's eyes. "Oh, Carl, pray to God."

The call of a mourning dove broke the silence following his words.

26

ONE SWEETLY SOLEMN THOUGHT

Thirteen days had passed and the smallpox victims fell prey to the ravages of the disease like rows of sunflowers falling before a violent wind.

First, they had buried little Wilhelm. Then Eli Schmidt. Next Aga Foth, followed by little brother Bejnamin. Three days later, Lusanna's mother, Catherine, and five others. It was as if an invisible hand reached in and raked indiscriminately without forethought or conscience. Family members left to grieve and handle their dead stood in shock at the devastation wrought upon the bodies of those they loved.

By the evening of each day, a wagon, drawn by two black horses, rocked up to the door of the storehouse to load the bodies, which had been placed in pine boxes, hastily nailed together by men holding back indescribable pain within their breasts.

Lusanna was grateful that the town mayor and his council approved of the gift of lumber, the wagon and horses, a driver to guide the team to the pauper's field, a lonely, windswept portion of land, west of the town.

"This we can do," the mayor had said, "to aid the suffering Anatofkins."

Lusanna was painfully aware that each day more and more space opened on the floor. The smallpox victims who had relatives to tend to them, lay on pallets with their family members. Those who had none to care for them had all been moved to the east and back of the building. The price for more room was so costly that Lusanna dared not think about it, yet at the same time she was grateful for space to walk without stumbling.

Numb. I wonder if I'll ever feel anything again? How can Father and I live without Mother and Benjamin? I feel like I'm naked and that all the skin has been peeled from my body. I can barely stand another person looking at me. Thank God Andrias is spared. Oh, what will he say, what will he do, when he finds out that....

Lusanna thought of Dr. Heppner's words to her and Elizabeth Dirks, the two who unfailingly changed bedding and clothing, brought broth and water to parched lips, comforted the dying. "There's not much we can do, once they come down with the disease."

She glanced back at her father, head in his hands, sitting in their space, his back against her mother's hope chest. She had no more tears.

I'm beyond that, she'd said to herself. I'll do what I can to help Father survive...Oh, God, what waters. What deep, deep waters.

The verse from Isaiah flooded her brain, verses that Preacher Eck had read more than once in their morning devotions.

When thou passeth through the water, I will be with thee; and through the rivers, they shall not overflow thee...

There was little time now for Lusanna to focus upon her grief or the unnamable, stark numbness of her body. Yet she took out a new piece of brown cloth from her mother's chest, folded it, then threw it over her hair, drawing the front down an inch over her forehead. She tied the corners behind her ears and headed to the back of the room to the wash benches. Here she scrubbed her arms and hands with the lye soap that townsfolk had left off before the two ugly signs announcing *QUARANTINED* had been nailed to each side of the door.

A verse she had memorized back in Antanofka thrust itself into her mind:

If any man will come after me, let him deny himself, take up his cross, and follow me.

It was not a decision made in her head, in her thoughts. It was a decision made long before in her soul. This she knew. Finished with scrubbing her hands, she grabbed a water pail and a dipper and headed for the nearest row of the stricken ones.

The one with his face turned to the wall seemed beyond any stirring. She waited. Then she said, "I have some cold water, wouldn't a sup be refreshing?"

Still no answer. She mentioned the water again. There was a rustle, shoulders moved, a face turned her way, eyes almost completely swollen shut. She stared straight at the angry boils bursting with pus. She waited.

A voice, old and cracked, whispered, "Mercy, yes, water."

She knelt beside the stinking man. *Who is this unrecognizable man?* She lifted the dipper cup to his fevered lips, holding it with a steady hand.

The ravaged victim uttered a gasp, "Thank you, Lusanna."

The way he said her name. She knew him. *Schoolmaster Heinrich. God, have mercy.*

Pity overwhelmed her. *No. It can't be. He taught us all, Elise and Jacob, Andrias and I, Henry Voth, Jake Unruh, Tobias and Eva....* Their names came at her like June bugs zooming toward a lantern.

"Is there anything I can do for you, Heinrich?"

There was a long pause before he replied. He lifted his head again and asked, "Mother, is she still alive?"

"No, Heinrich. They buried your mother last night with seven others. Cornelias Wedel read a little service, I'm told. Very few of us are allowed to go out to that burial place." She didn't tell him that both of their ministers, Eck and Unruh, had died at least two weeks ago.

Heinrich lifted a scabbed hand.

Seeing it wobbling before her, she reached to steady it. "I'll bring you a bowl of broth, Heinrich, when it is warm from the stove. I'll pray for you. The doctor is coming again this afternoon, they say. You'll be better soon."

"No," he rasped. "No, I won't make it. Lusanna, when I pass over, there is a box of books. They're yours. You are the one to be the teacher in the new school."

She saw that he attempted a smile, but it was too much. He collapsed upon his pallet.

Gone were her furious thoughts about his invasions into her life. It came to her in astonishing clearness.

What a person demonstrates externally does not reflect all that is within the heart.

The realizations flooded her mind.

Sure, he was hounded by the boys for his posture, for his strictness. Girls snickered at him because of his looks. I turned away when I could have been kinder. I passed him by, sometimes, even when he greeted me.

The leprous-looking man turned her way again: "Lusanna, I want to ask you to forgive me for calling upon you to read that Bible passage back in school. I, I," he coughed and struggled. "I thought only of myself that day. I wanted to test you. I was wrong. It was most inappropriate. Most inappropriate."

He fell to his blood-spotted pallet.

"Yes, Schoolmaster Heinrich," she paused. "I too, thought the passage was not appropriate. I felt humiliated, reading it. But, now, I can forgive you, now."

She stayed with Heinrich a few minutes longer before moving along with her water bucket.

He was one of the loneliest persons on our ship. He must not always have appreciated his difficult mother, Gerda. Often, he overlooked her jibes and rudeness, going about his tasks.

Heinrich had a good voice - leading our singing, and he was intelligent. In many ways he had been a good teacher. Strict, but thorough. All of us Antanofka youth benefited from his instruction.

I know that he suffered. Suffered the pain of many rejections. Most of us turned away from him. God, forgive. God forgive.

***

But there was more. It struck just after the caretakers had finished rolling up the pallets and filling the waterbuckets. They had taken time to look up at the sky outside by the well, noting that spring had come.

The Death Angel visited again.

Late March rains fell in torrents. Winds whipped. Rain swept off of eaves and shed roofs, rolling, rumbling in the streets toward the river. The building shook with thunder. Hail pounded.

Outside in back lots and yards the water swirled around privies, swept through barnyards, ever heading for the lowest levels.

Behind the brick storehouse, outhouses punctuated the darkness with their ungainly roofs. The water descended, soaking, swishing. *The well. The drinking water.*

When Dr. Heppner came this time with his black bag and his work-worn face, he leaned over another line of the fallen.

First came the fierce headaches.

"Lusanna," her father had said. "I feel..."

By evening he was vomiting. Not he alone, but a dozen others. Nursemaids and helpers looked on in disbelief. *Not again! What is it this time?*

Though Lusanna tried to lift the dipper to Joseph's lips, no amount of water would quench his thirst. He lay back upon his pallet, curled in a ball with stomach cramps.

Then the diarrhea. Fierce, unstoppable.

"It's cholera, Lusanna. I grieve to tell you we have an outbreak of cholera here." The doctor closed his bag.

Lusanna stared, unbelieving. *First Benjamin, then Mother. I can't possibly lose Father. Oh, God. Oh, God.*

Her pleading eyes shifted to the doctor's face. They stared at each other in the silence.

Cholera swept its scythe, gathering 36 more Anatofkins who had survived the smallpox plague, including Carl's father, Berent Jantz.

***

By late March, buds were bursting from shrubs alongside the river and creeks. Forsythia bushes in yards in little Florence bowed with the brightest gold.

One didn't have to listen long, when stepping out back for more water or to stoke an oven, to hear the call of doves, the sweet chirp of cardinals, and, would you know, meadowlarks on the fence, breasts bursting with song.

And, if one drew in a deep breath, one got a whiff of the promise in fresh spring air. Air filled with the freshness of a shower drifting in from the southwest or coming up off the river below town.

Ah, the river. Yes, she'd sneaked out to the river, defying the ugly sign nailed to the wall. *Let them hunt me down*, she'd said to herself, after Father died.

She had washed his hands and face, glad that he was released from his suffering. Even Dr. Heppner said, "Dear Lord, my girl, you'll have to let him go. You must prepare yourself. He won't make it through another night."

Now here by the willows, the breeze soughed through the tiny upper limbs of the cottonwoods like angels playing hymns upon their harps.

A song flooded her mind. *One Sweetly Solemn Thought.*

One sweetly solemn thought
Comes to me o'er and o'er
Nearer my home, today, am I
Than e'er I've been before.

One thing she had learned. God was secretly in all things, just as the blessed Jesus had said. He had been with them when they were torn from a homeland in Antanofka. He, with them, felt the pain of the separation from relatives and friends left behind. God was a suffering God. This, she knew. Jesus, the man of sorrows, acquainted with grief.

I'm sure that suffering and death are never the end of the story.

She thought of Mary Magdaline racing to the tomb planning to anoint the cold, still body of Jesus. Instead, she was startled by an angel who announced, "He is risen."

Even she and Elizabeth found a sureness and a strength as they had gone about their nursing duties, night and day. Tens, scores of people they had ministered to in their simple ways. Fluffing pillows and pallets. Lifting hips or limbs for ease of pain. Extending the dipper to cracked lips. Reading from the German Bibles, when requested to do so by the dying.

And I was the girl who couldn't stand crowds. The dreadful trip on The Vaderland. The packed, cold trains. The crowding-confusion in Hutchinson. Box car nightmares. Freezing cold. Packed into a brick storehouse in Florence, where already almost 300 have died.

I who always had to have a plan and be busy. I had difficulty learning to wait.

Wait. Wait. Wait for refuge. Wait for the robbers to ride away. Wait for food. Wait for the train. Wait for a place to lay down one's head. Wait for the privy door to open. Wait for the grave to open. Wait for the bishop to come. Wait for Brother Warkentine or Elder Krehbiel to come with money to keep us from starving.

Who knew? Maybe some of the survivors are still waiting for Elder Tobias Unruh.

Now, we wait for the revelation of a path that will lead us out of, what for us, has been the house of desolation.

Oh, little town! Not of Bethlehem, but of Florence. Did you grieve with us?

Here there was no star, no dazzling light. No angel song. Who covered your window eyes with black crepe when you saw our suffering? You with the lovely name. Isn't it said that Florence is fair? Very fair? City of angels?

But in their way, the angels came. Came in our misery. We remembered the passage in Romans:

For I am persuaded that neither life,
nor death, nor angels, nor principalities,
nor powers, nor things present,

*nor things to come. nor height, nor depth,
nor any other creature shall be able to
separate us from the love of God,
which is in Christ Jesus our Lord.*

*Perhaps the angel who hovered over us in our sorrow
will extend a wing and show us the road to our new homes.
Truly, that would be a resurrection.*

Many times now she had been to the cemetery to that
very, very common plot of land. She made herself look upon
the raw earth, the layers stacked one upon another, orange,
brown, black. Stones, like sores interspersed.

She had inhaled its rawness and fecundity. Its promise
of renewal and hope. The shock of grass torn away, the
awful gashes where they lay. There had been so many deaths
that the survivors couldn't keep up making the pine coffins.
The only solution had been to bury as many as twelve
bodies, wrapped in quilts or blankets, in a single grave.

*Tomorrow, new green and tiny blue flowers will lift
their faces from the grass. Soon the violets. Then the glory of
summer daisies. In the fall, wild marigolds.*

*A place where rabbits will romp and play. Even when
the wind whips down, it will be only to freshen and sweep
away last year's twigs and withered leaves.*

It had felt like her heart was twisted, wrung by an
invisible hand when little Benjamin's body was laid down.
But when her mother's quilt-wrapped body was lowered
beside him, she had said to herself, "I praise God for mercy.
I thank God for this ground, and for these good men whose
backs ache from digging through frozen ground to ease these
bodies into the earth with harness reins.

Rest in peace, Mother. Oh, Papa. Oh, Benjamin.

A trembling Brother Cornelius Wedel read from
Preacher'Eck's handbook, holding it with swollen hands: *"I
am the resurrection and the life," saith the Lord: "he that
believeth in me, though he were dead, yet shall he live...."*

From nursing the seemingly endless pallets of the sick, both she and Elizabeth had taken courage from the way many of them had died.

Prayers on their lips.

Sweet and peaceful resignation.

A youth, whose forehead she bathed, looked up at her face and said with the utmost clarity, "I see - I see --why, I'm going home." A smile relaxed his pale face.

When Father breathed his last, he handed me our family Bible from Antanofka.

Blessed book, traveling far, and, like us, you're worn. Pages dog-eared, cover scored and soiled. Within, you bear The Light that bores through our darkness, illuminating the blessed words, "Be not afraid. Come unto me, all you who labor and are heavy laden."

Oh, no wonder so many lay down in peace.

Out of the bitter comes the sweet.

27

ANDRIAS ARRIVES

Lusanna and Eva Ratzlaff stood on the platform of the Florence Station awaiting the arrival of Andrias, Carl Jantz, Agnes Unruh, and other young folk who had been spared the months in the Florence pest house. She stood alongside an English woman named Louise, who had organized women from her church and who had brought them towels, soap, staples, and even dried vegetables. The woman smiled and greeted her and Eva.

Lusanna smiled back. "Good morning," she said, in broken English.

"I'm waiting for my daughter from Emporia," the woman continued. "Maryanne, and her new son, Jefferson."

Unable to understand the words, Lusanna got the drift of the message, nodded again and continued smiling.

She noticed that other English, too, stood waiting back near the wall of the station. Polite, mumbling morning news to one another. A few could not restrain themselves from staring at the "Polish" girls.

For just a second the thought coursed: *What do they actually think of us? Our thin, raked bodies, our pitiful clothes, our bare legs?*

She quickly dismissed the thought, realizing that her focus now needed to be directed toward Andrias and Carl and the sharing of an unweighable sorrow.

The April breeze flapped their homespun skirts against their bare calves.

What will it be like when they arrive? Brother Warkentine tried to notify the ones who had left for Summerfield
about the plague, and the deaths. Still, I have not heard from
Andrias or Carl. Agnes? Nothing from her, either.

"If they aren't already prepared, Lusanna, I don't know
what we can do; the tragedy here is too shocking," Eva said,
looking at her.

"We have to live these hours, Eva, no escape. Minute
by minute. Surely the blessed Lord will lead us through."

I will be with you. The rivers shall not overflow you...

Lusanna adjusted a foot encased in her felt schlorre
(slide-on shoe), which she had dug out of her mother's chest.
The breeze tickled her calf.

Both girls had taken the time, with the warming of the
days in late April, to wash their hair and dry it in a balmy
wind as their eyes feasted on the angelic white of a plum
thicket in bloom.

They had boiled their soiled garments in the black
kettle, perpetually bubbling on the fire behind the
storehouse, throwing in one of the chunks of the gift lye
soap. Next they had dug them out with a stick, rinsed them,
and after wringing them out, flung them over budding bushes
to dry in the sweet spring air.

"It's good that it is spring. If the ground was still snow-
covered, and that frigid wind still blowing, our task would be
much, much harder," Lusanna said.

"I hear a whistle." Eva stepped closer to the edge of the
platform to scan eastward down the tracks. Alongside the
gravel and stones of the roadway, dandelions sported their
yellow heads among the greenest of spring grasses.

Lusanna's heart began to pound. She felt tears crowd
the corners of her eyes. She made herself hold her lips tightly
to keep them from twisting. No one needed to tell her that
her eyes would tell the story.

Around them, the waiting folk murmured and leaned
forward in anticipation.

The train wailed and the black engine grew larger each moment, its plume of coal smoke drifting behind it. It wailed again and rocked toward them, steam hissing from the sides. Memories zipped through Lusanna's mind. *In Ostrog, boarding the Russian train. The long, crowded passage to Antwerp. Little brother Benjamin, eyes bulging at all the newness. Andrias and Jake, unable to hide their pleasure and excitement. Oh, what was sandwiched between those events and now. Years hence, people, when they read of it, will shake their heads. Others will fall on their knees and pray.*

Lusanna and Eva, among the other survivors, stood silent. She noticed that some of the mothers were twisting handkerchiefs. Two grandmothers who had risen from death-bed pallets openly wept.

Tall men, thin as newly split rails, took off their caps, holding them at their breasts. Their chests drew in and shoulders lifted as they breathed anxiously. They shifted their feet in wooden shoes, which they had dug out of their baggage as the weather warmed.

Lusanna's heart pained as she recognized the heart-rending absence of children. *Oh, the little ones falling before the scythe.*

Andrias, Andrias. Lusanna shook her head, then lifted her chin.

I'm not certain that I can bear these moments which weigh like the heavy soil pressing upon the bodies of those so recently laid down.

A heavyset woman in a long lightweight coat and a hat that matched the black wool of her coat, stepped down first. She gripped the hand of a small girl who said, "Mama, where is Grandpa?"

Others descended, some aided by the conductor. Folks on the platform called to relatives they spied, greeting them cheerfully. By the hitchiing post, horses neighed.

Then Lusanna saw Carl Jantz first. He was wearing a new gray felt hat. *An American hat. Where on earth would he have gotten money for such a hat?*

She noticed, too, that his feet were encased in a pair of shiny boots. Good-looking leather boots. *The face of Mercy must have smiled upon him.*

Her heart began pounding even harder. She swallowed. *Oh, I hope I'm not going to faint.* She looked down at the bosom of her dress, recognizing that it was dingy, needed the mangle, bearing as it did the traces of their misery.

When Carl lifted his hat and raked back his yellow hair, she noticed that he had gained weight, his body healthy, straight. He lifted a hand upon seeing his mother, Elske, her head lowered as she wept. He edged through the crowd to clasp her to his chest.

Then Andrias.

He stood on the platform looking at her as if seeing her after an absence of years. She wanted to run and hide her face on his shoulder. He was wearing a new short coat with brass buttons. She could not even move her schlorre-clothed feet.

He's taller than I remembered. His skin, healthy, a blush in his cheeks. His hair, must have had it cut.

She could see a faint, dark beard on his chin and a thin mustache.

Then her eyes cut to his.

Oh, God. He knows. Look into his eyes.

Oh, what we must say to each other, God help us. Give us words. Give us...

Andrias dropped a small suitcase and ran toward her. "Lusanna, Lusanna..." He broke into sobs. His chest heaved, his body quivered in his anguish.

She buried her head in his shoulder and for the first time since she saw her father's body dropped into the cold earth on that patch of prairie did she allow such racking sobs.

They held each other without words. Others stepped down from the car, eyes searching, then meeting friends and loved ones.

Sobs and cries of weeping ones circled in the air.

176

The English, gathering their own arrivals and their belongings, stepped back in respectful silence, lowering their eyes.

The prairie wind ceased as if Mother Nature herself had heard a whisper from Providence, saying:

Bless them with the cloak of silence. After the silence, may the wind kiss them with the fragrance of the grasses along the river.

Let the face of Christ, enmeshed in the world, weep with them. Bless them with the balm of mercy.

28

WHERE WILL WE LIVE?

Now that Agnes Unruh, Carl, and Andrias were back, the days could be measured by how fast new leaves covered the arching branches, and how the weeds, and grass shot up in the brightest sunshine Lusanna had ever remembered.

The big Stucky fellow, engaged to marry Agnes, after seeing the situation in the warehouse, climbed up and forced open the gable windows, allowing a fragrant southeasterly wind to blow through, along with a few warbling pigeons. Below, the young people clapped.

If there are strange ideas about fresh air still among us, let those cleansing breezes sweep them away.

With brooms and makeshift mops the able ones swept, mopped and scrubbed. The principal challenge was how to organize all the stacks of small items - hoes, rakes, bags of seed - though some of the seed wheat and millet had been boiled for porridge.

Lusanna anticipated Brother Warkentine's arrival tomorrow. He had promised that he would have some kind of plan for settlement. She could hear Andrias and Carl out back, as they talked, burning soiled, old bags of straw that had served as pallets for the sick.

Lusanna wondered what the land would be like when they made the move.

"We'll have to load up on the train," they said, but after that it would not be far to a place called Moundridge, where they would load their belongings in wagons and the oxen would draw them out onto the prairie.

Home. Blessed Lord, home at last.

She remembered Brother Warkentine mentioning someplace called Lone Tree Township.

Maybe I'll find my tree. Dear God, could it be?

She thought of her tree in Antanofka, the smell of it, the greenness of its leaves in spring, their bright gold in the fall. The leaves whispering blessings in a breeze, giving its comfort. She could almost feel the way the rough bark tickled her palms when she, Anna Jantz, and Agnes Unruh clasped hands and tried to encircle the tree.

Was it still there, towering above the other trees and thatched roofs? Did some careless woodsman lay his ax to its side? Was there a boy, a girl like her, who loved it as she had?

Agnes, a cloth tied tightly over her hair, swept furiously. She stopped in the middle of her strokes to tell Lusanna another bit about her Peter Stucky.

"He asked me to marry him, Lusanna." Agnes chuckled loudly, her cheeks blushing red. "I'd have stayed back in Illinois, but Peter said that he always wanted to come west to Kansas. This is his chance."

"Well, Agnes, anywhere, anywhere but *this*." Lusanna wondered if the taint of the place, the smell and the spirit-deadening air would linger with her forever.

Since I'm spared, Dear God, she vowed, *I'll give the rest of my days my best. Only give us some land and sunshine. Rain for the crops. A roof over my head. An oven so that I can bake zwieback like Mother did back home.*

Wasn't it written somewhere in the Old Testament?

Then I will give you rain in due season,
and the land shall yield her increase,
and the trees of the field shall
yield their fruit.

The survivors, gaining strength each day, piled their salvaged belongings together, chests, trunks, packages, and boxes. They seemed to recognize that, when finding themselves upon the wide, lonely prairie, their meager possessions would be paltry indeed. Miniscule, when measured against their need.

It had taken Andrias a full week to break the silence that had overtaken him upon his arrival back from Summerfield and to adjust to the shattering news regarding his family.

Carl, however, wanted to talk. Lusanna was surprised at how he found moments to seek her out, his eyes searching into hers as if he found surcease there, a resting place to ease his sorrow.

Only yesterday, he'd taken her by the arm. She followed as he guided her out of the building at twilight, heading toward the river. They'd sat in silence beneath towering cottonwoods watching the water, its ripples, its flow. Now and then a fish flopped up, giving evidence of life and vitality. A raccoon slipped through the undergrowth on the opposite side, staring at them, then slipping along the bank and back into the waving grass. A whippoorwill called for its mate.

When Carl finally spoke, it was with utmost gentleness as he reached for her hand.

"Lusanna, I'm nineteen, already. Father lies buried in that cemetery. We're going to have an opportunity to have some land, God willing."

"Yes, Carl," she said. "Yes, it's the new beginning so many of us looked forward to, but now..."

"Now, Lusanna. You and I. Yes, I'm asking you to marry me."

The cicadas chirruped, the breeze rustled the cottonwood leaves. The fragrance of the Sweet William at their feet filled the air. The raccoon nosed through the bushes again.

"Carl, why, I..." Lusanna wondered if her heart would melt.

A rolling tumble of thoughts coursed through her head.

How? Where will we live? Can I tackle homemaking on the prairie? What about Andrias? Where would Anna and his mother, Elske, live? Would I have a chance to be a teacher?

Then she remembered that their Antanofka families were broken now, like puzzles; pieces lost and scattered. Never would their family groups resemble the circles they had in Polish-Russia. Now, there would be all kinds of arrangements, relatives, cousins, aunts, uncles, grandparents, the few remaining children, all re-grouped. Re-clustered, mustering courage to tackle the tasks waiting for them upon that endless prairie.

"You haven't answered me, Lusanna." His arm slipped behind her back as he drew her closer.

"Oh, Carl. Yes. I want to marry you. But you are not of age. How can we? What can you do about that?" She blinked her eyes to hold back her tears.

"We'll seek advice, Lusanna. I think my Uncle Cornelius might be able to give permission for a license to marry. Yes, I believe, maybe even with Brother Warkentine's support or Elder Krehbiel's, we would be able to jump that hurdle."

Lusanna looked westward at the sky, a Kansas sky, layers of orange, pink, deep red at the horizon as the sun slipped behind the hills. She looked into Carl's eyes and saw his love, his waiting.

"Yes, Carl. Yes, let's build our new home together."

***

Again, it was Brother Warkentine from Halstead, and Christian Krehbiel, who had come all the way from Summerfield to unfold the new plans for their final settlement.

The biggest challenge was how they would rearrange into families. With so many gaps torn through family circles by the scythe of death, *just who would live with whom?* They had gathered that last afternoon in the open air outside in front of the infamous building, echoing ghastly memories.

Ezra Dirks volunteered to lead the group in the hymn: "Come, Thou Fount of Every Blessing." At first the singing halted, voices thin as if faith itself had sunken like a stream, burying itself beneath the sand in a parched land.

But then, Carl, standing beside Lusanna and his mother, lifted his chin to sing the phrase, "Tune my heart to sing thy praise."

Andrias, behind him, began on the second verse with a mellow baritone, balanced by Lusanna's and Elske Jantz's pleasing sopranos.

To the left rose Agnes Unruh's low, complimentary alto, her eyes fixed upon the sun-gilded tree tops across the way. Suddenly the wind stopped as if it silenced itself so that the harmony of the hymn might prevail.

Across the street, a group of the English halted their steps, turned to look at them. An older gentleman removed his hat.

When they came to the second verse:

Here I raise my Ebenezer,
Hither by Thine help I'm come;
and I hope, by Thy good pleasure,
Safely to arrive at home...

Here and there sobs broke through the soaring stanza, tears streamed down the singers' faces.

Home. Home.
To arrive at home.

Lusanna could think of no more blessed words.

Following the hymn, Elder Krehbiel announced that the men who had drawn up the plans were called *The Kansas Aid Committee*, which included Christian Hirschler, David Holdeman, and David Goerz. However, it was evident that both Warkentine and Krehbiel knew that their shoulders would still be needed in bearing the weight of the resettlement.

Lusanna was certain, from their serious faces, that the assignment shook even them. *What about us?* She stood beside Carl, both of them listening intensely.

She and Andrias, Carl, Anna, and Jake Unruh had discussed the move, trying to control their anxiety and the tones of their voices.

Are we prepared for this? Aren't we mostly weavers, day laborers, woodsmen, house domestics, a few surviving millers? Which of us has ever ripped open such Kansas prairie? Carl and I? Can I live with his mother, Elske? What about Andrias? What about his sister, Anna?

Get ready to move. The plans were made.

In spite of trepidation, folks cleared their throats, attempted forward looks and suppressed their worries.

The brother, David Holdeman, had announced, "We've arranged for the Santa Fe Railroad to transport you and your goods to the depot nearest the land sites where you will construct your new homes. The new lumber will be placed upon the sites of your homes. The Aid Committee will try to have volunteer carpenters to assist those who need help in building their houses."

Lusanna saw Andrias lean forward. *He looks older than his years. Oh, God, what we have endured, yet you did not abandon us.*

"Each family, or family group, will be allowed forty acres."

Holdeman cleared his throat. "I know that doesn't sound like much, but we were able to get the land for three dollars an acre from the railroad by bargaining. We'll advance loans of two hundred dollars for every household. You will have ten years before repayment is required. By that time, surely, all of you will be on your feet."

Holdeman smiled nervously as if a part of him realized it would be a long stretch. A long stretch, indeed.

Farm? Plow, sow wheat, oats, barley, whatever they sow? Oh, Father, Father.... She knew Andrias knew little about such ventures. How about Carl?

Excited, yet at the same time fearful.

She realized that, indeed, they needed their Elder Tobias.

We were the largest Polish-Russian group, yet you never planted your foot in Kansas. What are you doing in South Dakota? Do you think of us? Does your conscience burn?

Carl lifted his chin, straightened his shoulders and took her hand in his. His warm touch gave her the comfort she needed to calm her fears.

Let Elder Tobias eat his beef and noodles in Dakota. In a few months, I'll be making zwieback and churning my own butter. I'll open my own door and windows and let the balmy winds drift through. I'll throw open my arms and welcome this dazzling light from the seemingly constant sun, and I'll say, "I'm a Kansas girl, now."

29

BEFORE THE JUDGE

It sounded like a lot of land allowed for the over one hundred families ready to be transported to the wide new prairie. Four thousand four hundred and eighty acres, to be exact. Each "family group" would be settled upon forty acres of virgin prairie land under the wide sky and burning summer sun.

In addition, they would share ten wagons and seventeen sod-breaking plows. They would be expected to work out arrangements concerning a milk cow for every two families, a yoke of oxen for every two to three families.

D. S. Holdeman, along with others in the Kansas Aid Committee, worked tirelessly for the Anatofkins. "No matter how we divide this money, there's not going to be enough. Maybe for the time being, they will have to put up some temporary housing."

"Well," said Warkentine, "we'll be there to help them with the construction. Surely, those who worked in the woods as lumbermen will have some skills."

"And," said Holdeman, "we've put letters in the Mennonite papers for more contributions. For the brethren who live around here, Moundridge, Hesston, Newton, McPherson, or Marion Center and Hillsboro, we are asking for small items and even larger ones, stoves, lamps, tools. We probably will have to provide the wheat flour for at least the next nine months or so."

"Nevertheless," said brother Hirschler, "one cannot but appreciate the joy in their faces as they anticipate seeing the land."

"It is a great venture for those who were never land owners. Nothing like it. It is almost a holy experience," said Warkentine, who had extended himself so tirelessly in these people's behalf.

"Yes," Holdeman said, "It will be like the Israelites first seeing the promised land."

It had taken the Antanofkans several days to sort out just who would be living with whom. They had discussed among themselves which ones would be signing the notes for the two hundred dollars each "family" had been allowed for lumber to build some kind of dwelling. They had been told that the plot of land lay south of a little town called Canton and north of Moundridge, a town that was almost totally surrounded by a colony of Swiss Mennonites.

They'd settled it this way. Lusanna and Carl Jantz, along with his mother, Elske, and sister, Anna, constituted their family. Elder Krehbiel would perform the marriage cermony before they "moved in."

Carl's sister, Anna, would start out living with them, helping to establish the farm. She was eager, however, to launch out, maybe be hired to aid a father with children who would need a domestic worker to cook, labor in the kitchen, garden, and take care of the children.

Though Anna wouldn't *think* of mentioning it, Lusanna knew that it wouldn't be long before Anna married Jake Unruh.

Andrias? Lusanna saw how it was with her brother. Though he talked more freely now, his face still bore signs of the shock of what they had endured in Florence: the earth caving in beneath him at losing all his family but his sister.

Just yesterday he'd come to her: "Lusanna, I've been talking to Uncle Gerhard. Since Aunt Helga and three of his children died in the sicknesses, he wants me to live with them for now, at least. He needs me, Lusanna. You'll have Carl."

At first the words shook Lusanna. *Another loss?*
That was a universal experience, wasn't it? Jacob
marrying Rachel, Rachel leaving her home and family....
She stood speechless, staring at him.

"I know it must surprise you, Lusanna. You'll be well
taken care of. When Carl needs me to help him, I'll be near
by. We're still a community, aren't we?"

Are we? Still a community, after Death has wracked us
so?

She saw the longing in his face, an eagerness to sink his
toes into the good earth. To tangle with training oxen. *Who*
could be a better substitute father than Uncle Gerhard
Jantz?

She swallowed the lump in her throat, knowing that
there were many words unsaid. It would take time - months,
years, and even decades - for what they endured to work its
way from inside their souls out into the world. Perhaps, even
the world itself could not yet contain the sounds of the
funeral dirges, the mind-numbing experiences of seeing their
loved ones' bodies stacked in frozen graves, one upon
another.

She stepped forward, drawing Andrias to her, her arms
around his shoulders.

"Yes, Andrias. Yes, take Uncle Gerhard's offer."

She smiled through her tears. "And remember, I'll be
here nearby. You may even be able to see the smoke from
my chimney."

But as soon as she said the word *chimney*, she wasn't at
all certain that there would even be one.

What had that man said? *Probably have to build out-*
door ovens made of bricks from the soil. Outside the house?
At least for a season.

Lusanna was greatly aware that, as of now, she would
be sleeping under the prairie sky until the pile of new boards,
deposited at each of the over one hundred sites, could be
constructed into shanties or houses of some kind. *Then, only*
then, will Carl and I be married. I want to step into my new

home. If Carl insists on carrying me over the threshold, that will be fine, too.

***

It hadn't taken the judge at the McPherson County Courthouse long to assess the situation. A stalwart young man, nineteen-years of age stood alongside a comely Dutch-looking girl who spoke one of the German dialects around Moundridge.

Who could keep up with the thousands streaming to the prairies from Russia, Poland, Germany, and other places he'd forgotten about?

The young man, named, Carl Jantz had brought along his uncle Cornelius to sign for him.

Underage. Oh, these underage ones. At least these ones appear to be honest. Who knew? Who would contest it, knowing what happened in the pest hole in Florence?

The judge smiled and looked up at the bearded clergy-man standing by, who had introduced himself as an elder among the Mennonites in Halstead.

With Elder Krehbiel's black suit, beard, and his august bearing, the judge accepted his testimony as to the veracity of the situation. He sent them on to the county clerk for the marriage license.

They don't know what they're in for.

Three other couples applied for licenses, too. One, a large redheaded girl, her feet stuffed into old boots of some kind. She had trouble containing her laughter. Her man? Big stocky fellow claiming to be from Summerfield, Illinois.

God forbid. Why on earth would a young farmer from that settled community and fine land want to start again on these hard prairies? Wait until he tries to train a pair of oxen, then grab the handles of a sod buster. He won't be smiling long.

The judge turned, sauntered back into his office, shaking his head.

30

TOWARD THE LONE TREE

Seven large wagons, each drawn by two teams of oxen, wrenched and rocked along the trail northward toward the prairie land chosen for their settlement. Lusanna decided to walk behind the wagon loaded with all the chests, boxes and goods salvaged from the Florence desolation.

In a couple of hours, she knew, it would be noon. She wiped her neck with a kerchief and planted her feet, clad only in the thin schlorres, on the tracks left by the wagon wheels. The sun shone like the pancake pendulum of her mother's clock. The grasses, bruised by the rolling wheels, gave off a spicy fragrance, filling the air.

"Whew!" she said, turning to Agnes, who tromped along with her and a half-dozen other friends. "I like the sun, Agnes, but I'm heating up."

"Suits me, Lusanna, the warmth. I was beginning to think, after the winter we've had, that I would never be warm again." Her cheeks were rosy, her eyes, bright with anticipation.

Lusanna lifted her eyes to scan the four other wagons ahead, where some of her people were seated on top of the baggage and chests, heads moving from side-to-side, shoulders rocking. *They've been so quiet.*

More than a pang of sadness suddenly shifted through her breast. She remembered. *Wasn't it a hundred years ago?*

Rocking along on top of loaded wagons. Rounding the bend in the road. Crowded, weeping as we were. Mother and I. Little Benjamin, turning to catch a last glimpse of our thatched-roof home. My tree. My stalwart, beautiful tree. Our words: "Farewell, dear home. Farewell, forever."

She felt tears crowd at the corners of her eyes. She plodded on.

A meadowlark fluttered just in front of her, its golden breast matching the flower she had almost stepped on.

We're all much quieter than before... before....

What is happening to us?

In her reverie she thought of the fact that now they had no minister, no kindly preacher to unfold the scriptures, to hold a rod, not to beat them, only to move it from time to time, showing them the way.

She could see it. Feel it. Some of her people, losing faith. She could hear the suspicious tone in their voices, indicating that they were finding it hard to trust.

Almost all of them were still grieving. Angry at pestilence. Angry at frozen gashes in the earth called graves. Though some of the people probably weren't aware of it, she knew that they were even angry at God, feeling forsaken by man and their Heavenly Father.

Others, like Enis Schmidt, bargained with God: *If you save me from this plague, and redeem me from death, surely, you will plant my feet in pleasant places, WON'T YOU? Then, I will serve you forever.*

I can't blame them or judge them. Our faith, our inner spirits have been put to the fire. But oh, God, do not let me give in to resignation.

She saw it, felt it, the depression. The lowering of the heads. Marita Wedel, Freida Koehn, Henry Voth. The listlessness in their eyes. The long sighs and periods of sitting, slumping on a chest. Their silence.

Who would call them out of it? Where is the Balm of Gilead, that heals the sin-sick soul?

To steady her spirits, she focused her eyes upon Carl's shoulders rocking back and forth, as he sat on the wagon bench beside the driver. Before long, she knew, Carl would slip down, and with a rod in his hand, walk alongside the good-natured giants who drew the creaking wagon.

Carl. Yes, Carl and his father knew how to train and work with oxen. She smiled.

And, she knew that, with oxen, the rod must be a gentle rod. Their big trusting eyes, glancing at it, knowing it as their guide. *Only a guide,* as the master lifted it kindly from side to side to show them the way.

Thy rod and thy staff, they comfort me.

Somewhere ahead, a horse neighed. Meadowlarks were singing now. Goldfinches darted from one high-topped plant to another.

Oh, these plants, this lush thick grass. Will I ever learn the names of these growing things?

A rubbery leaf brushed her bare calf. *Who had stockings?*

She looked down and saw a plant which captivated her full attention. Its leaves spread widely, like a fern.

But on this rather dry prairie, it couldn't at all be a fern.

Her eyes widened as she focused upon the indigo-blue flowers arranged on a long stem, thrusting upward.

She reached down to run her hand over the fern-like leaf. It felt soft as silk, tender and flexible as rubber.

What is its name?

She resolved to, in time, learn the names of these marvelous plants through which they were passing.

And, she thought, *they say that the name of this little province where we are to settle is called Lone Tree Township. Where is the tree?*

She saw that they were stopping up ahead in a small grove along the banks of a creek. She noticed that the drivers were allowing the oxen to refresh themselves with water. Beyond that in the distance something caught her attention. A canopy, a cloud-like shadow rose up, towering over the landscape. She fixed her eyes upon it. *A tree? The top of a large tree?*

Their drivers' oxen took their turn drinking from the flowing water, their gentle heads slowly turning from side to side, checking their master's hand. Carl had dismounted.

Holding the rod, he stepped back to her. A big smile spread across his tanned face.

She smiled and quickened her step to take his hand.

Oh, I wish I had better clothes for him. A shirt of fine cotton. Clean pants, that hold their shape, woven of substantial material.

In spite of his tattered shirt collar, pants bagging at the knees and a new rip in the left trouser leg, she wanted to kiss him. Tell him how much she loved him. Run her hand through his tousled goldfinch hair, now that he had removed one of the cheap straw hats Brother Warkentine had provided for the men.

"They tell me there's a giant tree ahead, Lusanna. Maybe you'll find your tree?

Lusanna pointed northward and toward the west. "Is that it? That towering canopy I see in the distance?"

"Yes, I think it is, Lusanna. The driver, Simon Schmidt, says that it truly is a marvelous tree, loved by the Indians, even used sometimes as a postal office."

"Well, Carl, tell Simon to get back over there and let's get these oxen teams moving again."

Is it possible that I've found my tree at last? Will its bark feel the same? Will it whisper to me, as did my Antanofkan poplar?

"Why, Carl," she said, then chuckling. "Why didn't we think about it? Why else would they name this township *Lone Tree Township?*

The realization dawned upon her. She could feel her smile spread even wider. Wasn't it said in *The Revelation of St. John*: "And the leaves of the tree were for the healing of the nations."

31

FROM ELDER TOBIAS

For several months, now, I have been here near Marion, South Dakota, among my people from Karlswald. Certainly, I was ordained a minister in the church in Russia in the year of 1868. Ordained, also, as an Elder. Some people call me "Bishop," and though that title is used among the Mennonites in Pennsylvania, I do not require it.

God knows my heart. My struggles. The times we lived through. Oh, the times!

Yes, we had a good life in Karlswald, our Mennonite schools, our churches, good people. Hard-working people, thrifty. Eager to perpetuate our faith, strengthen our communities. It is always good to live in community. The blessed Lord and the Apostle Paul so encouraged us.

We follow the principles laid out by the Savior. We give heed to the Sermon on the Mount, which for us is more of a statement of our faith.

But as life calls us, the changes come. Soul-shattering changes. Upheavals I never even dreamed would come about. And I, a leader of over twenty congregations!

There was, of course, that sizable congregation in that little village near Ostrog, called Antanofka. Those people?

Life was hard for them. Many of them preferred the shady forests and the tall trees there. It was backbreaking work, however, clearing and draining patches of land. Numerous of the men were excellent woodsmen. But the Russian Crown forced its hand upon these people. Ever cutting the ruble, pinching their budgets - forbidding them land ownership. Charging them up to one-half of what they earned to pay the Crown tax and rent. Besides that, their village was raided frequently by outlaws.

Hearts grieved throughout our prosperous Russian settlements in Molotschna, and Chortitza, those in Polish-Russia, all of us. We saw the paw of the Great Bear reaching into our communities, attempting to take away the heart of our blessed faith. Soon to follow, were our schools. Had we stayed, we would all have been required to pledge allegiance to the godless Russian Crown. Our sons would enter the military. This meant that we would have had to renounce everything dear to us.

Sure, I came to America. Visited Canada, too, along with those eleven other brethren. Graceful, blessed lands. I ate of the fruit of their fields. I sat around their heavy-laden tables, in the Mennonite homes, of course.

I even told the sisters of the churches, when I returned to Polish-Russia, of the flowers in the gardens I had been permitted to view. The fruit, the grapes, pears, and everywhere the luscious wild strawberries. I told them of the balmy Kansas climate. The good land. I had not been there. Others had borne witness of it. I had no reason to doubt them.

Oh, yes. The communities in the eastern United States were already well-established. Gardens. Haystacks. Great barns. Barn lots of sheep and hogs. Beef cattle and milk cows. Houses, some of which would satisfy members of royalty.

Oh, yes, it had been a good year. A year of promise.

But, the Antanofkans? I feel satisfied I've done my duty by my congregations. Shepherding them. Ushering them across the stormy sea to the new land. It was not unlike the experience of the Apostle Paul, shipwrecked, hounded, enduring plagues, sicknesses, and even threats of death. I have never been as sick as I was in crossing the North Atlantic in winter. God forbid!

194

But the Antanofkans, those from near Ostrog? I'm getting news, bits and pieces, telling me that they have met with the most severe kinds of hardship.

I'm not sure who changed the plans in Pennsylvania when they arrived. I believed that they would stay in Pennsylvania for the winter months. There is a part of me that twitches inside. Am I the one responsible? Could I have oversold the land? Did I embellish the truth about the easy fortunes the Mennonites had gained in the East? Did I forget to tell of their own long struggles?

Some are telling me I had no good reason to settle here with my Dakota brethren and sisters. However, when it comes to settling emigrants, look for free land. Look for easy water. That's what I said. Of course, here on these Dakota plains, water isn't near the surface as it is in the middle of Kansas where the Antanofkans settled. Here we have to drill seventy feet, at least, for a good well.

Then, too. settlers in Kansas had to purchase land from the railroad. I knew that the Antanofkans were the least-well-off of our people. I knew they wouldn't have money for land. But I trusted Brother Warkentine and the others on the Aid Committee to make the arrangements.

I shake my head and groan when I get news that the people from that little village of thatch-roofed barns and houses have had to suffer so.

I really can't accept it, now. They say over three hundred of them died? Died in a town named, of all things, Florence.

Oh, God. Oh, God, mercy, mercy.

Smallpox? Well, it struck my family, too. God knows how I sat beside my own beloved grandson in England. Quarantined off the shore. Ugly-sounding word. Yes, I know about smallpox, shipwrecks, and winter seas. That's why I was delayed.

Of course, I took advantage of the opportunity to spend the winter months around Lancaster, Pennsylvania. At the brethren's invitation, only. I preached in over twenty of their

James D. Yoder

large churches. How they affirmed me, giving me the kiss of peace.

I can taste the luscious dishes of butter beans and the beef and gravy. The seven sweets and the seven sours. That sticky, heavenly shoo-fly-pie. My mouth waters, even now.

What is this news? I must clarify it with that Brother Warkentine. The ministers of the Anatofkin group, Eck and Unruh? Have they succumbed to the diseases, too? Is it true that because of the frozen ground, and so many dead that they had to bury a dozen corpses in one grave?

What a scramble on resurrection day!

My wife, Helene, has just come into the room. She says my face is flushed. She places her palm on my forehead and tells me that she thinks I have a fever and that I should go and lie down.

Now that I think about it, I do feel a bit dizzy.

I hear from Elder Krehbiel that he has been extending himself to minister to those folks, stranded as they were in that Florence town. Fourteen degrees below zero, they say? I'm not certain that even I can believe that. Transported them in boxcars? Dear Jesus, what happened?

I remember that girl named Lusanna. Brother called Andrias. Good names. Names to last until old age, for certain. How winsome she was, the boy, handsome. Her parents, too, pious, God fearing.

I do believe that I should plan to take the train down to Kansas and call on those people, dear brothers and sisters, now without a shepherd.

Yes. I will call an assembly. I will clarify and set their minds straight. They probably are awaiting me for communion and baptisms. Marriages, too. could be, even a funeral.

Yes, maybe they will be glad to see Brother Tobias step through the Dutch door of their new houses, all in a row, catching the southern sunshine. Surely, by now, they are upon the land. Forty acres is a generous portion of land. Yes, Elder Tobias must go there and give a pastoral call.

Maybe I'd better take Helena's advice. I do seem unwell. Thirsty and unwell. Outside the Dakota landscape has shadowed as clouds begin to hide the sun. Yes, a chill may be coming.

What was it in the Book of Tobit? One of the books of the Apocrypha.

"Tobit," a name which means "blinded by pigeon dung."

My God, what a recollection.

32

ENOCH AND ADAM

Lusanna's heart beat in happy anticipation. This very day Carl and Andrias were making the trip with the wagon, drawn by the oxen all the way into Canton to bring back a cast-iron kitchen range.

Carl's sister, Anna, had found temporary work over at the Ratzlaff house, if they could call their board and sod construction houses. Olga Ratzlaff had given birth to twins last week. Carl's mother, Elske, was busy rolling dough on the makeshift table within the house.

Now, almost all of the Anatofkin Ostrogers were called upon to make do when it came to furniture. Most of them were waiting until they had cash from crops for money to furnish their houses. Lusanna had endured it, no beds, no tables, cupboards, chairs - such furniture required for houskeeping and decent living.

No, it hadn't been easy deciding where to hang the sheet at night separating her and Carl's portion. Elske and Anna lay on the floor to the right. Crowded, but nothing compared to *The Vaderland* experience. Don't even mention the storehouse in Florence.

They had fresh straw ticks, however, to place upon the hard earthen floor. There had been enough rain last summer for an abundance of fragrant hay.

For the entire last fall and winter, she had learned to prepare their meals, bake bread on the stove they built by stacking bricks made of the soil mixed with straw. She had drawn up her old homespun skirt and with her bare feet deep within the muddy mix, danced, hopped, and laughed as Carl built the little box forms for the bricks. Set them aside for a couple of days to bake in the hot sun - then, the fine bricks. Bricks that held the heat. And unless it rained too generously, the stove-oven would last for several seasons.

She was wearing a dress made of a common grayish calico from the bolt provided by the women of the Moundridge community. She had fashioned herself a plain apron to wear over it, stitched from one of her mother's old muslin nightgowns, which allowed her to wear the dress several days before washing it again.

Shoes? Would you believe that Carl surprised her, bringing home a pair of high-topped shoes with laces, soon after they arrived here? These, of course, he purchased from money he had earned back in Summerfield. She worried, though, about the two dollars he'd splurged for them. Her mind turned to her recent wedding when she first wore them. He had purchased them in Canton the day he and Andrias rode into town in the cart drawn by Adam and Enoch, the faithful pair of purplish-spotted white oxen.

Barefooted, she stoked up the fire underneath a large black kettle, filled with water from their well.

Thank God, that was a blessing.

The fellows had to dig only about seventeen feet down before the fresh water bubbled up. She smiled as she thought of the oxen and how Carl and Andrias labored to train them.

"We're sorry," Brother Holdeman had said. "We just couldn't afford better calves for you to train."

What had the Aid Committee done purchasing those wild-eyed young steers from the plains of Texas, expecting us to corral and train them?

Sure, the Committee needed to pinch their pennies. Look what they already have done for us? Carl and I wouldn't have this house had it not been for their help. I do have to say, though, it was slapped together with raw lumber, which shrank last winter, allowing the bitter wind to sail through. That's another matter. Carl plans to put a floor in this summer, add another room and fix those cracks with strips of lumber.

***

Out by the haystacks of dried prairie grasses they labored, Andrias and Carl. Lusanna could hear their laughing as well as words of frustration.

"They're really too big to start training," Carl said. "Usually one starts young. These cattle? Why they castrated them too late and there's a wild flicker in their eyes."

"That's the Texas longhorn in them, Carl. You're experienced. You'll show me how to do it."

"First thing," Carl said, "is to take this wooden rod and place it here by the side of the head of this - what did you say his name was?"

"That one's Enoch. The other one with the spot on his head is Adam."

"Well, first thing is to stand in front of Enoch and Adam, halter in one hand, the rod in the other, moving it forward as you pull. They have to move forward."

"Gentle does it?"

"Enoch wants to resist. See how he lowers his head trying to dig a horn into me?"

"What'll you do?" Andrias's eyes opened wide.

"Stay with it. Come on, Enoch, Adam. This way."

The half-grown animals lifted their dripping nozzles and stepped forward reluctantly. Soon they were waddling along behind Carl who walked with the rod held before him. Then he stopped. "Whoa." At that word, he held the rod across in front of the team. Enoch, to test Carl, gave the rod a hard nudge with his nose."

"No, Enoch." Carl ran the rod again in front of the calf.

"No matter how rambunctious he becomes, we always have to try to be gentle and low-key, Andrias. It's the only way to train oxen."

Andrias took his turn following Carl's instructions. They progressed through the steps, turning to the right while holding the rod and the halter, saying "gee," the same by saying "haw," while turning the rod and stepping to the left.

Adam seemed to enjoy the maneuvers, following faithfully. Enoch pulled back, trying to assert himself. Long strings of saliva dripped from his mouth and his wild eyes rolled as if to say, "You aren't going to tell me what to do."

Carl repeated the steps with the young calves, who by now were getting used to one another. Soon, they would not even want to be parted, giving each other the fullest loyalty and devotion, as well as, if they had a gentle master, the same devotion to him.

Next Carl showed Andrias how to train the team to back up. He turned around and faced the calves, then held the rod in front of their legs. "See, Andrias, they have to back up."

Just then Andrias noticed something twitch in the grass at the edge of the path on which Carl stood. *Should he say something? Would it startle the oxen?*

Then he saw it more fully as its body quickly coiled very near Carl's boot.

A rattlesnake. Big one. Would it strike and hit above Carl's boot?

He decided to call out his warning. "Carl," he yelled, "a rattlesnake, right by your foot!"

Carl's eyes opened wildly, his feet danced as he half-turned, searching this way and that. As he turned, and upon seeing the coiled snake, dropped the rod and yanked on the halter.

Enoch gave forth a loud bawl, lifting his head, shaking it menacingly. Perhaps Adam would not have demonstrated so wildly, but at his teammate's yank and pull of disobedience, he followed suit.

As Carl danced aside of the striking snake, Andrias raced to pick up the wooden rod to kill it. The Texas part longhorn oxen took off. They bellowed, snorted, manure streaked from their behinds as if to show Andrias and Carl just what they thought of them.

201

Andrias whaled at the rattlesnake with the wooden rod while Carl stood, hands at his hips, watching his team bumbling and bawling toward the creek.

After they made sure the snake was dead and had used the stick to toss it into a patch of prairie grass, they sat down, knees drawn up.

They howled. They laughed. Their guffaws carried to Lusanna's window, where she stood looking out.

Carl glanced up from his roost on the patch of prairie grass. He saw that she had observed the spectacle they'd made with the snake and the oxen.

"Hey, Lusanna," he called, "what's that verse in the Bible? 'His yoke is easy and his burden is light?' Well, you'd just better come out here and give this a try."

They laughed until they felt hollow, then ceased their rolling on the ground, Andrias realized how they had needed it: the laughter, the humor. The runaway young calves, not at all responsible. The entire episode freed them from the solemn situations they had faced for so long. For a moment, sadness, grief, despondency, and lagging faith, all seemed to seep into the earth.

"Come on, Andrias. We've got to teach them not to *giddup* unless we say it and use the rod."

They got to their feet and sauntered off toward the creek to retrieve the calves, foundering themselves on the lush grass.

***

Lusanna poked the boiling shirt and britches in the kettle with a stick, and she looked back at her house. Now, she was able to grin, after the frigid winter. Their house squatted on their patch of prairie, smacked between the Wedel house and the Unruhs' crooked, thatched-roofed dwelling to the south.

She checked their own prairie-sod roof, noting the flock of doves cooing and pecking through the dried grasses on top. She surveyed the unpainted boards, the one small window in front to the left of the door.

Smart idea, too, digging two feet down into the earth like they had done, scraping out the soil, leaving a packed dirt floor. By doing so, of course, the house was warmer, at least on their feet.

Sure. Many of the folks followed suit. Stretched the supply of lumber.

Lusanna grinned, remembering how she called it "my earth house."

Size of the house? Roughly, twelve feet by fourteen feet but she doubted that was correct. After they had arrived upon the land and each family learned the location of their forty-acre portion, the housing construction had begun.

We couldn't have done it, weak and depressed as we were, if it hadn't been for the host of Mennonite men from these other communities volunteering to help us. And, as recent settlers themselves, they didn't have much time to spare. It was truly a gift from God.

There was gratitude too, about the Aid Committee hiring those men to come in and help plow the prairie with their sod-busting plows. I saw how several of our men, weakened and discouraged, gave up when they tried. Some even refused because of their despondency and lack of skills.

Our wedding?

They hadn't waited until the house was constructed. Too many tasks clamored for their hands and shoulders. They both agreed that it made no sense to delay the marriage.

They had lived for a week in the dugout space in a hay stack at the back of their land, where it sloped toward a small creek. Actually, both Carl and Lusanna thought it was rather pleasant. The prairie hay was fragrant.

They chuckled and visited while looking up at the millions of stars in a cloudless night sky. The breeze sweet, and gentle, come evening, the bed, soft and fresh. Lusanna, Anna, and Elske slept to one side of the haystack, where they could still look up at the stars. Carl selected his sleeping place to the front. A sweet wind blew over the grass beyond, where the shared cow was tethered for the night. The cow was named *Mathilda,* meaning "mighty battle maid."

Agnes Unruh selected the name for the cow, who seemed to delight in planting her hoof into the milk pail. Or, when finished being milked, give one a painful butt with her head, if one was off guard.

"Once, I butted her back," Agnes had announced with a toss of her head. "After all, she needs to learn a lesson."

Lusanna didn't think it seemly, a Mennonite young woman behaving so. What about the blessed words of Jesus, "Do good to those who hurt you.?"

It pleased Lusanna, though, Agnes and Peter's house just to the north. She could even see Peter, shovel in his hands, digging in Agnes's garden plot.

Back to our wedding.

Carl and I saw the need to pitch in with every ounce of our energy to tackle the tasks awaiting us. Our neighbors, too. At first there were grumblings. A few quarrels over who would get which plot of land. Wives squabbling with husbands over where to place a window or a door.

Pity the poor Aid Committee and that blessed Warkentine. May God give him a choice place in heaven.

Reverend Krehbiel too. Why, he's like my grandfather, the one I remember who is buried back in Antanofka. That seems so long ago. Where are my Jewish friends, Esther and Laban? What happened to Elise and Jacob Wedel? Their parents, Helena and Amos? Did the Russian Bear consume them? Prisons in Siberia? Oh, God. I hope not.

They were married a year ago in late June. Carl had suggested that they hold the service, along with Agnes's and Peter's, out by the elderberry bushes along the creek at the back of their acreage.

"No, Carl. No. I want our wedding to be in front and under the shade of my wonderful tree."

Yes. She'd found it, the day of the move onto the prairie. She'd scanned the skyline, watching the canopy grow larger, the landscape surrendering to its dominance. Rugged, the giant tree beckoned her.

"A cottonwood?" she had asked the wagon driver.

"Yes," he replied. "And it is quite a famous tree. You know the Indians around here used to burn the prairies to keep down the brush in order for the buffalo to graze the prairie grasses."

"Did that have something to do with its growth?" she had asked.

"Why, yes, indeed. Yes, it did. It's located not far from Running Turkey Creek, which runs through there. That gave the roots their water supply. Plus the fact that it is on a little peninsula of land, somehow it was spared the prairie fires."

The wagon train began again. Others on top of the trunks and bundles started pointing toward the tree.

She had not seen it up close that day or have opportunities to smell the leaves, to feel the bark, to stand amazed in its presence and hear its own language and whispers. She had been forced to walk on, following the wagon carrying her possessions. She understood the drivers had very little extra time, surrounded as they were with immigrants so eager to catch sight of their homesites.

The more miles they walked and the wagons rolled, the prouder Lusanna became of Carl - Andrias, too, strolling easily alongside the stalwart oxen. Their liquid eyes and easy movements almost put her in a trance.

Surely they had been trained with gentleness.

It helped Lusanna when she, with the others, began the weighty tasks of unloading their possessions. It was painful, to set Mother's hope chest and the one made by Father right down into a patch of prairie grass. She couldn't control the flow of tears.

Carl, after he'd unloaded the last box and bundle, beneath the immense blue sky, did come over to comfort her, placing his hand around her waist. Fat, yellow grasshoppers scattered around their feet.

Elske and Anna stood waiting, looking into the distance. They watched the wagons roll on, stop and unload another immigrant family's scant possessions.

Oh, how small we are when compared to this expanse of prairie. Will we ever tame it? What will keep the grass from consuming us? Where do we go when the season changes and the winter wind comes blasting? There is no band of trees, no shelter...

And we surely have been introduced to Kansas winters in Hutchinson and in Florence. Oh, that night. Fourteen degrees below zero.

It had been then that Carl and Elske noticed the haystack down toward the creek. It was obvious that range cattle had eaten frequently from it. On the western side they could see a cave extending into the stack.

"Look. Lusanna, we have a home." He laughed, pointing.

"You mean...you mean a haystack?"

"Yes, until we get some kind of house built. Why, Lusanna, look at your first home."

It had given her some comfort, dragging the two chests down to the yellow mound rising up, the shadowed cave into the stack, facing her. When she got closer, she could smell the sweetness of clover and the other plants waving in the wind, their names yet unknown to her:

They bumbled around the first four days trying on their new identities as prairie people. When they were fully aware of the almost insurmountable tasks awaiting them, they were stricken to silence.

Finally, Carl found his voice. He took Lusanna by her shoulder and looked straight into her eyes.

"Lusanna," he said, "we can't wait. It makes no sense. Let's get married just as soon as Elder Krehbiel can come out to the prairie, here."

Startled at first, Lusanna stared back into his eyes, blue as the prairie flower beside her foot. She saw his trust, his faith, his longing.

She answered, "Yes. Carl. Yes. Tell Mother Elske and Anna. It makes no sense to wait. We'll have the ceremony when Elder Krehbiel comes. Didn't he say something about holding services for all of us next Sunday in that funny little schoolhouse?"

And considering that they had to sleep within the haystack, serenaded by strange animals roaming the grasslands called coyotes, the lonesome, shaky hooting of owls, and the cries of nighthawks, Lusanna thought yes, yes, indeed. Carl had the best solution. Especially when he mentioned that prairie wolves still roamed through here.

33

THE LONE TREE

There must have been a third of the people who ventured back toward the giant cottonwood tree by Turkey Creek the first Sunday in June. Many had walked. Others piled on wagons drawn by teams of oxen and horses, carrying as many neighbors as wished to participate. The Lone Tree was their reference point.

Lusanna understood that with all the suffering and hardships they had endured, many of her people would not have extra energy needed to make the effort. Then, too, what would they wear?

Everyone's travel clothing had worn to rags.

Lusanna and Agnes regretted that they couldn't celebrate the way they had back home with tables spread with verenika and pluma moos. The delicious pearl barley and oat meal cooked with sweet milk. Buttered bread and beef soup.

But this splendid tree makes up for that loss, she thought to herself.

Agnes agreed. Then, to their rescue, sisters Dirks and Peters insisted on aiding Elske with baking wheat bread. Olga Dirks promised a whole kettle of borscht, a combined venture with several neighbors contributing.

She had first experienced The Lone Tree fully on the day Carl and Andrias had ridden into Canton for seed, and of course, her shoes.

She and Elske had finished baking three loaves of bread in their outside brick oven. When she glanced up and to the east, the tree seemed to beckon her.

Finally, she was able to stand it no longer. "Elske, I wonder if you'd mind if I took a walk over to that big tree? She, Elske and Anna had talked frequently about their lives in Antanofka, and "Lusanna's tree" there.

"You're very much in need of a rest, Lusanna. Take a walk through the prairie, go find your tree." She smiled and nodded toward the door.

She could hardly slow her legs and feet as they tangled with the tall grasses, taking, as she did, a short cut across the prairie, abandoning the wagon trail.

Black-and-yellow butterflies swooped down, one resting momentarily upon her headscarf. She began to laugh at how the wind resisted her. She lowered her head and plowed on, checking her bearings by looking up at the broad tree canopy ahead.

When she arrived before the tree, she noticed that many people had gathered there as the grass was short, bruised, yet still green. Wild growth behind the tree outlined the creek. The monstrous living plant shook its leaves in greeting as if whispering to her: "Welcome, Lusanna. Welcome to the prairie."

She stood, head tilted back to scan the branches rising a hundred feet above her, broad as ordinary tree trunks themselves. Her mouth opened. She kept staring. She saw three black ravens on a top limb to the right. They lifted their wings, sailing off in the zephyr winds.

Billowing clouds in the deep blue sky provided a reverent backdrop.

A holy place. A blessed tree. Surely, the Indians bowed their heads and opened their souls here.

And he... no, not only "he."
She, too, shall be like a tree,
planted by the rivers of water....

Next, Lusanna stepped forward to throw her arms around the cottonwood. It was almost as if it knew her and was waiting her embrace. But her reach was small, minuscule when measured against its magnificent circumference. *Why,* she thought, *it would take five or six full-grown men to reach around this tree, maybe even more.*

She vowed, then and there:, *this is where Carl and I will be married.*

She kept drawing her palms over the corky bark, feeling the tickle as if the tree knew her love and responded. A sudden blast of wind shook the topmost branches with violence; the almost heart-shaped leaves on their long stems trembled.

A song for me?

Lusanna lost count of time. She lay down under the magnificent spread, looking upwards. She felt the tensions and weariness of her body ease into the earth. She closed her eyes and listened to the cottonwood rustle and murmur to her, accompanied by a meadowlark's song.

She drifted off into a heavenly sleep. Dreamed of a village, far, far, away called Antanofka. She, when finished churning the butter, ran out to her poplar tree to give it a hug and to listen to its whispering and what it had to say to her spirit. She saw the thatched roof and the chimney of their house and connected barn. She dreamed that she opened her arms to welcome the storks, Ichabod and Keturah, alighting there.

When she returned back across the prairie to her squat, rude home, she realized that at least a couple of hours had passed.

Dear God, I must have fallen into a deep, deep sleep.

Lusanna began to run, skip, and hop across the prairie toward the little sod-roofed nubbin of her house. Her feet tangled and she fell in tall clover. Bees zoomed about her, bewildered, yet they did not sting her. She rose, threw up her arms and laughed.

I can't wait to tell Carl. Under The Lone Tree, Carl. We will be married under The Lone Tree.

***

A five o'clock that Sunday evening, they had stood, the two couples and the four attendants, feet enmeshed in the prairie grasses, the canopy of the great tree gave them a wide, blessed shade.

Both Lusanna and Agnes had dug through their family chests, selecting dresses previously worn by their mothers. Lusanna chose a long, flowing, plain blue cotton, which fell to the very tips of her high-topped shoes. The dress, with its high collar, showed Lusanna's throat to its best.

She had pulled out her mother's black *haube* (covering for church) with the wide ribbons, tying them under her chin. Her sun bleached hair shone in contrast beneath the edges of the *haube*.

Agnes's dress was an off-colored brown linen, also from her own mother's hope chest. Agnes giggled, complaining that the dress was "too tight." Agnes donned her mother's haube with its black lace. "Am I an old lady, now, Lusanna?" She slapped a thigh as she laughed.

Oh, thought Lusanna, *the world needs people like Agnes.*

It seemed not to trouble Agnes at all that she was forced to wear boots that she had greased to cover the scars from the abusive wear.

The men?

Carl Jantz, his mane of yellow hair falling toward his twinkling blue eyes, shifted his feet in attempts to hide his anxiety. His shoulders lifted in a Russian white blouse-shirt from out of his family trunk. Obviously, it had been worn by his father back home for special occasions only.

His heavy, loose-fitting twill trousers would have benefited from better ironing, but that, indeed, was a small matter. *Who had time for that?*

Agnes's Peter wore similar trousers of black cord. His shoes, too, were worn and recently greased, his shirt, similar to Carl's, though one could tell, not of the same quality.

Elder Krehibiel read from First Corinthians, the passage about loyalty and commitment in the sacred ordinance of matrimony.

An evening breeze drifted through the branches of the cottonwood, which towered like an Egyptian pillar along the Nile, its leaves clapping, whispering in its own joy.

Then came the Elder's questions, requiring the *I do* from all four of the applicants. Whipporwills called to each other, far down the creek to the south.

Next Brother Unruh led the song which surprisingly filled the air with its harmony.

> *O happy home, where two in heart united in holy faith and blessed hope are one. Whom death a little while alone divideth, And cannot end the union here begun!*

The sun eased into a multiple band of oranges, purples, and light pink, spreading trailing fingers. The setting itself made a perfect cathedral, outlined by the flowering elderberries along the peninsula of land.

Women, whose hearts had been cheered by the service and the establishment of new homes on the prairie, with all their hopes and dreams, stepped forward, smiling broadly, tears in their eyes, to kiss the brides.

They spread a tablecloth dug from someone's hope chest across the flat bed of a wagon, drawn up by brother Schmidt.

They dipped the borscht into bowls from the kettle over the smoldering coals, a fire that they had built before the gathering.

With the spread of pluma moos made out of sand plums, which the women had discovered along branches and creeks, and the freshly baked bread, its rich aroma spreading as they sliced it, the wedding banquet proceeded.

Agnes was unable to contain her laughter, which startled the finches on the lower branches of the tree. She gave her new husband a tease-of-a-punch on his arm.

The wind circled about them, lifting the sounds of merrymaking.

It should be written down somewhere, thought Lusanna: *"And the Anatofkins laughed at last."*

34

THEY SETTLE IN

The year rolled on as most of the Ostrogers from Anta-nofka settled in. A few, facing the daunting tasks ahead of them, gave up, returning to Summerfield, Illinois. Some longed for Pennsylvania, scraping their meager resources together and saying farewell to their life-long families and friends with whom they'd striven and suffered. Others scattered to Missouri and Iowa.

Over a couple of hundred of us, still, thought Lusanna. She smiled as she dusted the dresser in her and Carl's bedroom. She was proud of the furniture, though it was secondhand. The little dresser with two curved drawers bellied out into the room gracefully, matching the veneered bedstead, head and foot. She had found crocheted table scarves in her mother's chest to place on top of the dresser.

She was rejoicing over the fact that instead of enlarging their first half-dugout house, Carl had scraped together enough money to buy lumber. By tearing down the old structure and reusing the lumber, he was able to build a good house, indeed. Four rooms. A substantial house where she could raise a family.

She glanced out at her black Home Comfort kitchen range, noticing that the teakettle was boiling. *Oh, that osage orange wood they bring in here builds the hottest fire.*

Her loaves had risen.

She stepped through the living room, noting the breeze came through the southwest today as it blew back her panel

213

curtains, which she had made from old cloth from the trunk. Green roller shades were halfway open.

She decided to dig out some sausage from the crock of lard out in the cool root cellar Andrias and Carl had dug a year ago. The way the Concord grapes were stretching their tendrils out in the garden, they'd soon have a few kegs of wine to tide them through the bitter winter, placing them alongside the crocks of kraut.

Yes, fix sausage, kraut, mashed potatoes and green beans from the garden. That along with her fresh bread and butter, the supper would surely pass muster.

She looked up at her kitchen shelf and saw the gleaming jars of sand plum jelly. *That'll finish off things, with the fresh butter and bread.*

By evening, the western sky was ablaze in the splendor of afterglow when Andrias came riding up in a springwagon, the dark-haired Esther Foth, wearing a bright calico dress, laughing alongside him on the bench.

Thank God, he's found someone to help take away the loneliness. How the time flies. He smiles, now. Andrias is going to make it. He'll be successful.

She thought about how Esther's father, Henry, had been able to purchase two more portions of land. *Think of it. A hundred and twenty acres!*

With the new machinery coming in, she saw the eagerness in Andrias's face. She thought of the ease with which he'd learned to train oxen in the community. Not only that, but young colts, too. *Wouldn't Father and Mother be proud?*

She thought of brother Benjamin. *Little, loving Benjamin. All our lives are better because of that child's love.*

Her hand automatically rose to her chest.

Oh, Carl, take me over to Florence. How far is it? Fifty long miles? I want to go and sit by their graves. Not I only, but many, many here whose grief surely has lessened but will always remain.

She stepped over to the cupboard, reached for a loaf pan and slid it into the oven of the cast-iron stove.

She began to hum a hymn based upon Isaiah 32:2. "And a man shall be as a hiding place from the wind, and a covert from the tempest, as rivers of water in a dry place, as the shadow of a great rock in a weary land."

O, Jesus is the rock in the weary land, the weary land...

All three loaves lifted their bosoms in the oven, browning gently on top. The savory smell of the bread spread through the kitchen. A breeze flowed through the back window, distributing the fragrance.

She sang the chorus of the hymn: *A Shelter in the Time of Storm.*"

***

They sat, Lusanna at the east end of the table, Carl, across from her. An evening amber light glowed throughout the combination kitchen and dining room. Lusanna had graced the table with a tablecloth from the hope chest.

My hope chest, she now called it.

She had taken time to snatch up some of those bachelor's buttons and break off three bunches of yellow clover at the edge of the garden. She could have gathered more luxuriant flowers; however, with the tasks of the day, she hadn't taken the time. The simple ones she'd picked added their grace and fragrance from the jar placed in the middle of the table.

Carl called upon Andrias to say the blessing, which he did quietly. Sincerity and seriousness registered in his youthful voice.

The plate of stuffed sausage, cut in generous sections, passed around the table. Lusanna liked it that she'd gotten her potatoes mashed quickly, and with warm milk from the fresh milking, they were hot and fluffy.

"Lusanna, you and Carl surely made good sausage." Andrias smiled and forked in another mouthful.

"I like the sauerkraut," added Esther. "I like it with the light taste of grape leaves one puts on top of the crock."

Outside, frogs croaked from the creek back of the makeshift barn. The saplings they'd planted weren't large enough yet to attract many tree frogs, yet, if one listened, one heard an occasional chirrup.

The conversation hinged upon their lived experiences, retelling stories all the way from Antanofka in far-off Polish Russia.

A sadness crept through their hearts as they mentioned the overwhelming losses and sorrows.

"But this land is a blessing. Truly a blessing. Only three dollars an acre from the railroad." Andrias looked at Carl.

"It's good land, too, Carl. Uncle Gerhard thinks that he is going to have enough wheat and oats this season to sell after threshing. He's counting on that money to build another house."

It was so. New houses sprang up as a modest prosperity took hold. There had been enough of chilblains, children with purple hands clinging to their featherbeds on earthen floors. Bitter winds slicing through the cracks left by withered and shrunken new boards. Broken families, regrouped clusters, widows and unmarried women, lonely on the windswept prairie.

"I like it, too, now that these Mennonites all around here think that education is so important. "Why," said Esther, that conference, called The Western Conference, insisted upon setting up a Mennonite school, teaching high German, advanced courses in the Bible. Singing, such singing. Reading real notes from hymnals. Music such as I'd never heard before." She forked another mouthful of kraut.

"Well, I'm sorry to say, Esther," replied Lusanna, "there are some of our people who feel these more established Mennonites with differing culture and ways are treating us with downward looks."

"You mean, like we are children?" Andrias asked.

"Yes. I think they say they are treated *paternalistically*, whatever all that includes." Lusanna checked the bread plate.

"Our people ought to hold their tongues," Carl said. "We wouldn't be alive if it hadn't been for Brother

Warkentine and Elder Krehbiel. Look what he's doing, bringing in ministers. A regular church, now, meeting in that old schoolhouse."

"But many of our people aren't attending." Lusanna's voice dropped, her tone, touched with sadness.

"I'm sad about that, too," Esther said. "You know, some of the young people found the work beyond their capabilities. They had no farming skills. You know, Carl and Andrias, how hard it is to break sod. Especially, if you never had the experience."

"Well," added Andrias, "It isn't just the prairie sod. It was the weather, the unexpected arctic blasts when we arrived. We will never forget it."

"That's right, Andrias," replied Carl. "But you have to remember, these young adults have to be responsible. They've been taught. Preachers Eck and Unruh, God rest their souls. Don't forget the ministry of Elder Tobias Unruh. He baptized us."

At the mention of Elder Tobias, silence reigned around the table. An evening hawk called. A lightning bug, darting hither and thither, could be seen when they glanced out the window.

"Well," Lusanna said, "that's another matter. Quite a few of our people still feel abandoned by Elder Tobias. They keep saying that he misrepresented the land, he and the railroad companies.

"It's true, Lusanna," Carl said. "The railroad companies purposefully overinflated their descriptions of Kansas land and Kansas prairies. Their descriptions didn't quite match the reality when we got here."

Moving the flowers back to a shelf, Lusanna rose to light the kerosene lamp on the table.

Esther told of her experience of attending the new Mennonite School, taught by Schoolmaster Dirks. "I feel truly blessed, Lusanna."

"I wish you could go for at least a semester, Lusanna. There are over one hundred students, and they have a wonderful chorus.

"But you know, Esther, I'm an old married lady, now."
She chuckled.

"I don't like it, the things I'm hearing. You know about
a dozen of our young people, both men and women, took
jobs off the farms to go over and help the Swedish people
over northwest," Andrias said, looking at the dish of pluma
moos Lusanna had just picked up.

"Yes," said Carl. "Quite a few of them took jobs in the
broom-corn fields. Good pay. Earning as much as fifty
dollars for their work. I guess, in a way, I don't blame them."

"The thing that hurts me," Andrias replied, "are the
reports in the Canton newspaper, about how they spend their
money foolishly. They even say that the English refuse to
believe they're Mennonites when they dress the way they
do."

"Dress?" asked Lusanna.

"Yes. Girls with fancy hats from the millinery shop.
Dresses frowned upon in our community. With so much
need here and in their homes, surely that's not the right path,
is it?"

"No," Esther replied. "That's not according to the
Bible: "be ye not conformed to this world; but be
transformed by the renewing of your mind. That's what St.
Paul said in Romans, chapter 12."

"I agree," added Carl. "But we mustn't judge them too
harshly. It's been too hard, just too hard for some among us.
They may have lost their way for awhile. We must treat them
with kindness, forgiveness. Keep every door open."

Murmurs of agreement circled the table. The pluma
moos, along with mint tea, capped the evening, as far as the
meal was concerned.

"I hear a wagon rumbling up, horses neighing." Lusanna rose to look out the front door and saw who else but
Agnes Stucky and Peter, rollicking and rolling in on a
springwagon. Peter leaped down to tie the horses to a fence
post.

"Everyone, come to the front. Agnes and Peter have driven over." Lusanna was the first to burst through the door, a happy smile spreading on her tanned cheeks.

"Oh, Lusanna." Angnes' laughter filled the air. Peter smiled broadly.

"Oh, it's so wonderful, Agnes and Peter, coming over to see us like this. Why, had I known I'd..."

'I know that, Lusanna," Agnes interrupted. "I know you'd have worked your... well, you'd slaved all afternoon with so many to cook for. I came over to ask you all if you wouldn't want to load up in the springwagon and head across the prairie to that giant cottonwood Lusanna's been boasting about."

"Oh, Agnes! Yes. Yes!"

Lusanna was the first to climb into the springwagon.

"It's going to be full moon, soon," Peter said.

Voices chorused together, "Full moon on the prairie. We can't think of anything nicer."

35

FAREWELL, LITTLE CHURCH OF ANTANOFKANS

It is now July, 1875. My dear wife, Helena, sits by my sickbed. I know the Lord will be calling me home soon. I am fifty-six years old and had looked forward to a long life, at least my three score and ten. However, I know, now, that it will not be His blessed will. My hours are waning. I have selected the hymn for my funeral, "One Sweetly Solemn Thought," which I know my Mennonite brothers and sisters will sing with the proper solemnity and reverence that I now feel.

One sweetly solemn thought
Comes to me o'er and o'er, -
Nearer my home, today, am I
Than e'er I've been before.

Do one's years slide before one as he lies upon his deathbed? Feverish. Unable to swallow or to eat. Not even sup of broth from the spoon Helena holds.
The years slip by in my mind. I dare not be so pompous as to, myself, utter the words: "Well done, thou good and faithful servant..." Those are for the Lord, only. It is my duty, now, to wait until the scroll is unrolled in the heavenly kingdom, and I see my Lord face to face.
I think of my own name, "Tobias." I remember it recorded in the book of Tobit. I smile when I recognize its meaning: "blinded by pigeon dung."

I know that my task with my churches was to ever see more clearly.

Oh, God, Heavenly Father: forgive me, when I failed to see.

The Lord gave me the calling to preach the gospel. He gave me the task, duly authorized by the church, to be an Elder. I have seldom used the word Bishop, however it has been attributed to me, from time to time.

My two sons and dear Helena are here beside me. They weep. They hold my hand. Though the chill of death creeps over me, I can still fill the warmth of their hands.

I bless them. I close my eyes, yet still the scenes of my life slide before me. Those villages, so far, far, away, Antanofka, Waldheim, Karlswald, Fuerstendorf...I know them well. I see their thatched roofs in my mind. I hear the hymns echoing from the churches. I see the young ones, kneeling as a deacon and I baptize them, one by one.

Sometimes, lying here, I can feel the rolling of the ship, The Kenilworth, which brought us, at last, safely to Philadelphia, blessed city of brotherly love.

The Lord appointed me to be one of the twelve chosen to establish the value of this new land, this America and its many broad states as sites for our new homes. I tried to perform this task with humility and proper obedience to the call.

We were beset by the evil one, the godlessness of the Russian Crown, forcing us to leave what was dear to us. Dear, indeed, but when compared the blessed ventures of obedience to the calls of justice, love, and peace, our homes there became as mere chaff.

I am not saying that we did not weep when we left our homeland. Nothing is more heart-rending that seeing maidens and their mothers weeping atop the wagons, saying, "Farewell, farewell...I'll never see my home again."

But I, like Father Abraham, were among those who "...looked for a city which hath foundations, whose builder and maker is God."

Eleven brethren and I were privileged to survey this land. We ate of its fruit, we sat amazed at its lands and rivers. You may bear witness that I described it as a pleasant place indeed.

Now, I think of my brethren and sisters, the Antanofkans. Brother Funk tells me in his letter that he visited your homes on the Kansas prairie and saw your suffering. I'm told that you ate watery potato soup, that your children huddled cold upon the earthen floors. That your homes were insufficient, the lumber shrinking, allowing the bitter winds to cause you great discomfort.

My heart bleeds when I hear it and I wonder if I had misguided you. Oh, my dear Antanofkan people, I pray for you. I pray for you upon my deathbed as I breathe my last minutes. "Lord Jesus, keep them in your care."

I did not speak for two entire days when I received word of the plagues that overcame you in that town called Florence. I, too, suffered by the bedside of our people stricken with smallpox. Quarantined off the coast of England.

Like the Apostle Paul, I suffered shipwreck, the tortures of seasickness, the perils of travel on the sea.

How shall I ever stop hearing those words, both of comfort and of sorrow?

> *Eternal Father, strong to save,*
> *Whose arm hath bound the restless wave,*
> *Who bidd'st the mighty ocean deep*
> *Its own appointed limits keep;*
> *Oh, hear us when we cry to Thee,*
> *For those in peril on the sea!*

I feel a numbness creeping from my feet, up my legs. I clasp my hands over my heart, waiting to greet my Savior.

I pray as He has taught us to pray, "Forgive us our sins, as we forgive those who sin against us..."

Oh, the blessed Lord. "Hallowed be thy name...."

I go to my fathers. I go to my eternal rest.

May evermore, evermore, I say, those words of that hymn we sang upon the rolling decks come from my heart and lips to you. To you, dear little congregation of Antanofkans: "Thus evermore shall rise to Thee, glad hymns of praise from land and sea."

***

Obituary of Bishop Tobias A. Unruh
(From The Herald of Truth, September, 1875)

Bishop Tobias A. Unruh was born May 5th, 1819. He came from Karlswald in Polish-Russia, last winter and settled in Dakota, and was called from his earthly labors by the hand of death on this 23rd of July, 1875. His whole family had been sick when at last he also was taken with severe fever, of which he suffered about two weeks. Six days before his death, he became speechless and remained so until the time of his death....

36

RETURN TO FLORENCE

Lusanna didn't think they should take the time for it, going back to Florence and to the cemetery. But Carl had insisted on it, after he had harvested his ten acres of wheat, a crop which more than pleased the both of them, the heads heavy, full of ripened grain. After stacking the wheat, they waited for the threshing stone and oxen. It would be their turn to use them next week. Perhaps it was time for this, what he had promised her.

When the five of them, Carl and Lusanna, Andrias, and Peter and Agnes, stood on the station platform in Halstead waiting for the train, a mixture of feelings tumbled within her breast. She knew they registered on her face. *Anxiety? Fear? Overwhelming sadness? Perhaps a mixture of all three.*

Agnes and Lusanna had packed a split-hickory basket with the ham sandwiches Agnes had made, slicing the bread from a fresh, savory loaf. Lusanna had caught a young Rhode Island Red rooster, wrung its neck, and, after plucking and gutting it and cutting it into pieces, fried it in her iron skillet.

The fragrances drifted from under the cloth covering the basket.

The train wailed and rocked toward them.

The car was only about half-loaded with mostly women passengers who obviously had donned their Sunday best, hats planted securely on their heads, no doubt on their way to Newton or Peabody to do some after-harvest shopping.

Lusanna and Agnes wore their traditional head scarves tied under their chins, duly noncomformed to this world as far as their attire was concerned.

"Good to see that most of the wheat is harvested," Carl said, leaning across Lusanna's side to glance at the passing fields and grassland.

"One thing we can be thankful for. Yes indeed. Had we come to Kansas in the winter of 1874, instead of one year later, we wouldn't be looking at such good crops." Andrias stared out of his window.

"You mean the year of the grasshoppers?" Carl asked.

"Folks are still talking about it, the spring and summer of 1874. Why, even the trains couldn't go. Wheels just sliding around with so many grasshoppers on the tracks."

"Yes. We, at least, were spared that, however..." Carl didn't finish the sentence.

When the train reached Peabody, four of the women descended from the train, their pocketbooks gripped firmly in their hands.

After three new passengers settled into their seats, the engine wailed, the wheels started rolling again. Off to Florence.

As the car rocked Lusanna scanned their faces. Agnes, Carl, Peter, Agnes, and Andrias. Their heads rocked gently as they sat in silence.

The land began to change from flat plains to gently rolling hills, land unsuitable for wheat and corn, but excellent grazing land. She had learned enough about Kansas that she recognized they would soon be at the edge of what they called The Flint Hills.

Lusanna swallowed. She reached out for Carl's warm hand, noticing the veins on the back of his hand. Feeling the calluses on his palm.

Will their voices overwhelm me? Are they carried in the wind?

Can I endure it?

She saw Andrias shifting his feet, leaning forward, leaning backward. He took off his cap and laid it on his lap.

He put it back on his head again. She noticed the whiteness of his brow, which had been shaded from the sun.

The loss. The broken circle. The everlasting silence when I so want to hear those voices.

Mother speaking. "Lusanna, could you check on Basha? I thought I heard Schoolmaster Heinrich bringing the cows back from pasture."

Oh, Mother. You, at least, would have enjoyed this sunshine.

Father Joseph. How he read the scriptures. "O Lord, you have searched me and known me. You know when I sit down and rise up. You discern my thoughts from far away..."

Benjamin. "Lusanna, Lusanna, come and watch the storks. Lusanna, let me take a turn on your linen loom."

Schoolmaster Heinrich. "Lusanna, you may proceed to the front of the class."

Elise. "Lusanna, Mother sent you folks some of her currant jelly. No, Lusanna, Jacob and I won't be going to America, we..."

Lusanna sifted her position on the seat, still clasping Carl's hand. The engine gave three toots as it approached a crossing.

Oh, dear Jesus, we'll soon be there.

Steam hissed and spread from the side of the engine as it puffed, waiting for their unloading at the Florence station.

They descended, heads low in silence. It was as if none of them dared to glance across the street. Without even thinking, Lusanna pulled a handkerchief from her small handbag, raising it to her nose.

"Wonder what they finally did with that building? What did they put in it?" Carl's voice had a nervous wobble in it.

Andrias was the first to take courage and look at the brick building across the street. He stopped.

The four others halted, staring.

Lusanna half-expected an overwhelming stench to encircle them. The wind, whirled dust in the street. *Didn't it pick up the wails of sorrow?*

They clustered together, almost unconsciously. Mouths open, eyes scanning the building. A wagon, drawn by a team of reddish horses, rattled by. A group of the English across the street halted, staring at them. Perhaps they recognized the survivors, remnants of the Antanofkans from Ostrog.

Finally, a man with a star-shaped badge pinned to his shirt stepped up to them. *Sheriff, constable?*

"You folks will have to move on. You can't just keep standing in the street like this, 'specially on a Saturday. You're in danger of getting run over."

His face grew solemn as if he was thinking: *You're those Polish-Russians, aren't you?*

Andrias was the first to speak. "Would you believe it? A hardware store. Look, Carl, look, Peter, out in front, garden things, rakes, hoes, baskets...."

Still, they stood staring. Alongside the building a row of sunflowers lifted buds, giving promise that in a month they would burst into golden yellow.

"What are you thinking, Lusanna," Carl asked, noticing her silent stare.

"Why, why, I'm thinking 'out of the bitter came the sweet.'"

"Would you want to step inside with me," Andrias asked.

"Why, Andrias," Lusanna said, clutched her handkerchief more tightly, "not right now, at least."

But Agnes took her hand. "Lusanna, let's go inside. I don't think we should spare ourselves this." She half-dragged Lusanna past the hoes and rakes, the rack of garden seed, wooden tubs and pails, and through the opened door.

The smells drifted to their noses. Pungent smells of iron and copper. The sharp newness of steel. Faint musty smell of various grains in bags, which had not yet sold. Kerosene lamps, stoneware dishes. Zinc tubs hanging on the walls. Horse collars.

The sounds? Warm voices of clerk and customers.

With Agnes's encouragement, and the clasp of her hand, Lusanna allowed herself to be led through one aisle and back toward the wide-open door.

The trip seemed a hundred miles to Lusanna. Within that short time she saw people heaped together, leaning on hope chests watching steaming kettles on the pot-bellied stove. She heard the wails of sick infants. A doctor's voice, "Smallpox. Quarantined. It's smallpox."

The coughs, the strangles of the dying. Her nose pinched at the overwhelming stench blasting her. She heard a man's voice calling harshly, "Shut that door, the outside air is bad."

She glanced toward the spot where Benjamin and her parents had taken their last breaths, surprising herself that her eyes could linger there. All she heard in her head was "Blessed are those who die in the Lord…"

She glanced through the back door - the line of privies, all but one, gone. A hitching post. Saddle horses, waiting teams. Birds singing. The wind, suddenly teasing and sweet.

Carl and Peter stopped before the new harness, the smell of the oil lifting from it as it hung on the wall. She heard their voices but was unable to comprehend their words.

***

Nearing the cemetery northwest of Florence, Lusanna looked back at the town lying in the flood-plains along the Cottonwood River. She turned her head back toward what lay ahead. *That patch of ground.*

Tired from the struggle up the hill, they all sat on the grass in the shade of a cedar tree. The westerly wind was warm, but not overwhelmingly hot for July. For this, she was thankful.

Her eyes turned toward the spot. The place in her memory. She felt Carl's warm body as he nestled closer to her. Agnes stood, hand shielding her eyes as she searched.

Andrias had plucked a stalk of bluestem and was chewing the end of it.

"This is actually a beautiful place." Peter was the first to speak. "Up here, out of the flood waters from the river. Someone must have thought of that, some years ago."

A cardinal called to its mate from the deep green cedar.

"I'm ready," Lusanna said, turning to Carl and Andrias. The others rose along with them. They left the basket nestled behind in seeming agreement that they would picnic later.

Andrias was the first to break out weeping. His feet, however, plodded on toward the graves, searching.

They all were asking, "Where? Wasn't it there? No, over there. There was a small cedar springing up which marked the place, wasn't there?"

As they scanned the stretch of grasses, spoiled by unhealed patches, some, yet raw, red earth and gravel showing through. Other gashes with thin grass where weeds had taken hold. Thistles. Milkweed. Prairie dock.

Lusanna stared. "Here it is. I know the spot. Yes, Carl, Andrias. They're buried here, Father and Mother. Little Benjamin over there. Before we moved away, I placed that round stone there until…"

Then her eye shifted back to the milkweed and there she saw butterflies. Gorgeous swallow-tailed butterflies. *God has not forgotten this place….*

Standing there, then sitting, they waited, allowing the tears to flow, the sobs to work their healing through their bodies.

Andrias had picked up some soil and gravel from Benjamin's grave. He rocked. "Oh, Benjie, so much I wanted to show you."

Agnes had stalked over to the fence by the road where she broke off a bunch of orange flowers that the English called butterfly bush, and placed the blossoms upon her family's grave-spots.

The great white clouds billowed as they drifted over-head against the purity of the blue sky. The wind itself seemed to whisper, "Be not afraid. All is well. All is well."

"Lusanna, are you ready to step back into the shade now?" Carl asked.

"I'm ready, Carl." She noticed that the others were rising from their positions. They wiped tears. They turned for another look. She could hear them whispering names.

"I have to tell you something, Carl," Lusanna said, again, taking his hand.

"What is that, Lusanna?"

"It's that verse Elder Tobias Unruh read the evening he told us all about America and balmy Kansas."

"You remember that?"

"Yes, Carl. Yes, I do."

She recited the verse. "'Do not remember the former things, or consider the things of old. I am about to do a new thing. Now it springs forth, do you not perceive it?'"

"Isaiah, isn't it, Lusanna. From Isaiah?" Carl asked.

"You remembered correctly, dear husband. From the prophet Isaiah.

Again, a zephyr wind kissed their cheeks and brows. Lusanna suddenly recognized that she was hungry. Agnes's ham. Nobody smoked ham better than Agnes.

"This way, folks. This way." Lusanna led the way back to the graceful spread of the cedar and the plump woven basket filled with what God and Mother Nature, plus the work of their own hands, had provided.

***

The sun had lowered in the western sky as Peter's springwagon bounced along on the trail heading to their land where they were called by the English, and other Mennonites, too, the Cantoners or the Ostrogers.

Though the team was anxious to draw them onward, Lusanna dared to ask Peter if he would mind driving off track a short distance to the west.

"We have time, Lusanna. It's the tree, isn't it? You'd like me to drive over to the big cottonwood."

Andrias and Agnes both chimed in, "Yes, do that. We do have time."

Already they could see the towering canopy to their left - a sentinel to the plains, seemingly everlasting, enduring.

Lusanna was the first to jump out of the springwagon, followed by Carl, Andrias, and Agnes.

Lusanna lifted her skirts as she raced toward her tree. She lifted her head, spreading her arms wide open in welcome. It was as if the spirit of the tree and her own spirit were waiting for each other.

She stopped, turned, making sure the others were coming behind her. She noticed that the sun hung at the edge of orange and purple clouds.

She strode on toward the pillar-trunk, looking at the massive gray-cork-barked roots stretching outward, holding it to the earth where it received its nourishment. Nourishment, too from the bright Kansas sun, despised by some, loved by many.

As she stood checking the branches of the tree, she could see the scars left by lightning bolts, the broken places where smaller limbs had split off and crashed from ice storms in winter. Her heart picked up its beat as she saw new growth at the ends of the branches, the clusters of shimmering, rustling leaves. At her feet, a leaf-cluster had broken off, leaves turning yellow. She picked up the cluster, twirling it in her fingers. Lifting it to her nose, she smelled the cleanness and purity of it, the pungent, spicy life of it.

From near the top of the tree, a hundred feet above her, she could see the tiny body of a red squirrel, who with his chatter, seemed to be making fun of her.

Andrias and Carl were at her side. Agnes strained her neck upwards, peering at the top. Peter, hands on his hips, waited. Lusanna said: "Let's see if we, all of us, can stretch our arms, hold hands and try to reach around the tree."

"You mean all five of us?" Peter asked.

"Go on, Peter," Agnes urged, "don't be a spoil-sport. Let's do it."

They gathered, careful not to stumble over one of the long roots that anchored the tree to Mother Earth.

Faces on the bark, hands outstretched, on tiptoes even, they reached. The evening wind circled about the tree. A rabbit bounced from the elderberry bushes, and another followed. From somewhere, a hawk screamed.

"Stretch. Carl, are you reaching as far as you can?" Lusanna asked.

"I'm stretching, Lusanna. We can't reach around it, not even the five of us. We're going to need at least another person."

They dropped their arms and hands, stepped back in reverent awe.

"Some day in the future," Lusanna said, surveying the faces of her dear ones, "there will be a church near here.. Surely it will be called, The Lone Tree Church.

She wanted to say more but held her words to herself. She wanted to say: "And the church, like the leaves of this tree, will be for the healing of hearts and nations."

As the sun slid through the gold-edged cloudbank, she felt Carl's warm hand at her back. "Come, Lusanna. We'll come here often. Now, I want to take you home."

"Home? Why, yes. Let's all go home."

They rattled onward, the horses stepping lively toward their waiting water trough, oats, and pasture. They saw ahead the rows of little huts, houses, sod roofs and walls. Here and there, they saw home-made brick ovens at the sides of the dwellings. The prairie grasses waved and nodded as they rolled down the trail. Meadowlarks lifted their wings and sang evening greetings to them.

"I see our house, Carl. *Home.* We're home, at last."

Lusanna allowed the sweetness of the prairie to enfold her as she rocked on the wagon seat, holding Carl's hand. She smiled to herself, thinking about how Agnes whispered in her ear, "Lusanna, there's a new gleam in your eye."

She wondered if she shouldn't tell Carl her secret just as soon as they stepped into their house.

ACKNOWLEDGMENTS

I am indebted to many persons and sources for the background material for my historical novel, *The Lone Tree*. These include: Leslie B. Allison's "Russian Mennonites in Florence in 1870's," *Kanhistique*. November, 1993, p.p. 7-9; J. A. Boese's *The Russian-Polish Mennonites Settling in South Dakota 1874 and Soon After*, Pine Hill Press, Freeman S. D., 1967; *Bernard Warkentine*, from v. III, part 2 of *Kansas: a cyclopedia of state history, embracing events, institutions, industries, counties, towns, prominent persons, etc.* Transcribed by Carolyn Ward, 2002; J. J. Goering's *A Short History and Tribute*. *http://.koehnfamily.com/mhistory.html*; Jacob D. Goering's *The Lone Tree*, Unpublished paper; David A. Haury's *Prairie People: a History of the Western District Conference:* Faith and Life Press: Newton, Kansas, 1981; Clarence Hiebert's *The Holdeman People: The Church of God in Christ, Mennonite, 1859-1969*, William Carey Library: Pasadena, 1973; *Histories of The Congregations of the Church of God in Christ, Mennonite*: Gospel Publishers, Moundridge, Ks., & Ste. Anne, Manitoba, 1975; Paul G. Jantzen's "The Lone Tree: Prairie Wanderings," Hillsboro, Kansas: *Star-Journal*, July 7, 2005; Kohn Family http://koehnfamily.com/manifest.html; Cornelius Krahn's *From Steppes to the Prairies*, Mennonite Publication Office, Newton, Kansas, 1949; Christian Krehbiel's *Prairie Pioneers*, Faith and Life Press, Newton, KS, 1961; Susanna A. Krehbiel's *Autobiography of Susanna A. Krehbiel, (Life of Christian Krehbiel), 1949*; Gustav E.

Reimer's and G. R. Gaeddert's *Exiled by the Czar:* Mennonite Publication Office, Newton, Kansas, 1956; Martin H. Schrag's *The European History of the Swiss Mennonites From Volhynia:* Published by Harley J. Stucky and others, Graphic Images: North Newton, Kansas, 1999; Helen B. Shipley's *The Migration of the Mennonites From Russia, 1873-1883, and Their Settlement in Kansas: A Thesis Submitted to the Graduate Faculty of the University of Minnesota, 1954;* C. Henry Smith's *The Coming of the Russian Mennonites:* Mennonite Book Concern, Berne, Indiana, 1927; Abe J. Unruh's *The Helpless Poles,* Pine Hill Press: Freeman, S. D., 1980; and David V. Wiebe's *They Seek a Country,* Pine Hill Press, Freeman, S. D., 1974.

In addition, I express gratitude to Darlene Schroeder of the Mennonite Heritage Museum, Gossel, Kansas, for her insights and help. I thank Ralph Lehman who first informed me of the account of the Polish-Russian Mennonites' travails in Florence, Kansas. It was through this sharing that I committed myself to writing this book.

I am also grateful for the excellent assistance I received from the library staff at The Hesston Public Library, Hesston, Kansas, especially Chris Buller, Karen White, and Ellen Voth. I also thank the Florence Public Librarian, Gayle Scriven, for her help. I thank my copy editor, Laurel Schunk, and my wife, Lonabelle C. Yoder, for her help in reviewing the manuscript. In addition, a hearty thanks to David Godshall for working with the manuscript formatting.

NOVELS BY JAMES D. YODER

THE YODER OUTSIDERS

SARAH OF THE BORDER WARS

BARBARA: SARAH'S LEGACY

SONG IN A NAZI NIGHT
(Published in hardback and large print as
Black Spider Over Tiegenhof)

LUCY OF THE TRAIL OF TEARS

A BRANSON LOVE

SIMONE: A SAINT FOR OUTSIDERS

ECHOES ALONG THE SWEETBRIER

MUDBALL SAM

THE LONE TREE

To order books go to **www.YoderBooks.com**
Contact the author at **James@YoderBooks.com**